EARTH DEEP

EARTH DEEP
DWARVISH DIRTY DOZEN™ SERIES BOOK SIX

AARON D. SCHNEIDER
MICHAEL ANDERLE

DON'T MISS OUR NEW RELEASES

Join the LMBPN email list to be notified of new releases and special promotions (which happen often) by following this link:

http://lmbpn.com/email/

This book is a work of fiction. All of the characters, organizations, and events portrayed in this novel are either products of the author's imagination or are used fictitiously. Sometimes both.

Copyright © 2023 LMBPN Publishing
Cover Art by Jake @ J Caleb Design
http://jcalebdesign.com / jcalebdesign@gmail.com
Cover copyright © LMBPN Publishing
A Michael Anderle Production

LMBPN Publishing supports the right to free expression and the value of copyright. The purpose of copyright is to encourage writers and artists to produce the creative works that enrich our culture.

The distribution of this book without permission is a theft of the author's intellectual property. If you would like permission to use material from the book (other than for review purposes), please contact support@lmbpn.com. Thank you for your support of the author's rights.

LMBPN Publishing
PMB 196, 2540 South Maryland Pkwy
Las Vegas, NV 89109

Version 1.00, August 2023
ebook ISBN: 979-8-88878-536-2
Paperback ISBN: 979-8-88878-537-9

THE EARTH DEEP TEAM

Thanks to our JIT Team:

Zacc Pelter
Jeff Goode
John Ashmore
Peter Manis
Jan Hunnicutt
Paul Westman

If we've missed anyone, please let us know!

Editor
SkyFyre Editing Team

DEDICATIONS

This book is dedicated to those readers who have been willing to take a chance on this series, along with everything else I've written, thus far. You place in me a trust to use your time well, and it is my hope that you feel it has not been time wasted. May we continue to meet together between these pages and share dark and heroic tales together for years to come.

— Aaron

To Family, Friends and
Those Who Love
to Read.
May We All Enjoy Grace
to Live the Life We Are
Called.

— Michael

ACKNOWLEDGMENTS

I'd like to acknowledge this book and more broadly this series would not have been possible without the dedicated efforts of my fantastic and faithful editor Lynne. Your patience, your honesty, and your skill have set me straight and bolstered me up so many times I struggle to remember them all. You exceptional abilities as an editor made us co-labourers, but your wit and wisdom have made us friends. Thank you so much, ma'am. I really do appreciate you.

SOUTHERN YSGAND VALE MAP

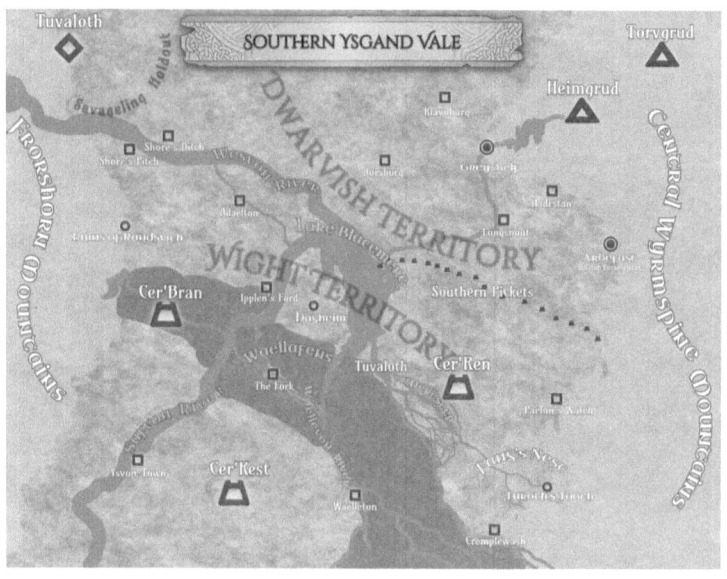

You load sixteen tons, what do you get?
Another day older and deeper in debt
Saint Peter, don't you call me 'cause I can't go
I owe my soul to the company store

—*16 Tons*, Tennessee Ernie Ford

I am the captain of my soul.

—*Invictus*, William Ernest Henley

PROLOGUE

"Do you think it's true?"

The question from the dwarf made his commander twist around as though it had stung him.

"What's that supposed to mean?" the tweldwan of the 6th Division snarled, his voice warning enough without the dramatic posturing. The dwan's eyes found something interesting on the dirt floor of the hovel they were standing in and remained fixed there. His superior officer's eyes gleamed dangerously when he leaned forward, refusing to be dissuaded by the dwan's sheepish posture or the wood shavings sprinkled about. The previous occupants must have been woodworkers of some ilk.

"I said, what is that supposed to mean?" Tweldwan Okmur Kallson of Clan Brydwif repeated, pressing forward until the honor guard was forced to shuffle back. The motion was uncomfortable and unfamiliar.

The other two honor guards moved to one side, ostensibly to make room for their commander and their unfortunate comrade. Having the motion put some distance between them and the other dwan was surely a coincidence.

"I-it's just th-that we've heard so many things," the dwan stammered, the brittle creak in his voice at odds with his weathered and scarred face. "M-my apologies, Tweldwan."

This was no dusty-eared youth from the tunnels or even one of the few sun-kissed Vale-born younglings. The dwarf was a worthy veteran of the battle line, yet he was cowering beneath his tweldwan's accusing glare. That was the effect that Okmur "Peak-Breaker" Kallson had on most dwarfs.

A head taller than any dwarf and a handspan broader at each shoulder, he was a colossus among his people. Even the longshanks he met viewed his obvious physical potency with wary admiration. This, combined with his reputation as a storm of destruction in the press of battle and a temper as violent as a tornado, there were few who could stand before the tweldwan without feeling a quiver of trepidation. When faced with his ire, most crumpled.

"The only things that matter concerning Torbjorn *Kinslayer* are these, " Okmur growled, the room crackling with tension. "It is said that he is an oath breaker, faithless, and a traitor. That's all that matters, and you'd do well to remember it."

"Yes, Tweldwan." The honor guard nodded, but despite the beseeching looks of his companions, he added, "But if that be the case, why are we here?"

Every dwarf in the rustic cottage waited with trepidation as the Peak-Breaker stood in what might have been a pensive silence for any other creature. Then the behemoth's face adopted an expression even more unsettling than his most tempestuous frown: a smile.

"Because I want to watch the light bleed from his eyes as I

crush the life out of him," Okmur rumbled, licking his lips. "I'll drag his corpse to the Grimmoth's Rock so the ol' Fiend can have his heart, but his last breath is mine."

The honor guard was dumbstruck. Their war harness clinked as they shifted from foot to foot. Another member of the guard confirmed the grim implications of the words.

"So, we are going to betray a banner of truce." The dwan swallowed.

"There is no truce with traitors," Okmur declared, his declaration absolute. "If the Kinslayer is stupid enough to come here thinking I will parley with him, then he's a fool as well as a traitor."

The dire words hung in the air as the tweldwan moved to the small window on the front wall of the borrowed domicile. The setting sun blazed its dying hues over the fallow farmland, and the very sight of it insulted Okmur. Given the surge of the wights and then the chaos of the re-annexation, the rich lands of the Vale—the lands he and so many others had paid in blood for every meter of—had not been worked. After the last of bandits and revolts had been subjugated, the time had come to see if the Vale would provide the bounty it had promised all those years ago.

Then Torbjorn Kinslayer—Torbjorn the Traitor—had begun his revolt.

Once little more than a dark specter lurking in the Holt'Dwan's periphery, Okmur had been as shocked as everyone else when cries of being chosen by the Shaper had catapulted Torbjorn to leadership at Greyshelf, but the tweldwan had been thankful that Ondwan Glastuc had been deposed. The old fool had gone from complacent to negligent, and no dwan worthy of the name had been sorry to hear that the Shaper had struck him down.

Yet, for all that, Okmur would have served another century under Glastuc if he'd known that the dwan who had commanded them at the siege would use that to set up a rebellion. Not only did it prove the guile behind the previous "miracle," but it now tainted every dwarf who had served under the traitor's command at Greyshelf. It was a stain on their honor, on their very souls, so Okmur had sworn to see it expunged.

For months, Ondwan Ashfer had denied him the chance by sending other divisions against Torbjorn's fledgling rebellion in the west. This had proved disastrous. One division, the 8th, had been sent limping back, and then a pair of divisions, the 4th and 5th, actually joined the rebellion.

Ashfer, not as debauched as Glastuc but apparently just as incompetent, had dithered away most of the good campaigning weather by being indecisive until the rebels began to advance across the Valley. No word had yet come of the 3rd, which had stood in their path along the banks of the Wesvon River, but silence did not bode well.

Finally, with the first chill of autumn in the air, Okmur was to lead a coalition of divisions, 7th, 9th, 10th, 11th, and his own 6th—nearly all the remaining Holt'Dwan's forces in the Vale—to bring Torbjorn to heel. Only the primping dandies of the 1st were held back, their arses planted firmly in Greyshelf to protect the primary access to the Wyrmspine Mountains. Seemed Ashfer didn't much like the idea of Torbjorn's forces being able to threaten his beloved Heimgrud.

"Let him cower," the tweldwan of the 6th whispered, grinding the words between his teeth. "I'm going to end this here and now."

Okmur's honor guard shared glances but held their peace. They knew better than to interrupt their superior in one of his dark moods, which had become more frequent through the dwindling days of summer. They held their places as the light morphed from the brilliant shades of orange and pink to the glowering reds giving way to bruised purples, not even daring to suggest lighting a fire in the hearth. In truth, the room was suffocating, though it had little to do with the temperature.

"He's coming!"

The declaration from the dwan set to watch at the door drew soft sounds of relief from the guard. Their ordeal was nearly over. One unshouldered his duabuw and pumped the priming arm before a sharp look from Okmur froze him in place.

"How many are there?" the tweldwan called to the watching dwan.

"Just him," was the answer. "Stepped out of the hedge line at the edge of the field and headed this way on his own."

Okmur frowned. "How do you know it is him?" He swept past the guards to shoulder through the door.

The guard on watch pointed at the lone figure trudging across the overgrown fields. Dwarvish eyes made the twilight as bright as morning sunshine, and it was easy to see the dark, shaggy head and the sturdy profile of a well-built dwarf. Those were not enough to convince Okmur that he'd not been played false, but the sight of the dark, gleaming left hand, a blasphemy of living wood, was solid evidence.

Understanding that he'd been spotted, the dwarf raised the peculiar hand and waved it wearily at the dwarfs at the cottage. He kept marching forward, empty fields stretching to either side and a hedge falling farther behind him. Even if the rebel had an entire division stowed in and behind the thick bushes, he was quickly moving beyond a point at which they could save him from attackers. Avenge him, yes, but that would be cold comfort to their leader's corpse.

"He really is a fool." Okmur scoffed, his sapphire blue eyes squinting at the hedgerow to spy even a twitch.

"We could drop him with a few bolts," the dwan with the crossbow in hand proclaimed. "A few more steps, and even if the first round misses, we'd have plenty of time to put one in his back if he ran."

Okmur measured the distance with a practiced eye. The tweldwan preferred to face an enemy face to face, where his size gave a clear advantage, but long years of experience had trained him to have a good idea of distance as far as dwarvish crossbow volleys were concerned.

Torbjorn's situation would be bad if Okmur's guards launched bolts at the rebel. That didn't include the squad of rangers that was skulking in the barn behind the cottage. Torbjorn was as good as dead at Okmur's word. Given what he'd seen of Torbjorn's leadership at Greyshelf, the tweldwan knew the approaching dwarf understood that as well.

"Very brave, or…" the commander muttered, then his voice trailed off, and his eyes narrowed. Okmur's lips puckered as he saw the drag of Torbjorn's feet and the way the mane of dark hair hung limp around a bowed head.

What if the traitor wasn't brave but just tired? Tired from marching or perhaps weary from prosecuting his rebellion.

Something resembling sympathy squirmed in the back of Okmur's mind, but a potent brew of hate and indignation rose in its place.

"Bastard," the tweldwan spat. "He better put up a fight when I crush him. He's taken enough without taking that."

The dwarfs standing around Okmur looked at their muttering superior, none daring to move. Several heartbeats later, Okmur stopped staring at Torbjorn and noticed the unsettled hesitation of his guards.

"What are you all gawkin' for?" he bellowed, causing the quartet of dwans to jump. "How can I enjoy smashing the grem-spawned wretch under my boot if you fill him with bolts? Shoulder those duabuws and stay out of my way. I'll do this in my own time."

Okmur caught the quickly smothered scowls of the guards but decided not to comment since his quarry was nearly within earshot. He didn't doubt his dwans' loyalty, only their own eagerness to visit vengeance on the traitor who was undoing all their hard work. The tweldwan could understand that. He would be sore about the matter as well, but *some* privileges came with rank.

Torbjorn closed the remaining distance with agonizing slowness. Okmur and his guards stood in silent vigil the entire time. When he finally stopped before them, he looked even wearier than his sluggish movements had indicated. His dark eyes were sunk into their sockets, and his face was slack.

"Got a chair in there for a tired dwan?" Torbjorn asked as he stood before them, shoulders bowed. "I could use a chance to sit and rest my bones for a bit."

The honor guards swiveled as one to their massive superior, whose teeth clenched behind his resplendent beard. A tempest of dark emotions swam in the huge dwarf's pale eyes, but when he finally spoke, his tone was steady and gentle, almost soft.

"I'm sure we can find something for you," Okmur replied with the barest bow of his head, then swept an arm in a welcoming flourish. "Come in, please."

The dwans of the 6th fought to keep from casting curious glances at their tweldwan as Torbjorn trudged into the cottage with a grateful nod. Once the traitor was within the walls of the cottage, they stole glances and exchanged minute shrugs before they came to a silent consensus to be quiet and watch.

There was a pair of chairs and a small table tucked into one corner, quickly vanishing into shadow as the last light of the sun left the window. Okmur dragged the table over while instructing one guard to bring the chairs and the other to light a fire in the hearth. It wasn't long before Torbjorn Kinslayer slumped in a chair at the table, watching flames crackle across dry logs in the fireplace.

Okmur put a hand on the other chair, and the rustic furnishing creaked. It was clearly for the best that the tweldwan didn't sit on the thing. Given its protesting noises, the chair would give out spectacularly if the commander's armored bulk settled on it, and that would hardly set a proper tone for this meeting.

"Thank you." Torbjorn sighed, not looking up from the fire, though one hand pawed at his belt before coming away empty. "You wouldn't happen to have any food or water, would you? In my rush to get here in time, I managed to scuttle out of camp without either."

Okmur smiled broadly even as his eyes narrowed, wondering what manner of game they were playing. Torbjorn continued to watch the flames as he waited for an answer, his face reflecting his fatigue.

The tweldwan found it hard to believe that this was the same dwarf he'd seen striding across the battlements during the defense of Greyshelf. This dwarf was smaller and eons older. A fighter once, maybe, but now shrunk by the ravages of time and labor—a shell. Suspicious but determined to get to the bottom of things, he decided he'd come this far with his charade, so why not maintain it to the very end?

"Of course," Okmur responded, motioning to one of his guards without taking his eyes off Torbjorn. "I'd prefer that we all be clear-headed and focused during this...discussion."

Hard cheese and bread appeared in short order, along with a water skin and a short jug of ale. Torbjorn repeatedly offered his thanks for everything placed before him and consumed it ravenously.

"Supply troubles?" Okmur asked, doing his best to sound sympathetic rather than prying. If Torbjorn's rebels were running low on supplies—supplying three divisions of dwans and their support staff was no mean feat—Okmur's efforts would be all the easier.

The proverb that an army marches on its stomach was painfully real and even more true when talking about those who'd placed themselves beyond the logistical reach of a standing army. That alone could explain Torbjorn's weary, almost despairing behavior.

Unfortunately, Torbjorn didn't seem interested in answering the question, though he did offer his thanks a final time before he drew back from the table and settled himself against the back of his chair.

"You've been more than fair," Torbjorn began, motioning at the empty skin and jug. "I expect you're itching to get to the killing-me part. Why don't you go ahead and try so we don't waste any more time?"

For several heartbeats, there was not a sound in the cottage except the crackle of the fire. Finally, the chair Okmur was leaning on squeaked, and the big dwarf, his genial smile slipping, leaned toward the seated rebel.

"I'm not sure I know what you are talking about," the

tweldwan lied through his flashing teeth. "I thought we'd come to this meeting with the intention of seeing if there might be some way to put an end to this without the need for more dwarfs to die."

Torbjorn nodded his shaggy head as though he'd expected every word he was hearing.

"If that was true, I'd have come dressed to the nines and ready to talk," Torbjorn declared, spreading his hands. "Who knows what we could have worked out between us? Two old boars jockeying tusk to tusk before settling on common ground."

Okmur's smile dropped, and his eyes shone as he looked at Torbjorn. "Then what did you come here for?" His free hand settled on the axe that hung from his belt. "You don't seem to be in very good shape for a fight."

Torbjorn nodded as a slow smile spread across his face.

"I don't suppose I do," he intoned, looking himself over with a disapproving grimace. "But I've been out of sorts since I was pitched into a cell in Greyshelf the first time, and I don't imagine that things are likely to change much. Not until we finish this ugly business."

Okmur shoved the chair he'd been leaning on, and it scooted across the packed earth to butt against the table. Rising to his full height, the colossus leered down his nose at Torbjorn.

"What *is* that business?" he rumbled. "There are some who think your goal is to take the Ysgand Vale for yourself, and others who say your goal is much grander than that."

Torbjorn picked a few crumbs from his beard in quiet defiance of the menacing giant as he paused to consider his response.

"I haven't sat down and plotted this out from beginning to

end," Torbjorn admitted with a shrug. "I'm not going to say that it was all an accident, but I didn't intend for things to end up this way."

Okmur swallowed the scoff that welled up in his throat, but he couldn't do much to keep disgust from his tone when he spoke. "A victim of the Wyrd, then? The plaything of the Shaper's will? Not something I expected to hear from the likes of you."

The guards around Okmur shifted, but Torbjorn didn't seem to notice. He kept his eyes on the fire. "I'm surprised too." He nodded. "But I've given up trying to explain why things are the way they are. In the end, the only question is what we choose to do when each choice is given to us."

The Kinslayer's gaze finally swung to Okmur, deep, dark eyes smoldering with an intensity that seemed to have been stolen from the depths of the fire he'd been staring at.

"So, what is your choice going to be, Peak-Breaker?" Torbjorn asked, his tone flat and cold. "We goin' to keep talking, or are you going to try to do what you promised to do ever since Assface sent you out here to kill me? Or you got jelly in your joints?"

Okmur's fury overshadowed the nettling question of how Torbjorn could know such things, and his axe leapt in his hand. It was brutal, like its owner. One side was a flanged maul, and the other was a broad grin of hungry steel. It rose, but Torbjorn kicked out and flipped the small table into Okmur's face. The axe sent the remnants of the table spinning away as kindling as the massive dwarf commander barged through the splinters.

Torbjorn, his semblance of exhaustion shed like a loose garment, was already moving, magsax tugged from his belt and the chair he'd been sitting in hoisted in one hand as he spun away. Blade point and chair legs danced before him as the rebel did his best to keep the other dwarfs to one side of him. Seeing the bared steel, the honor guard reached for their swords, but Okmur's voice prevented that.

"NO! He's mine!" the tweldwan of the 6th roared, advancing toward Torbjorn with his axe raised for another cleaving stroke. "I've been looking forward to this for months!"

The behemoth advanced to strike the rebel, but Torbjorn thrust the chair legs toward the other dwarf's face, and it struck the wood instead.

"I'm flattered." Torbjorn chuckled as two chair legs flew away. "But I'll be honest. I didn't think about you until we heard the 6th was finally done hiding around Longsnout."

In response to the taunt, Okmur launched a series of slashes that reduced the chair to splinters. Torbjorn skittered toward a corner. The Kinslayer's eyes darted toward the door, but the dwarf commander blocked any hope of escape. After another step, he had Torbjorn's back against the cottage wall, and a sneer curled beneath his mustache.

"Really?" the tweldwan thundered with a mirthless laugh. "All that bravado, and you run so soon?"

Instead of retorting, Torbjorn lunged forward with unexpected swiftness. The magsax hammered every seam and joint in reach, the battle-hardened dwarf knowing every possible vulnerability in dwarven war plate.

The first few blows staggered the hulking tweldwan, but they didn't bite deep enough to trouble him. Okmur laughed and plunged forward. His only truly vulnerable spot was his bare head, but his height and proficiency with his weapons rendered Torbjorn's attempts to reach that ineffectual.

Batting a sword stroke aside with a gauntlet, the big dwarf

came on, arm winding back for a crushing blow the traitor couldn't hope to block. Okmur told himself to check the swing so Torbjorn was maimed but not dead so he could make good on his promise to squeeze the life from the dwarf.

The crushing blow didn't connect.

In his haste and wrath, Okmur hadn't noticed that this close to the wall, the conical roof of the cottage was lower, and there was a stout joist over the traitor. The tweldwan's axe bit deep into the wood and stuck, and the shock threw the massive dwarf forward. The Peak-Breaker, his face thrust forward, had only a moment to register Torbjorn's smile before the hilt of the magsax struck his ear. The heavy blow sent the colossal dwan staggering to one side, leaving his axe lodged in the joist.

This was the opening Torbjorn had been waiting for. He sprang forward and lashed out with his blasphemous left hand. There was a sharp smack when that hand met Okmur's jaw, and the hulking dwarf went down on one knee.

Rather than pressing the attack, Torbjorn darted around Okmur, who was already staggering back to his feet, and made for the doorway.

"Stop 'im!" Okmur gargled around a mouthful of blood and bits of teeth. His vision was still blurred, and he wasn't steady on his feet. Grimmoth's Grin, the pipsqueak could hit! But the tweldwan spun to pursue, hollering after the retreating coward.

"Don't let 'im—"

Okmur jolted to a stop for the second time when he saw two burly dwarfs standing over his guards, duabuws leveled. The hard eyes gleaming above the heavy scarves wrapped around their faces promised they'd not flinch if it came time to loose the deadly bolts pointed at him.

Between them was Torbjorn, who scooped up the crossbow of one of the fallen dwans at his feet. The hulking tweldwan tried to make sense of what he was seeing. Where had these dwarfs come from? If more had come, why hadn't anyone raised an alarm? And where were those damned rangers?

"Cutting it a little close, don't you think?" Torbjorn asked as he finished the third pump of the duabuw's lever. "That monster nearly had me for dinner."

"Half an ogre, for sure," said one of the dwarfs, dark eyes smoldering under red brows. "And from the look of him, he still might be hungry."

The other dwarf, who looked large even to Okmur, gave a low chuckle before motioning over his shoulder. "Stout lads back there took a bit longer to bed down. One even stumbled across Waelon before they were all out cold."

Okmur frowned, trying to piece together what they were discussing. He noticed that his guards were still breathing. One was just stunned, his wide eyes blinking.

"Waelon?" Torbjorn called sternly, eliciting another chuckle from the broad dwan. The one with the fiery eyebrows gave a sulky shrug.

"He'll wake up with a headache," the dwarf groused without taking his eyes or aim off Okmur. "But he'll wake."

Torbjorn nodded and turned back to the tweldwan.

"There you go. All accounted for, and no one permanently damaged. I've got to say, that is a good deal gentler than what you planned. I mean, what did you plan to do with those rangers, eh?"

Okmur squared his shoulders, uncertain of how he'd been outfoxed so handily but sure he could turn things around. Many made the mistake of thinking that with his size and physical prowess, he was dull. Most of those who'd made that mistake had learned their error in judgment at great cost. Careful not to let his eyes stray to the signal horns on the belts of his guard, Okmur spread his hand with a placating shrug.

"I was going to meet the legendary Torbjorn Kinslayer," he intoned, then nodded at his stricken guards. "It seems I underestimated how dangerous you were."

"Too right you did," the one called Waelon hissed with a voice like a rasp on granite. "Amateurs."

Okmur stuffed the sneer that rose at the barb, keeping his eyes fixed on Torbjorn. He was the leader, so he was the one who mattered.

"I was only taking precautions," the tweldwan continued as though he hadn't been interrupted. "But you had me beat, and I'm at your mercy now. So, what is it to be, Torbjorn Hralson of Clan Cyniburg? Am I to go the way of the 8th, sent crawling back naked and ashamed? Or are you going to do with me what you did to the 3rd Division?"

This was the most ticklish bit of the whole business. A gesture from Torbjorn could see him punctured by three bolts, and at this range, his armor and bulk would not prevent the violence. However, the tweldwan didn't see murder in the Kinslayer's gaze. If anything, the traitor seemed in elevated spirits at the mention of the vanished division.

"The 3rd?" He chuckled and glanced at his comrades without his aim wavering. "You hear that, lads? Sounds like our job's done. I thought the Peak-Breaker would be a harder sell, but it seems he's willing to consider joining up with Vormo's lot."

The guffaws of the other two dwarfs were nearly as

grating as the implications of Torbjorn's words were disconcerting.

"You're saying the 3rd *joined* your rebellion?" Okmur asked, the revelation rocking him nearly as hard as Torbjorn's hilt had. If it was true, his task force would face nearly equal numbers. The 3rd and the 5th had both recently come off refitting and retraining, so they were the closest to a full-strength division in the entire Holt'Dwan.

That nearly made up for any difference one more division would create. Also, most reports stated that Torbjorn's forces were supported by contingents of savagelings. The primitives may not have counted for much on the field, being disorganized and poorly armored, but if they acted as scouts, skirmishers, and raiders in tandem with the army, they would be much more dangerous.

Okmur wasn't a coward. He also wasn't a fool, so he felt a sinking sensation in his stomach as he envisioned what would be waiting for him on the battlefield, assuming he ever got there.

"So, how about it, Tweldwan?" Torbjorn called, drawing him from his thoughts. "You looking to join up after all?"

Okmur looked at the duabuws leveled at him and felt the answer form in the back of his throat. It wasn't what he'd thought he was going to say, but it was ready to spring from his mouth, especially with three gleaming bolts aimed at him. His heart hammered as the unfamiliar sensation of gripping fear surged through him, and he glanced around. He knew what he needed to say to dismiss the fear, and the pressure was mounting. The words were nearly formed.

Then he glanced at the little window, and through it, he saw the night-swaddled fields. The fallow fields.

When Okmur looked back, something must have shown in

his eyes because Torbjorn's teasing, jovial tone evaporated like drops of sweat upon a forge.

"Steady now, Okmur," Torbjorn warned, one hand coming off the duabuw to pat the air placatingly. "No need to rush this and doom a lot of good dwans to death."

Okmur's heart twisted at the mention of those who would die, a further disgrace in this mounting indignity. For all that he was hard on those under his command, he did not wish them ill. He deeply, if quietly, cheered their successes, not unlike a stern father. What father would want to see those under his leadership needlessly die in the meat grinder of war?

Then he remembered the fields. How many had fallen for those fields? How much blood had been shed, yet they still stood empty? The harvest should have been underway, but they were bare because of Torbjorn Kinslayer.

The fire blazed anew in Okmur. Any who met his eyes would see it flashing in them. Without faltering, he advanced one step, then another. He met the eyes of each armed dwarf, his head high and his bearded chin thrust forward.

"I'd rather die," the tweldwan rumbled, the sound reverberating through the cottage. "I'm no traitor, and neither are those who will stand with me."

"That can be arranged," the stout dwarf remarked. Torbjorn frowned, and Waelon glared. "You're getting closer if you keep stepping in this direction."

Okmur felt as much as saw the renewed scrutiny Torbjorn leveled at him, but he took another step.

"A signal horn can't signal no one with an arrow through your gob," Waelon warned, and Torbjorn nodded. Another step, and he was within reach of the horn lying on the floor.

The leather cord that bound it to the belt would snap easily enough, or so he hoped.

"Okmur, please listen," Torbjorn urged, his voice softer as he lowered his duabuw. "I didn't want to start this, and in many ways, I *didn't* start it, but regardless of what history will say about it, this is not the betrayal you've been told about. The Sufstan was founded to be the strong arm in the south, but we've just become another extension of the corruption festering the heart of the Empire. I know it, you know it, and so do many others. Those others need us to lay hold of this opportunity and—"

"And betray everything you ever swore yourself to? Turn your back on oaths you made to Emperor and the Shaper and the Holt'Dwan?"

He was almost there. One more footfall, and he could spring.

"He's going for the horn," Waelon observed, his tone chillingly calm.

"Don't shoot," Torbjorn commanded and turned back to the tweldwan. "Okmur, please! I'm beggin' you. Just let me—"

Okmur sprang forward in answer, a wild laugh ripping from his throat as he closed his fingers around the horn and raised it to his lips.

"*NO!*" Torbjorn shouted and advanced until there was little chance of striking the tweldwan with a bolt that wouldn't also skewer him. With that cover, Okmur didn't bother to shield himself as he blew a thunderous note.

The renegade dwarfs spat rough oaths before Torbjorn spun on his heel and instructed both to go make ready for battle.

When Okmur lowered the horn, only Torbjorn remained. The hulking tweldwan considered hurling the instrument at his enemy's face as he charged, perhaps taking Torbjorn unawares with the sudden action.

When he looked down, he saw the Kinslayer's duabuw leveled at him, as well as the hate he'd expected on their first encounter. It burned white-hot in Torbjorn's dark eyes, eclipsing the fury Okmur had felt.

"Damn you," Torbjorn growled, his voice shot through with a pain that gnawed on Okmur. "I don't want to do this."

Before the tweldwan could twitch out of the way, the duabuw sang.

CHAPTER ONE

"We should've killed him before he blew that stupid horn."

Gromic's declaration was lost on his compatriots as the trio tore across the field, legs pumping. All three dwarfs could hear horn blasts echoing in reply from beyond the low hills. It seemed Okmur's vanguard, mostly blotferow cavalry from the 9th, had managed to creep closer than they'd anticipated. If the sun was up, a glance over their shoulders would reveal plumes of dust rising as the dwans' mounts' hooves churned.

They pelted toward the low wall in front of the hedge from which Torbjorn had emerged not long ago. Above their panting, they heard the rumble of the battle swine approaching, only moments away.

"Come on," Torbjorn snarled as he squinted through the black tangle of the hedge. "Faster!"

Not slowing, all three dwarfs made to vault the low wall. With a curse, Gromic tumbled onto the path just before the packed flora.

"Come on, tub," Waelon growled as he snared the still-rolling dwan and yanked to set him on his feet. "I'm not goin' to tell Haeda we left your fat arse behind because you'd rather roll than walk."

The broad dwarf managed a grunting laugh as he was half-dragged to his feet, then both paused as they stood before the hedge. Looking up and down it, they frowned into the dark. They couldn't see where their commander had gone. All they saw was a wall of brambles with no breach to allow them through.

"Torbjorn?" Waelon called, reaching for the axe at his belt. "Commander, is there a way through?"

Gromic went for his magsax to hack a path.

"Majesty?" the stout dwarf called, broad-bladed sword whispering out of its sheath to gleam in the glow of a waning crescent moon. "Where are you?"

A shout of rage thundered from the cottage, and both looked over their shoulders to see a massive silhouette nearly block the orange light spilling from the door. Behind the building, they saw the dancing light of many torches like angry, swollen fireflies preparing to fall on them.

The dwarfs spat oaths as they spun back to the hedge and hewed with feverish vigor. Their armor was not the line dwans' full field harness of plate and mail, but the studded gauntlets and iron-banded bracers wrapped in stout worcsvine leather were more than enough to ward off the scraping thorns and the sharp ends of branches. They made quick progress through the hedge, halting only for a moment when they heard a whistle informing them how to adjust their course.

A few hammering heartbeats later, they burst through to the peculiar sight of Torbjorn securing the harness to a pair of tall, long-limbed equines hitched to a wagon. The dwarf commander's unfamiliarity with the arrangement made the task difficult, and the jagged spines that sprang from their brows with which they raked toward the beleaguered dwan made things worse.

"Blasted stabhorns! I'm trying to untangle you!" Torbjorn growled as he narrowly avoided catching a bony spike in the thigh. "No good being faster than a swine if you can't keep from being impaled!"

Both mares—as evidenced by their more elegant and needlelike horns, among other things—reared in indignation.

"No worries, Yer Majesty," Gromic called, shuffling over. "Just have to know how to talk to 'em is all."

"Well, talk fast." Waelon spat. He gave the creatures a wide berth as he boarded the wagon. "We need to get moving now!"

With much firm but gentle shushing, Gromic approached the irritable equines, hands at his sides and shoulders squared. Torbjorn stopped trying to untangle the straps and let the former fordwan have his chance. Having a hundred iron-shod swine bearing down on them chafed his patience, but a hasty failure would be fatal. He had to be patient.

"Though, Shaper help me, not too patient," the commander muttered as he watched Gromic make a low bow to the dangerous beasts of burden. The big dwarf continued to whisper and coo as he held the prostration. Eventually, the fitful mares quieted, and with almost languorous slowness, they dipped their spiked heads in return.

"That should do it," Gromic stated as he straightened. He then approached to stroke their arched necks. "They're sensitive creatures, is all."

Torbjorn could think of other descriptors for the creatures, but he decided he'd settle for rigging them up. If he made it out of this alive, he could share his real thoughts, then never trust his life to the wretched creatures again.

"You been spending too much time with Haeda," Waelon grumbled from the wagon bed as he fitted a specially prepared bolt to his duabuw. "Though I'm not sure even she takes to these elf-besotted, gangly, sharp-faced—"

"Waelon," Torbjorn hissed as he noticed the unicorns twisting their long necks to glare balefully at the dwarf in the wagon. The commander nearly had the situation managed, but the last thing he needed was one or both of the beasts acting up. After the sharp word, Waelon finished his business with the duabuw and hefted it to his shoulder.

"Ready when you are, Commander."

"There," Torbjorn crowed when the harness fell into place. "Come on, Gromic. Playtime's over. We're off!"

Gromic gave each sharp-crowned steed a last caress on its cornsilk-fine mane before bobbing another bow, then scuttling over to clamber aboard the wagon. Torbjorn was on the bench, reins in hand, eyes glittering as he selected a path to the tree line. The enemy vanguard was nearly on top of them, and Waelon's special bolt's load was going to draw their attention.

"Let's hope you're as night-eyed as they say," Torbjorn muttered under his breath before looking over his shoulder. "Let 'er fly, Waelon."

The deep-throated twang of the crossbow sounded an eyeblink before Torbjorn cracked the reins, then the unicorns gave one of their peculiar lyrical cries. Despite their spindly forms, the beasts pulled hard enough to send Waelon flat on the wagon bed as his signal bolt became a silver streak overhead.

Like a shooting star in reverse, the projectile cut an eye-searing path across the night sky. At its zenith, its sparkle matched the stars'. As Torbjorn and company hurtled toward the forest, the impostor star winked for the last time before detonating with a roaring thunderclap and burst of light. The spiny heads of the unicorn mares flew back, and they gave heart-wrenching screams of surprise and fear before redoubling their speed.

Torbjorn didn't steer so much as hold on. The other dwarfs gripped the rail and sideboard with white knuckles as the wagon bounced and juddered across the landscape. The shrill horns of the charging blotferow riders signaled to one another to converge on the site of the signal bolt's launch. The dwarf commander thought he could hear the protesting squeals of the swine and the snarling oaths of their riders as they fought to plow through the hedge.

"Well, we got their attention," Gromic offered, though his face was ghostly as he clung to the seat beside Torbjorn.

"It's not their attention I'm concerned about," Torbjorn shouted over the wagon's rattles and squeaks at every dip and furrow. Fighting an urge to adjust the unicorns' chosen path, the commander peered at the forest. His stomach tightened against his ribs as the seconds bounced by until... Yes! There!

At first, it was barely more than a flicker that might have been blinked away, but then they came like a glimmering wave, silver bolts streaking out from both arms. The sight had Torbjorn ready to throw his head back and roar until a blow as hard as any Okmur Peak-Breaker could dole out struck his heart.

Dwarfs, good stout dwans, were going to die tonight.

"That little tick still hanging on, sister?"

"If the pinching at my sides is any proof," Bella called to

her brother over the thrumming hoofbeats of the unicorns. "He's not going anywhere."

"From the look of things," the shapechanger replied, "we'll have to chisel him off you when we arrive. Isn't that right, little tick?"

Ober might've returned a sharp reply to Hukka's teasing, but he was currently too focused on staying attached to Bella as their steed galloped on. Feeling like a parasite clinging to the wosealf didn't help his attitude, but it was secondary to not being unseated as the riders of Tuvaloth sprang across the ground to encircle the enemy vanguard.

The dwan had no illusions as to what would happen to him if he lost his seat. The slight skinchangers were riding the spritely female unicorns, but around them, the cavalry of the last savageling bastion was astride mighty stallions.

Despite his better judgment, Ober looked to one side and saw sharp, iron-hard hooves, each wider than his face, shredding turf as they galloped. The mares would dance over him disdainfully, but their brutish counterparts would reduce him to pulp in a storm of passing hooves. The thing living beneath his skin might not allow that to be his end, but Ober didn't want to find out. Even if death had eluded him, pain never had.

His hands tightened around the elfess, and she winced and twisted in his grip.

"Easy," Bella called over her shoulder, a hint of a pained yelp in her throat that vanished quickly. "You don't need to worry. I'll not let you fall."

Despite his fear of being trampled, Ober felt a sudden confidence in the elf's words that he understood even if he couldn't explain. She believed it, and that made it so. Not for the first time, the young dwarf marveled at her serenity. It wasn't just different from the hot blood of her people, but it was also unlike his inner turmoil. The wosealf had helped him achieve an equilibrium, a partnership of sorts with the thing that shared his body, which he'd never thought possible when he was first stricken with its presence. The mental and spiritual oneness the elf skinchangers experienced was still far beyond him.

Never was that clearer than in moments like these when the thing inside him, the thunderblood, could sense the coming fight. It was pressing the edges of his body and mind like a swimmer testing the water.

"Not yet," Ober muttered, his will coaxing rather than pressing the thing back into its fitful doze. "You'll get plenty soon."

"What's that?" the elfess asked as a group of yelping puppies swirled ahead. They were closing on the enemy, and it was time to tighten ranks. The riders of Tuvaloth had come out in an open formation, and now the lancers would close ranks as their gleaming spears were tucked in for an impaling charge.

The three skinchangers would also take their positions.

A rider beside them howled, and Bella and Hukka replied. Trying to stay close without crushing the elfess, Ober looked around and saw the elven riders moving closer together. They stopped when they were almost knee to knee, forming a wall of elf and equine flesh ahead of the skinchangers while the riders moved to the flanks and the rear.

Ober got anxious when Bella jerked the reins to one side, but he saw they were only shifting to accommodate the formation of a pocket in the midst of the charging cavalry line.

They were the payload, the poisoned parcel, about to be

delivered into the heart of the enemy vanguard. The lancers, pinching in from either side, were only the method of delivery, though as he watched the spears sink into their battle positions, Ober pitied the dwans they were about to fall upon.

The reminder that those they were about to kill were dwarfs stuck in Ober's mind like barbs. The intellectual hooks were embedded deeper now than the last time they'd been forced to face their own on the battlefield.

"Are you ready?" Bella asked, and Ober felt flesh ripple across her body. The thing inside him perked up, sensing the eagerness of the monster that lay beneath Bella's skin. There was nothing he could do now to convince it to subside again. Dark bristles spread over his arms, and his hands thickened and twisted. He gave a soft grunt when the flesh of his fingers split to accommodate the tips of his claws.

"How close are we?" he managed through teeth that no longer fit in his mouth. That would soon be rectified by a jaw that was less than amenable to speech.

"Nearly there," Hukka reported, close enough now that if he'd wanted to, Ober could have sharpened his claws on both elf and unicorn. After the tick comment, the thought was appealing.

"Hold on," Bella warned, leaning forward over the neck of her steed to whisper to the creature in Elvish.

Ober told himself the plan was simple. He needed to follow it, not just for himself but for the others. However, the thunderblood had different ideas, and it was all he could do to keep the body-twisting, mass-increasing changes from seizing him.

"A little closer," Bella called.

"A little closer," Hukka replied, his spine arching in a way that suggested it might pull itself out of his skin. Up ahead, between the moonlit lance points, Ober could make out the bucking mass of dwarvish cavalry fighting to wheel around or maybe retreat. As much as it hurt his ears to hear their cries and screams of confusion, the thing inside enjoyed his foes' terror.

"A little closer," Bella howled, and it was a true howl, a long, hungry sound that no dwarf, elf, or human mouth could produce. The dwarvish part of him shivered at the sound and watched in horror as the elfess' face stretched into a muzzle. Then the dark lips peeled back from the gleaming teeth, and the young dwarf knew they hungered for dwarvish blood and dwarvish meat. She wanted to rip and tear at dwarvish bodies to savor what lay within.

Welling up within him on a sweeping storm of exultant rage was the same desire.

Just ahead, the elvish lancers sheared through the disrupted dwarvish formation. Spear points bit deep, and hafts flexed and splintered. The sharp-crowned mounts, their jagged blade-like horns armored in brass or silver, had ample opportunity to rip and gouge. Everything was chaos and blood.

Then the wall of riders was gone, and Ober heard someone shout, "*NOW!*" He was already in motion.

As he hurled himself off his mount with a graceless eagerness, his skin split, his weight multiplied, and his frame swelled. When his feet hit the hoof-scored earth, he looked not like a dwarf but like a rolling mountain of muscle and fury. A roar that was part ursine, part tempest blasted from his jaws, and he sprang upon the first dwarf within reach.

Metal buckled and warped, no protection against something so elemental and savage. When that dwan's mount made to defend its slaughtered master's honor, it was put down by a single paw stroke. Bone snapped as the head spun to an impossible angle.

Ober told himself he had to steer the beast. Not dominate it but guide it, but the point at which its joy in slaughter and his dark impulses merged seemed impossible to distinguish. They wanted this, they needed this, and if he was given a choice at this moment, they would never stop.

Claws as long as an elf's hand swept out, sending rider and boar tumbling end over end, blood splattering as they fell. The smell of it filled his snout, and a roar swelled his chest and erupted from his maw.

The primal sound set dwarfs and their mounts screaming and squealing. Those closest to him made futile attempts to shield their ears. A few, either braver than reason or driven mad with fear, made a fumbling charge over the mess of tangled swine and broken dwarfs. Weapons raised and wailing wild cries, they sought to strike the furred mountain moving among them. Their blows descended like hail and proved as effectual as ice hitting a mountain's face. Lances snapped and swords and axes were torn from nerveless hands. Hammers and maces rebounded to send their wielders lurching back.

Then the beast that was and was not Ober showed them what a true storm was.

The first dwarf's helmet inside his jaws, and its hardened steel crumpled like tin. With a sharp twisting shake, the helm and the head inside it went one way while the rest of the body went another. Then a paw ripped the leg of a rider off at the hip and snapped the spine of his mount.

A roar signaled another raking sweep that unmounted three riders. When the bodies landed, it was hard to tell where one mangled form ended and another began. Their mounts, fatally faithful, slammed forward, iron-shod tusks and hooves gouging and ripping. Another bellow tore from the beast's throat, and crushing paws whirled in a gory dance. In the wake of this performance, nothing was left except jutting spars of bone amid a mess of offal.

A heavy blood-streaked head drooling crimson spittle searched for more foes, but the vanguard was in flight. Those who could do so rode and others ran, but all fled. The ursine warrior saw two lupine shapes dart after those retreating. One snared the leg of a dwarf or a blotferow and twisted it free with a wrench of its long muzzle before darting after another. The other bore down upon a rider sporting a dogordwan's crest.

The bear followed the retreating dwarfs. Some looked back and screamed before putting spur to mount or ducking to run faster, while others, seeing the oncoming avalanche of bestial fury, surrendered. Barely slowing, a snap of heavy jaws or a raking claw took them out as the thunderblood rolled on.

Beyond the vanguard, the Sufstan loyalists formed up in orderly squares, their broad shields facing the cardinal directions. Duabuws were hefted to rest on the rails in the shields, but no bolts flew. The ranks waited for the order. Fordwans stalled, unsure of what to do. Death was coming for them, red in tooth and claw, but any salvo from their crossbows would harm the retreating dwarfs as much as the trio of savage horrors ripping their way through the routed dwans.

Those farthest from the skinchangers adjusted their aim toward the wheeling savageling cavalry, but their efforts yielded little fruit. The wosealfs had turned their mounts around and were streaming into the night. None doubted that they would try to take the dwarvish flanks unaware, but stout formes with a spear for every crossbow watched those approaches, and the wild riders of Tuvaloth would pay dearly if they tried to force the issue. The frustration was enough to see veteran dwans grinding their teeth as fordwans swore and stamped. When the first members of the vanguard rebounded off the edges of the squares, this frustration swelled into a groan that ran down the lines as they watched the trio close.

Then, just beyond the oncoming monsters, a battle force appeared that matched their opposite number. The forces of Torbjorn Kinslayer had advanced without torch or lantern, with a thin line of savageling skirmishers moving ghostlike ahead of them. They materialized like an army of phantoms.

The call went out to adjust aim and loose a storm of bolts upon the new arrivals, but those calls were drowned out by the hissing storm of quarrels that descended on the loyalist position. Stout dwarvish shields fended off the worst of it, and the dwarven mail defied much of what got through, but here and there, a dwan staggered back, clutching at a jutting bolt's shaft.

The volley the loyalists unleashed in response left much to be desired. Many formes were uncertain if they were firing at the oncoming beasts, the creeping skirmishers, or the looming line of dwarfs. Most bolts went wide of their mark, and fordwans bellowed conflicting orders as they strained to see or hear what they were to do: hold or advance?

What was their target priority? Did they follow the directions of the first tweldwan to answer or their commander? Where was the tweldwan of the 6th? Where was the Peak-Breaker?

At the center of the line, the thunderblood launched into a forme, flanked by its lightning-quick lupine escorts. As claws and fangs ripped and tore, bolts fell, bouncing off plate and digging into mail, but they found no purchase in the pelts of the skinchangers.

Moments after contact, the central forme bowed and flexed outward, then its formation came apart. The skirmishers ranging ahead of Torbjorn's battle line crept forward to take advantage of the chaos, hurling javelins and axes at the beleaguered loyalists.

The most daring of their number raced forward to hew and gouge the confused dwarfs. Some learned the error of their ways when a magsax took them in the belly at their approach or a bolt skewered their back as they withdrew. Many howling elves danced back from the formes, blades wet with dwarvish blood.

The central formes got mauled before the order came from behind the frontline. Horns blaring and drums pounding, the secondary line pressed forward while the formes on either side of the carnage moved inward. The remaining squares melted into the ranks that were surging into the fight, and their efforts prevented further slaughter.

The thunderblood and his companions ran into a wall of dwarvish steel. The line flexed but held firm even as more dwans were dragged to a savage end. Then, step by shuffling step, they fought beasts off. Empires had been worn down and crushed by the press of a dwarvish line, and for all their fury, the skinchangers couldn't help but give ground, though the loyalists paid for each inch.

It was a small victory, but behind the monsters, the other dwarvish line was approaching. Its dwans were untroubled by the horrors, and none of them were weary. Even with the loyalist volleys, hardly any had been bloodied. Every loyalist dwan who knew his danglers from his duabuw understood this didn't bode well for them.

Then a fresh hammer stroke fell.

A chorus of pipes shrilled on the southward flank as the Kinslayer's blotferow cavalry swung about. Behind them, the lancers of elvish cavalry were massing, and the wall of armored dwarfs on metal-shod pigs was a mobile bulwark. If the charge came, the dwarvish riders would guard the cavalry. Then the swifter savage elves would tear through the heart of the loyalist line.

It was a bad situation for the loyalists, and a call for retreat sounded. Slowly at first, but with mounting speed, the loyalist formes withdrew across the fields in good order. A single voice raged against the withdrawal, but it was swallowed by the jingle of armor as the dwans trotted back. The divisions moved back the way they'd come, as unstoppable as the tide. If they kept cohesion, their losses from the coming charge would be painful but not catastrophic.

The call for the cavalry charge did not come, the moment slipping away like grains of sand in an hourglass. If delayed much longer, the cavalry would be out of position to execute the attack effectively, and the enemy would escape intact, or mostly so.

The front line peeled back, leaving the skinchangers to frolic among the retreating formes. They stalked like Death among the broken, ending the wounded and cowering. Eyes shining in the dark, they found and felled dwan after dwan, whether they fought, fled, or begged. Fangs closed over throats, and with a sharp twist, it was over, and the hungry wraiths sought more victims.

The thunderblood was far less subtle.

Anything that so much as twitched was mauled, and ravaged corpses lay in heaps. Then the beast looked around and found no one else to vent his fury upon. Something that might have been prey moved farther away, but they were only retreating shadows at the edge of his red-shaded field of vision.

With nothing to stoke its gore-fed wrath, the beast paced in fitful circles around the slaughtered before settling on blood-smeared haunches. Jaws stretched wide, but instead of a roar, a yawn emerged from the cavernous throat. The heavy head swept around one last time before sinking low and hinging there, almost in embarrassed disappointment.

Then the monster shrank. Viscera-smeared hanks of fur fell off shriveling sinews as bones popped and twisted inward. When things finally settled, Ober sat upon bloody earth churned to mud.

The young dwan slowly rose to his feet, blinking and stretching. Despite his eyelids threatening to sink lower with each flutter, he managed to take in the ruin around him, then look at the retreating dwans. His view of the field was limited, but there were still a lot of dwans on the loyalist side, yet no one was giving chase.

Scratching his side and stifling another immense yawn, Ober frowned and glanced at the dwans standing at attention a duabuw shot away, none bothering to pursue the withdrawing enemy.

This peculiarity demanded investigation, so he swept his gaze around the battlefield. On the northward edge of the field, he could see a line of dwarvish cavalry with savageling spears behind them. The sight sent a thrill of concern through him, but he reminded himself that the elves were their allies, which was as befuddling now as it had been months before in Tuvaloth.

Continuing his sweep, he saw a knot of his erstwhile-enemies-turned-comrades standing a dozen yards from him.

They were engaged in a lively discussion with two smaller examples of their kind. Eyes widening, he recognized Bella and Hukka. Ober fought off the drag of lethargy on his limbs and moved toward the impromptu gathering.

As he drew closer, Ober could make out the tones of the elves, even if the words escaped him. These wosealfs, who had served as the forward skirmishers for the dwarvish battle line, were not happy. Their musical tongue was lyrical gibberish to the dwan, but he could pick out the notes so sharp they threatened to cut the ear. When he saw them jabbing long fingers at the retreating loyalists, sharp teeth flashing, his sluggish mind pieced together the source of their irritation.

"Bella, Hukka!" the young dwarf called, picking his way around the messy remains between them. He tried not to look at the faces of the dead, but here and there, an accusing corpse stared at him with glassy eyes. The fatigue of the transformation numbed him, but it wouldn't last. He dreaded the broken faces that would find their way into his dreams.

The dwan called to the elves again, and both waved at Ober, though whether it was to beckon him over or prevent him from coming closer was difficult to tell. He'd become familiar enough with the elf siblings to tell that they were tense.

Ober slowed his advance to give them a chance to settle things, and when he reached them, the elves were trading a few last curt words. Some had padded off to scavenge the bodies. Given the looks several gave him, they were leaving in a foul temper. The instinct to be on guard around them rose, but he tamped it down. They were allies now, brothers in arms.

Shaking his head at the thought, Ober stopped before the siblings, who had fixed their eyes on the retreating loyalists.

Neither looked at Ober, and they spared him the discomfort of asking the obvious question.

"They are angry," Bella stated, jerking her pointed chin at the other wosealfs. "They don't understand why we didn't press the advantage."

Hukka made a soft sound at the back of his throat that might have been a growl. "We had them by the throat," the savageling declared, pointing north. The riders were bringing their mounts around. "He could have ended it, yet he stopped and let the enemy quit the field."

"Maybe the commander wanted to limit the number of dwans that died," Ober offered. "Now that they know they can't just roll over us, he might have a better chance of getting them to listen."

The elves regarded Ober soberly, and he had to suppress a shudder.

"Perhaps," Bella said, though her flat tone suggested the answer, even if it was correct, was unsatisfactory. "Though that is little comfort to warriors who faced death with hardly any plunder to show for their efforts."

Ober saw savagelings picking through the mangled remains and wondered if they would find anything worthwhile.

"More than that," Hukka called, drawing Ober's attention back. "Many of them wonder if the prince would have exercised such restraint if he had been facing elves."

Ober didn't dare hazard a guess on that score, even if he thought he knew the answer.

CHAPTER TWO

"They still at it?"

Haeda heaved a sigh as she moved to the tent flap. She'd hardly parted the canvas when sharp elvish voices underscored by dwarvish growls rolled in.

"Sounds like it," the driver declared redundantly, squinting at the blushing sky. "Sun's nearly up, and they're still shouting. Commander's more patient than I am."

In the center of the tent, where a brazier burned low, Gromic nodded at the glowering coals. The other Bad Badgers were strewn about the spacious tent, sitting or reclining in a facsimile of rest. Despite their positions and the suggestion that they should steal some slumber, each strained to make out what spilled in through the flap. All except Ober, who was snoring at the rear of the tent.

When the young dwarf's droning threatened to drown out the argument in the command tent, Tomza gently but firmly rolled him onto one side. Her brother didn't so much as snuffle at the repositioning, though his snores did lose some of their ferocity.

This adjustment came a heartbeat before the pitch of the argument rose. It sounded like someone was pounding on a table, followed a second later by the clatter of metal vessels. Some of the Badgers started, and all looked at Haeda for an explanation.

"Doesn't sound like things are going to be sorted anytime soon," the dwarfess offered, her brows furrowing over her brilliant green eyes.

"Should we head over?" Waelon asked. He hadn't moved, though he was as tense as a coiled spring. "Just in case."

Gromic wagged his head as he poked at the coals with a stick.

Clahdi spoke up from across the tent. "Commander was clear." Her fingers played over her rune-etched axe haft. "We can't be seen in the command tent unless we are called. Having a bunch of non-command staff there would send the wrong message."

The fiery-maned dwarf gave a low rumble and spat into the brazier's glowing depths. When Waelon joined Gromic in staring into the coals, more than one dwarf raised an eyebrow at the silence in place of the expected argument. Tomza and Haeda shared a look, and Gromic coughed as he stole a glance at Waelon, then returned to the coals as he sucked his teeth.

"Clahdi's not wrong," Haeda declared when the uncomfortable silence stretched beyond bearing. "But I'm with Waelon. I'd feel a good deal better about things if one of us was there watching his back."

There were nods around the tent, except from Tomza, who had to adjust Ober again. She looked at the flap as she chewed her lower lip. "I don't like being shoved to the outside either," the young ascedwan agreed and added: "But he's not in any direct danger in there. Those are tweldwans and wosealf war chiefs in there, right? Folk that know what is at stake here."

"Maybe." Gromic shrugged, pausing to shake out a tongue of flame climbing his impromptu poker. "But every one of them would've been happy to put a knife in Torbjorn's back a few months ago."

"Some less than that," Clahdi reminded, leaving off her listless tracing to jerk a thumb over her shoulder. "Those lads from the 3rd haven't been with us more than a ten-day, if that."

Waelon nodded a touch too eagerly, drawing more stares from beneath tented brows. Noticing the scrutiny, he scowled back before growling an explanation. "If anyone was having second thoughts about Torbjorn, those are turning into third and fourth thoughts after he let the loyalists get away.

"And if any of the tweldwans in there were thinking of *fixing* his mistake in judgment, bringing the head of Torbjorn Kinslayer to Ondwan Arseface would go a long way toward easing back into the Holt'Dwan."

None argued the observation. Their gazes swung toward the cacophony in the other tent. For another handful of heartbeats, the Bad Badgers strained to pick out the words and their crisscrossing arguments and counter-claims, not admitting it was of little use. At this point, the storm of voices was an entity unto itself.

Gromic muttered into the strained pause after returning to mind the fire. "I thought we were calling Ashfer 'Assface,' not 'Arseface.' Did I miss that changing?"

"Is that really the most important question right now?" Haeda asked with a laugh. "I mean, 'Arseface' is news to me, but it hardly seems a pressing concern."

The red from the brazier's depths seemed to have climbed

into Gromic's cheeks as he rocked back. He drew in a breath and spluttered it out as he rocked back.

"I don't suppose it's life or death right now," the stout dwarf replied. "But it helps to know what we're talkin' about. What if, since we're now callin' Ashfer 'Arseface,' you take to callin' someone else 'Assface' since the name's freed up? I don't want to be confused about which Assface we're talkin' about, especially in a serious situation."

Waelon barked a laugh, which drew a bemused look from Gromic and a scowl from Haeda.

"What's so funny?" Tomza asked, looking up from giving Ober another shove to try to quiet him.

"I'm just trying to think of what sort of *serious* situation knowing which Assface Haeda's talking about might apply in," Waelon offered, the statement becoming a question as Clahdi leveled a flat-eyed stare in his direction. The former rangers regarded each other for a moment, then Waelon blinked and shifted around.

"I'm just asking," he muttered, fixing his eyes on the fire after throwing a glare at Gromic. "Just sounds stupid to me, is all."

The broad dwarf frowned, either ignorant of or unmoved by the glare as he considered the question.

"Well," he said after a moment, "what if suddenly one of you runs up and tells me to get ready to put a bolt between Assface's eyes? Then around the corner comes Ondwan Ashfer and some grem maggot who has a donkey-ish face. Which Assface am I supposed to shoot?"

Waelon opened his mouth, then shut it with enough force to make his teeth click. Tomza looked at the two brawny dwarfs incredulously.

"Let's be honest," she began. "That's a pretty contrived scena—"

"No," the red-bearded dwarf interjected, and a thoughtful scowl settled over his face. "I think suet-seat has a point."

A sharp cry, perhaps of pain, came from beyond the tent, and further discussion of the point ended. The dwarfs, sans the snoring Ober, scrambled to join Haeda at the canvas portal. Then the Bad Badgers got to see a dwarf fly firsthand.

The flight was short, but given the stout physique of the dwarf and the weight of the battle armor he wore, it was a feat. The event's termination was less grandiose; the unlikely projectile met the earth with a dull thud. For one anxious second, the grounded dwarf lay motionless, no breath stirring the bulky frame. Then, with a wheeze, he rolled onto one side.

Haeda chortled, eyes glittering. "Looks like Torbjorn's getting it sorted." Once he pitched onto his side, all in the tent could see the runes scored into the dwarf's cheek. An airborne dwarf was rare enough, but a flying tweldwan was a sight of near-mythic proportions.

"Sounds like he's not done yet," Gromic stated with a nod at the command tent. Sections of the canvas were bulging and rustling, and there was another sound of a shocked cry. This one was higher and longer, more of a keen.

An eyeblink later, something came bouncing and rolling out of the tent and careened past the flattened dwarf. What had appeared to be a tangle of limbs resolved into the tall form of a bare-chested wosealf. His glittering ornaments and bangles were askew, pale skin and garments smudged from his course to where he now lay. Despite that, it was clear that he was adorned as only a war chief among his people would be.

Sprawled on his back, the elf's lean chest rose and fell

rapidly as he stared at the sky. The rosy hues were giving way to pale blues, and the celestial palette was reflected in the savageling's wide eyes.

Dwarf and elf lay within arm's length of each other, neither moving except to keep their breath steaming in the air, which had not yet been warmed by the new day. Had the means of their arrival at their present location not been known, the Bad Badgers might have thought the pair were weary brothers in arms who'd sank down to rest after a long march.

"Oh, no, you don't," thundered a voice that was strong if hoarse. "You get up and settle this business now."

The Bad Badgers' commander stomped out of the other tent. Every dark whisker bristled with irritation as he made for the stricken pair. Behind him was a procession of frowning dwarfs and inscrutable wosealfs, some whispering but none letting their eyes stray from the scene.

Torbjorn stopped before the flattened tweldwan, boot tapping, then bent and seized the dwarf by the cuirass. The dwan started to scramble to his feet, but Torbjorn was hauling faster than he could push. The result was the dwarf's feet scratching and scrabbling on the earth before Torbjorn gave him a hard shake.

"On your feet or shame your ancestors, dwan!" Torbjorn barked in a parade-ground thunder. "You started this, so you better be ready to finish it."

The dwarf managed to find his feet just before Torbjorn released him, and the Bad Badgers recognized him.

"Borttr Brakson of Clan Orref," Clahdi murmured. "The 5th."

"And you!" Torbjorn snarled, advancing on the prostrate elf. "Same goes for you, longshanks."

The wosealf blinked rapidly. Then his sharp features reacted to the sight of the oncoming dwarf. With a litheness and speed that were at odds with being flat on his back, the savageling got to his feet.

He looked down his nose at the dwarf who marched up to him but was not quite able to leverage his height. When Torbjorn matched that stare, the elf froze. Then, with the barest twitch, the elf's eyes darted to the congregation from the command tent that watched him without comment.

"On your own, blade ear," Waelon rumbled. "Nothing between you and a dwarf's boot in your scrawny arse, you filthy—"

"Shut it," Haeda scolded, jabbing an elbow behind her. "Torbjorn's talking."

Torbjorn had been silent as he matched the wosealf's stare, but now he pivoted one foot to face both the elf and the unsteady dwarf. "Good." Torbjorn snorted, alternating between glaring at each. "Now that we're out here in front of the entire camp, you two can make good on your words in *my* command tent."

To illustrate the point, Torbjorn pointed at the canvas pavilion in question. As he did so, the Bad Badgers noticed the way both troublemakers flinched.

"Has 'em shaking in their boots," Clahdi muttered, her admiration obvious. "I know what that's like."

The other Bad Badgers nodded solemnly but made no comments as they watched the drama unfold.

"You can start on each other, or you can come straight to me," the shaggy-headed dwarf growled, biting off each word. "Just know that however this shakes out, you are going to have me to contend with at some point, so let's just get it over with. I've got an army to command."

It seemed for all the world as though the war chief and the tweldwan weren't aware of each other. Their eyes were fixed on Torbjorn, though whether their gazes reflected hate, fear, or confusion was hard to tell. Fingers curled and uncurled and weight shifted, but they stayed put, breath dancing in white plumes.

"No? *No?*" the commander of the Bad Badgers asked, looking from one to the other and back with his head cocked. "You weren't so quiet before when you were taking turns questioning me and threatening each other. You have a change of heart? I have you picking dirt out of your teeth, and you don't want to at least take a swing at me?"

The elf and the dwarf exchanged looks before staring at Torbjorn, disbelief stamped on their faces. The war chief's long fingers curled. The tweldwan's fists clenched into trembling balls.

"You want to take turns, is that it?" Torbjorn asked, leaning in the elf's direction, then shifting to lean toward the dwarf. "Come on, then. Someone's got to go first. Don't be sh—"

With the fluid quickness of his kind, the elf suddenly had a dagger in his hand and sent it plunging toward Torbjorn's throat. The audience and the Bad Badgers drew a collective breath as the bronze blade flashed in the dawn's light but had time for naught else.

There was a loud rasp and a cry of pain, and every witness realized that Torbjorn had managed to interpose his wooden left hand. The magically strong fingers had closed around the dagger and the hand holding it and bent the blade sharply. The fingers of the hand holding the dagger had fared little better than the blade.

"Not your best idea, lad," Torbjorn mused as his grip tightened. The elf sank to his knees. "You try to turn this into *that* kind of a fight, and you won't like how it turns out."

To illustrate the point, Torbjorn's grip tightened, and the *twang* of metal snapping was accompanied by a chorus of wet pops. The elf screamed and clawed at Torbjorn's peculiar limb with his free hand, which resulted in split and bleeding nails.

"Don't play the game if you can't pay the price," Torbjorn warned before releasing the war chief's hand with a shove. A shard of blade tumbled to the earth and the elf fell, all grace gone as he clutched his mangled hand.

"I'll be paying that blade ear a visit soon," Waelon promised.

Gromic seemed ready to second the idea, but Tomza retorted in a sharp whisper, "And undo everything Torbjorn's doing? Look at those war chiefs. They didn't just see one of their hotheads humbled. They also saw him spared. You can see that they understand that. Look at their faces."

Waelon made a sound that suggested he'd rather press his face to a grinding wheel than look at the wosealfs, but the rest obliged. Many of the elves were whispering among themselves, but the ice had gone out of the stares. Some even nodded.

"Communicating across cultural barriers," Gromic announced proudly, beaming at his leader. "Commander's exercising royal diplomacy here."

Soft chuckles arose from the Bad Badgers, though they shielded them behind their hands to keep from drawing the eyes of the command crowd. They quieted when Torbjorn turned from the squirming elf to the tweldwan of the 5th.

"What'll it be, Brottr? Eh? Here is your chance to show that the son of Brak doesn't speak idly."

The tweldwan's mouth twitched beneath his long

mustache, clenched fists vibrating against his sides. The sturdy dwarf was a few fingers shorter than Torbjorn, and there was little doubt that those knuckles would deliver bruising impacts. However, the Bad Badgers might as well have been watching a piglet square off with a boar.

"Come on, Tweldwan. Get on with it," Torbjorn growled in Brottr's face. "I don't have all day to wait for you to make up your mind, seeing as I've got an army to lead."

Brottr continued to stand voiceless before Torbjorn. As he did, his mouth twisted, and his hands trembled.

"Is he havin' a fit?" Clahdi asked. "Looks like he is."

Gromic and Waelon shook their heads.

"Dwan's trying to weigh which would be worse," Haeda answered when the younger dwarfess looked at the company for an explanation. "The shame of staying still and quiet or the embarrassment and pain of Torbjorn stomping him flat."

"Torbjorn needs to be careful," Tomza muttered, mostly to herself. "He may have earned the respect of the savagelings, but I'm not sure the tweldwan learned the lesson."

"He can't be weak, though," Clahdi countered, looking confused. "If they think he can be pushed around, things are going to fall apart."

"Maybe," Gromic shrugged, studying the dwarvish officers. "But remember, they all joined because they wanted to or they feared the mutiny of their dwans if they didn't. Old rules of command don't quite apply. It's all personal now."

Waelon nodded and jerked his chin at the watching tweldwans. "Not one of them watching likes the idea of being in Brottr's boots, and there's not a one that isn't thinking about standing in his place."

"Don't push it, Torbjorn," Haeda whispered so softly that

those beside her could barely hear her. "Shaper be merciful and let him not push it."

Whether it was the plan or he was moved by the driver's quiet prayer, Torbjorn took a step back. After a few moments of eyeing Brottr, he heaved a low sigh.

"Fair enough," he grumbled, turning away from the tweldwan to address the crowd from the command tent. "I'm not going to waste any more time on this. What's done is done, and we've got more important things to do than stand about."

Torbjorn looked at Brottr again as though checking to see if the dwarf had changed his mind before stepping away to address the crowd.

"You are to go back and get ready to move. We can hope that Okmur's forces scrambled back into friendlier territory to keep us from outmaneuvering them again, so we need to move and not give him time to dig in. I know no one likes taking to the field so soon after an engagement, but the more distance Okmur puts between us, the more chance for mischief. Get what rest you can and be ready to strike camp as soon as the scouts come back. Understood?"

The dwarfs muttered affirmatives and the elves nodded, which seemed to satisfy Torbjorn.

"All right, then," he growled, his tone as much as his words signaling the conclusion of the gathering. "Get to it."

The tweldwans and their subordinates filed toward their divisions, including a stiff-limbed Tweldwan Brottr. The wosealfs dispersed in an order and direction only they understood. Torbjorn watched them all depart. Finally, a small knot of war chiefs moved to the side of their stricken compatriot.

The Bad Badgers watched as their commander stepped toward a tall, spindly chieftain who seemed to be the leader of the gang. The elf had an impressive collection of bleached braids spilling over his shoulders, laced with bone ornaments that rattled as he nodded at the dwarf. Torbjorn returned the nod, then gestured at the wosealf still clutching his mangled hand on the ground.

"If the lad's hand needs tending, let me know, though I somehow doubt it," the shaggy dwarf stated, his voice weary. "Just remember, there's to be no magic inside the camp."

The elf said something in his fierce, melodious tongue. Torbjorn seemed to understand the intent as much as the language.

"Aye, you're welcome." The dwarf stepped away after a last look at the felled elf. The wosealfs saw to their business as Torbjorn trudged back toward the Bad Badgers' tent, head bowed. His steps were slow and his gaze was fixed on the ground, so he didn't see the other dwarfs clambering away to hide that they'd been watching their commander.

Torbjorn entered the tent to a taut and sheepish silence. Gromic looked up from where he sat before the brazier. Waelon fiddled with a whetstone without honing his axe. Clahdi was probing a hole in her ranger cloak, and Haeda was rummaging through her pack. Tomza was the only one moving with a purpose, which was to pummel her brother onto his other side so his droning snores didn't get on her last nerve.

"You all got a show just now, didn't you?" Torbjorn asked as he stepped over to his pallet. He'd been offered proper accommodations more than once, but he had refused to bed down anywhere except amid the Bad Badgers.

"What are you talking about, Yer Majesty?" Gromic asked with a touch too much false bemusement.

"Don't start that nonsense. I saw you lot tittering over

here." Torbjorn groaned as he sank down on the pallet. "And can we please remember the rule?"

Gromic's cheeks blossomed red over his yellow beard as he shifted uncomfortably. Around the tent, the Bad Badgers muttered abuse at Gromic for giving the game up.

Torbjorn tugged at his bootlaces.

"No 'Yer Majesty' inside the tent. Yes, sir," Gromic recited, then cleared his throat and raised his voice to address the whole tent. "But I'm sure I speak for everyone here when I say you handled that matter with Brottr and that savageling in a truly princely fashion."

Torbjorn waved off the ensuing grunts of affirmation and positive statements. "Very kind of you all," he began and yanked one boot off, then paused to squint across the tent. "But did any of you hear what the actual issue was?"

There was a noticeable pause before Haeda confessed on behalf of the group. "We heard shouting, and we figured it was about you letting the loyalists retreat. Though about the war chief and Brottr also having issues with each other, we've got no idea."

Torbjorn nodded, his suspicions confirmed.

"We need to stop calling them loyalists," Clahdi put in, tossing her cloak over her shoulder with a huff. "We are loyal too, just to something else. Calling them 'the loyalists' makes it sound like…well, the opposite of it."

"It makes us sound like traitors," Tomza offered after the former ranger's voice trailed off. "That's the worst thing a dwarf could be."

The senior Badgers nodded grimly, their eyes distant and hard.

"Liars," Haeda added.

Gromic snorted. "Oathbreakers."

"Scum," Waelon declared.

Clahdi's face paled, and her jaw dropped as she looked around the tent. Every other dwarf wore a hard smile that defied their somber words. Even Ober's sleep-slackened face bore the ghost of a grin. Then he snored, and Tomza shoved him to one side with her boot.

Torbjorn cocked his head and eyed Clahdi, his tone gentle in the face of her confusion. "We learned a long time ago that what others call us has little to do with who we are, lass. Every dwarf in here has been called those things and worse, though they're the bravest and best the Holt'Dwan has ever seen. We are what we do, not what others call us."

The dwarfess frowned as she sank down on her palette and took up her long-hafted axe. As she touched the runes etched on it, she nodded and even managed to smile.

Torbjorn watched her for a moment, concern wrinkling his face, then decided to interpret the smile as acceptance. The lass had been through a great deal in the last few months, and he worried about what was happening beneath the surface, but his concern wasn't enough to circumvent the weariness stealing over him.

He almost surrendered, but he felt the press of his belt and magsax and the weight of the brigandine he'd worn to the meeting. He'd slept in less comfortable attire, but there was no reason to do so now since he needed to get quality rest if they were going to strike camp after the scouts came back with word of Okmur's movements. Shedding armor and belt might take minutes, but getting proper rest would be welcome, even if it was just for a few hours.

Stifling another groan, Torbjorn climbed to his feet and unbuckled the belt, his vision blurring at the corners. His fatigue made his movements clumsy, and he hadn't completed the effort before Gromic was at his side. The broad dwarf muttered something obnoxiously relevant that Torbjorn didn't have the energy to refute, and then the blade-bearing belt was free.

Torbjorn muttered his thanks and tugged at his armor. Before he could make serious inroads, Gromic and Waelon stepped in. The brigandine was unclasped and removed with gentle words of admonishment regarding trying to help.

Then Torbjorn sank down. Haeda and Tomza smiled beatifically as they guided his descent to the embrace of his pallet. "Make sure to wake me," Torbjorn murmured, his words almost inaudible. "Need to be ready."

When he stretched out, his back gave several pops that made dazzling lights flare in his eyes. The commander could feel every inch of their fast march across the Vale to where they now camped. Time had been against them in more ways than one, and he'd had to keep moving up and down along the advancing forces to ensure they remained cohesive. Now he had to heed all the warnings his people had given him that he would exhaust himself.

Torbjorn felt his companions' thoughts, cares, and fears, but they were all insubstantial compared to the warm tide washing over him. He was borne away, and nothing else could gain purchase.

Finally, he slept under the compassionate guard of his Bad Badgers.

CHAPTER THREE

"You've got to be joking!"

The sharp words intruded upon Torbjorn's consciousness as he lay there, desperately willing himself to return to sleep. He'd been ensconced in the immeasurable gift of dreamless sleep, only to be dragged back to consciousness. A groan escaped his lips, but then a firm hand took hold of his shoulder and gave it a hard shake. His limbs were slow to respond, as heavy and clumsy as though they were made of lead.

"Easy now," a familiar voice called before Torbjorn's turgid swing impacted something solid. "Sir, you need to wake up."

The dwarf commander wanted to tell whoever was talking what they could do with that idea, but his throat was dry, and his tongue wouldn't cooperate. What came out was a thick cough, then he made another effort to swing his arm.

His hand was captured, and he was hauled upward. Torbjorn swung the other hand, but that only resulted in him flailing and lurching to one side. His knuckles smashed into uncompromising metal, and he cursed. Whoever had pulled him up seized the other hand and kept him from falling over.

"Keep him up, and let's get his armor on," a voice as familiar as the first one instructed. "And someone should mix liquor with cold water."

"Tub o' guts always has something," another familiar voice put in. "Keeps it tucked in *there*."

"I'm all out," the first voice declared, and the commander saw that Gromic was holding him up on one side. "Besides, why would I keep my stash next to my danglers?"

"Keeping it in the shade of your gut keeps it cool." The second voice was Waelon's. He was propping Torbjorn up on the other side. "That, and if you keep it down there, no one'll find it by accident."

Gromic chuckled, and the third person cut in, her voice sharp and imperious. Torbjorn blearily peered into Haeda's face. The dwarfess was holding the hauberk that was the first layer of his full battle harness. She had the fitted plates ready at her feet.

"The brigandine," Torbjorn muttered, but Haeda dragged the mail over his head. Before he could protest, Gromic and Waelon slid his arms into their respective positions.

"Not an option, I'm afraid," the driver declared as she finished situating the mail and set to lacing the open neck. "You've got to look presentable for the troops if nothing else."

Torbjorn frowned, then winced as Haeda hauled on the leather cords. His head wasn't clearing quickly, but little bit by little, he was piecing things together. His eyes swung toward the tent's door, and he saw sunshine through the open flap.

"Did I sleep through the whole day?" he asked, afraid to process what this would mean for his army. He was embarrassed, but then anger stole over him. An entire day spent in slumber. Hadn't any of them remembered what he'd said? Had the scouts decided not to give their reports, or worse, had they made their reports to someone else? A tweldwan perhaps, in a crude attempt to curry favor or undermine him?

Torbjorn saw that the other Badgers were gone, even Ober.

"How long have we been camped?" Torbjorn asked with more force in his voice. "Why was I allowed to sleep so long?"

Haeda was attempting to fit his breastplate over his head. She gave him a sharp look as he moved to get a better look outside.

"Would one of you please help me?" she snapped. "I think the commander can stand on his own now, so make yourselves useful."

Gromic and Waelon released their grip on Torbjorn with such speed that he nearly lost his balance. Luckily, his wrath sharpened his mind and body.

Torbjorn righted himself and looked Haeda in the eye as the breastplate was secured. "Haeda. Tell me what is going on. Did the scouts ever come back?"

Haeda swore as a clasp pinched a finger, and she left Gromic and Waelon to see to the rest.

"The scouts came back, but you're confused, Torbjorn. You didn't sleep the whole day. You were barely asleep for an hour before the scouts scrambled back. Seems Okmur's lot hardly made it a mile down the road with their tails between their legs before they turned right back around and marched back, or at least most of them. From what the scouts reported, a goodly number of the 11th and what's left of the 9th took to the road. The rest are heading back for us."

Torbjorn blinked. "Okmur divided his force and then

decided to charge us," the dwarf muttered, shaking his shaggy head. "That makes no sense."

"Maybe he didn't have a choice about the split," Waelon suggested after tightening a strap beyond what Torbjorn thought was necessary. "After the mauling Ober gave those prissy porkers from the 9th, they might've just buggered off, and the 11th might've been sent to make sure the pig-bummed dandies got where they needed to be without being robbed blind by bandits."

Torbjorn was still having trouble understanding that he had not had a full night's sleep. It explained his lack of mental acuity.

"Sounds fanciful," Gromic retorted as he motioned for the next piece of armor. "But I don't see what else explains it. Maybe it's just wishful thinking, but I expect it's all to do with that bully's pride. Can't stand losing to the likes of—"

"*SHUT UP!* Both of you!"

Gromic and Waelon both ducked and focused on outfitting their commander.

"Haeda," Torbjorn began after a long breath. "You're telling me that Okmur's forces, or most of them, are marching toward us right now."

"Yes, sir." Haeda nodded, shoulders squared.

"Do the elves and divisions know what is happening?"

"If they don't, it's not for lack of us sending runners and telling them to get ready."

Torbjorn nodded and took a deep breath. Then he took another.

"All right, good work." He swept a glance over his war harness. "We played tricks on him before, but we've got the advantage of numbers now. He's going to have to commit his dwans to keep us from pulling the same things again."

"We going to finish the fight this time?" Waelon asked, earning a sharp look from Haeda and a hard shove from Gromic. "What? It's a fair question?"

Torbjorn nodded, trying not to remember the bodies that littered the field after their last clash. War was an ugly business at the best of times, but waging it against his own people was sucking the life out of him. He knew the fatigue he felt was only about his body in part, and he was not sure it was the major part.

"If Okmur is bloody-minded enough to turn right back around after the chance we gave him," Torbjorn's words got heavier with each syllable, "we have no choice."

Gromic patted Torbjorn's shoulder to signal that his body armor was in place and to hold still so that the helmet could be seated. Torbjorn saw Haeda hand the helmet to Gromic, and he eyed the alterations the 2nd Division's schildwan had ordered. A series of sturdy spines worked in dwarvish steel rose in a rough fence around the brow of the helm, each one of the seven sacred metals. It was a simple adjustment that made the helm a crown, with more skill displayed in the sturdiness of the spikes and the seamless lamination than in the quantity of material.

But if that was the case, why did it feel so heavy when the helmet/crown was settled on his head?

"Awaiting your orders, Your Majesty," Gromic intoned as he stepped away with a bowed head. Haeda and Waelon bowed their heads as well.

He almost angrily reminded the stout dwarf about the rule, but he couldn't bring himself to do it. "All right then," Torbjorn muttered. "Let's get this over with."

"That's odd, isn't it?" Mordah Jorridottr of Clan Febir, the fordwan of the 2nd Division, Third Forme, pointed at the advancing battle line, or more accurately, the lack thereof. In place of the disciplined ranks of the dwarvish legions was a wall of bodies.

Torbjorn squinted from his vantage point on the rocky hillock he'd set up on with his command staff, which was mostly Mordah, a handful of runners, and a small group of ascedwans trained in signals and direction. As he watched the loyalists advance, he could make out a semblance of order, with formes' banners jutting up here and there to signify the different groups.

"Doesn't look like they're making room for maneuvering," Mordah observed, her brow furrowing. "And if my eyes are working, I don't see them upping shields to receive a volley."

Torbjorn had to agree that it looked like the mass of dwans was coming forward without taking even the barest precautions. As the lines drew closer, he saw cavalry forces trudging at the back of the formation. "Trudging" was the word for it since each rider was on his own two feet, leading his blotferow forward.

"Dwans marching without order," Torbjorn muttered, part of his mind telling him he must still be asleep. "And cavalry dwarfs walking. What in Erduna's leaky dugs is going on?"

From various seams in the earth below came a series of blinking flashes—sunlight on bared steel.

"Forward ranger positions requesting direction," the dwarfess stated after a nod from one of the ascedwans. "Do we break up their advance with sniping bolts, Your Majesty?"

The question didn't demand an answer. Command structure was not being observed. Mordah's title was fordwan, yet she had acted as lardwan and vindwan in equal parts during the past few battles. The answer was simple; the rangers should start shooting. They would have their pick of targets, and with no shielding, those shots would be telling.

It would either throw oncoming dwarfs into confusion as they tried to protect themselves, or they'd trample their dead and charge their attackers. With the latter option, they'd have trouble doing significant harm to the rangers before the forward line of Torbjorn's divisions unleashed a hail of bolts. If that was the case, Okmur's forces would die quickly, and he'd have a rout on his hands, not a retreat.

"What are you playing at, Peak-Breaker?" Torbjorn growled, irritation nibbling at his mind. Okmur was proud, rash, and even volatile, but he wasn't stupid, no matter how badly he'd been embarrassed last night. The tweldwan would have learned from their previous encounter and thus would know that such a reckless ploy, if you could call it that, would be tantamount to suicide.

"Your Majesty," Mordah prompted, her voice unhurried while also being insistent. "The rangers require your direction."

Torbjorn opened his mouth to issue a command but spied something strange near the center of the oncoming mass. A handful of dwarfs was moving, or staggering, ahead of a larger group. The larger group formed a cup around the rear and sides of the smaller group. This was extraordinary since it was the closest to an actual formation the group had, but it also seemed like the larger group was herding the smaller.

It was hard to make out details from this distance, but Torbjorn couldn't help but notice that one of the people in the smaller group was much taller and had broader shoulders. As Torbjorn watched, the tall dwarf lurched, clearly struggling not to limp across the fallow fields.

"Have them withdraw to the flanks," he ordered almost before he'd organized his thoughts.

"Majesty?" the fordwan asked as Torbjorn moved to the edge of the hill to peer at the oncoming assembly.

"Signal the rangers not to shoot and move to the far flanks," he clarified. "Have them reposition so they can watch for anything trying to sneak along the rear or edge of their formation. I don't want any surprises, though I don't expect any."

"Y-yes, Your Majesty," Mordah replied and relayed the commands to her staff.

Torbjorn's voice rose again as he clambered off the hill. "Tell the line to hold their bolts as well," he called over one shoulder. "No one launches a shot without being fired upon. Is that understood?"

"Yes, Your Majesty," the fordwan shouted, torn between following and relaying the instructions. "Where are you going?"

He was heading for the base of the hill where the Bad Badgers waited, the closest thing he had to an honor guard. The company was leaning against the wagon, scowling at the disorganized enemy advance nearly as hard as Torbjorn had. At the sight of their commander advancing toward them, they straightened and saluted.

He didn't slow down to return the salute. "Get me to the front," Torbjorn commanded, his tone absolute.

From atop the craggy hill, Mordah repeated, "Majesty, where are you *going*?"

Torbjorn mounted the wagon, which started moving before most of the Bad Badgers had put both boots on the wood.

"With any luck," he shouted back, "I'm going to go accept a surrender."

"Well, if they had to wake me up, at least they brought me gifts."

Despite his fatigue, Torbjorn smiled at what he saw.

Okmur Peak-Breaker, amid a collection of far smaller dwarfs, stood panting and wheezing from their forced march across the field to stand between the would-be loyalists and Torbjorn's army. Okmur had gotten the worst of it, given a shoddily bandaged foot that hurt with every step the big dwarf took. Torbjorn felt a tug of sympathy and a smaller tug of guilt since he'd put the bolt through Okmur's foot to conclude the parley the night before. He had told himself it was to protect him and the lads from pursuit, but Torbjorn knew it had really been about putting the screws to a tweldwan who was willing to put an axe in his skull under a banner of truce.

Not that Torbjorn hadn't done far worse while serving in the Shabr'Dwan, but weren't "true" officers supposed to be better than that? Wasn't that why they'd cursed him and his Bad Badgers and treated them worse than they'd treated grem slaves? Hadn't it been implied that members of the Holt'Dwan were right to treat them with disdain since they would never act in such dishonorable and duplicitous ways?

His indignity was in danger of being poured out then and there, but Torbjorn forced himself to take a steadying breath. This looked like a mass revolt among the loyalist ranks, but there was still much to be concerned about, not least of which was how the leaders of his divisions saw him handle this.

As he looked at the harried and hobbled tweldwans and command staff, he imagined what it might feel like for them. If he was thinking this, so might others.

"Torbjorn Hralson of Clan Cyniburg," someone shouted from the ranks of the former loyalists. "We present these, your enemies, as tribute."

Mutters and whispers blossomed through the ranks behind Torbjorn and his Badgers. He'd been right, but the declaration had a weight Torbjorn couldn't deny. These dwans were the last serious threat in the valley, and if they joined Torbjorn…

The commander tried to keep his mind from accepting the dizzying potential. He stepped forward, and Gromic and Waelon twitched due to his proximity to so many potential assassins.

"I hope you all understand what this means," Torbjorn began, meeting the eyes of the dwarfs beyond the panting and shuddering wretches before him. "Do you really understand what you are doing?"

There were more murmurs from his dwans, but Torbjorn let them wash over him. He doubted this was the sort of welcome many of his people wanted him to offer, even though he had told them this was his intention not long ago.

I should write it down, he thought, smiling. *But I'd better pay attention right now, or I might not get to give a speech like this again.*

No answer came from the mass of disenfranchised dwarfs. They watched him with flat expressions but were clearly confused.

"I'm asking because I want to make sure you understand," Torbjorn boomed. "I won't have any dwan coming to me some dark, bloody day to tell me I promised him ease or comfort, living off the fat of the land as a cadre of petty tyrants."

The confusion showed on their brows as the dwarfs behind the disgraced tweldwans frowned.

"All of you have forsaken your bonds to your ondwan, to the Holt'Dwan, to your emperor, and to your very blood!" The words rang like a hammer on an anvil, each strike harder than the last. "You are deserters! Traitors! Oathbreakers!"

Torbjorn paused to let the words sink in, and in that pause, he felt a presence in his awareness. He looked around and found Okmur's eyes blazing hatred at him. Torbjorn felt a sudden urge to step back, as though he expected the hulking dwarf to charge across the intervening ground in the blink of an eye.

Not with that foot, he thought, but the realization brought him no satisfaction.

The dwarfs beyond the stricken tweldwans muttered and exchanged anxious, angry looks. The pot would boil over if he didn't act soon.

"That's what they are going to say in Greyshelf," Torbjorn shouted, adding heat to his voice to get their attention. "Then the news will get to Heimgrud, then to Torvgrud, and before long, it will echo through until your names are cursed on Mount Smarthdun itself."

Torbjorn always hated the transformation that happened on the faces—no, the eyes, always the eyes—of every dwarf staring at him.

Worse before it gets better, Torbjorn reminded himself, but it felt like a hollow promise.

"Your fathers will come forward with shaking hands to have your names stricken as your mothers weep," he continued, his voice thick. "Your family members, if you have one, will bow their heads, and they will foreswear you now and forever, and generations from now, not one of your line will hear of you. You will be a ghost without a name. A shade denied the eternal rest of the stone that cannot welcome those without a people."

Torbjorn met those eyes again—hard eyes glittering with unshed tears.

"All of this and worse is what awaits you, and nothing can undo it," he declared, his arms sweeping out as though to cast a net of damnation over them. "Even if we let you fall on us and take our heads to Ondwan Ashfer, it will not change this. There is no escaping this fate, this doom."

One...two...three... Torbjorn counted, his heart thundering in time with the tally.

"Unless..." he began, his voice gentle despite the volume he projected, "unless we win."

The dwans leaned in. He saw the desperation in their stares and heard the rasping in their breathing as air was sucked through clenched throats. The rush of the powerful moment was almost matched by the disgust that came over him.

It shouldn't be like this, playing on honest dwans' emotions. That wouldn't stop him, but it gripped his stomach each time.

"I don't know what you were told about what the Kinslayer's Traitors were up to, but let me make this clear. I didn't want to start this rebellion, but that choice was taken from me by your masters when they declared that I and those with me had to die for no reason other than that I'd served well and faithfully.

"That was when I realized oaths should not silence and enslave. We pledge our loyalty in the belief that those we pledge to are worthy of it. What good is talk of oaths if they do not bind them to us as we are bound to them? Why do we risk so much for the likes of Ondwan Ashfer, who only offers us more death?"

Torbjorn straightened and stood tall. He usually despised preening, but in this case, the effort would be well-rewarded. He felt them change around him. He'd offered a promise, so he had to look like someone who could make good on it.

"That was when I decided...no, that was when I *knew* that whether through the Shaper's will, the twist of the Wyrd, or pure happenstance, I had a chance to change things for the better. I had the opportunity, the training, the bloodline, and everything else to be he who has been denied us for so long.

"I've lived my whole life as though I wasn't the king's son in the hope that by doing so, I would be worthy. It's only now that I see how incredibly stupid and wasteful that was. I've squandered the time gift given me, but no more. Here in this valley we've all fought and bled for, I came to understand that I've insulted all of you by not learning the lesson until now."

Torbjorn saw heads nodding—no small thing—but more than that, he saw their eyes. The anxiety, the anger, and the fear were fading, and with their departure came something incendiary: hope.

"I'm not promising you anything different from what you've faced so far. There will be more battles, more dying, and more suffering, but as we face those things together, I will strive to be worthy of you. I will listen to you, and I will suffer with you.

"I will see you fed and equipped. You've honored me with your trust and choice, and I will honor you by leading you as best I can until we've wrought change in the Holt'Dwan and those who sent us to die here in the valley are faced with the consequences of their actions. They will *pay*!"

A cheer, soft at first, swelled and was joined by others. It got stronger and deeper with each voice that joined. Within a heartbeat, it was raucous. Within two, it was a deafening roar, and within three, Torbjorn was rocked back on his heels by its force.

Again he felt a presence, and again he turned to find Okmur's eyes boring into him. Torbjorn stared back, refusing to surrender. The moment stretched on as the Peak-Breaker tried to will his wrath into Torbjorn. Torbjorn just stared back with the ghost of a smile on his lips.

In time, maybe he'll learn. Maybe once he sees—

"Make them pay!"

The cheer had become a chant. Only now did Torbjorn hear it, and its significance was lost on him.

Then the front rank of dwans rushed forward, magsaxes drawn, to seize their ousted leaders by their throats and beards.

"MAKE THEM PAY!"

CHAPTER FOUR

"Hold him down!"

With a bellow like a wounded aurochs', one dwarf hurtled back while a second staggered and fell on his buttocks. Tomza would have sworn at the display, but she was too busy trying to throw together a potent combination of herbs and fungi. Her deft hands plucked sprigs as she watched the situation with a critical eye.

There were still two dwans with pale faces in the fray. Behind them, the two dislodged dwarfs were slow in getting to their feet and even slower in moving back to the task. Tomza wasn't sure that any of the attending dwans would have the heart, much less the strength, for the job at hand. If she wanted to keep things from spiraling out of control, she was going to need more help.

"Gromic!" she shouted. Her voice cut through the commotion outside the infirmity tent. "Waelon!"

She heard their grunts a heartbeat before the pair ducked through the entrance, and two heartbeats before her instincts proved prescient. With another roar of pain, Okmur Peak-

Breaker rose from the operating table, his body smeared red with ugly lines, forming a web.

The two remaining dwarfs skittered back like someone had greased the heels of their boots. Okmur's furious shove left one slumped against the side of the tent as the other toppled over backward alongside a tray of battle barber instruments. Neither seemed ready or willing to come near the bloody giant again.

"Get 'im," the young dwarfess shouted as her fingers kept up the frantic pace. "Before he ends up walking over his own guts."

As though to illustrate the point, Okmur's hand fell to his broad, muscle-knotted belly as he lurched to his feet. A wet red mouth gaped under fingers that could do little to staunch the flow of blood. Despite the obvious pain of the injury, Okmur doggedly managed to take two steps before Gromic and Waelon reached him. The tweldwan's trousers were soaked with vital fluids, yet he fought when the brawny pair made to seize him.

"Get off of me, scum!" Okmur howled, and a fist as big and hard as a mallet's head swept left and right. "Don't touch me, traitors!"

Waelon ducked one sweeping blow, and Gromic, who was beside him, caught the strike on the cheek. The stout dwarf staggered to the side, starbursts going off behind his eyes. Waelon threw himself at the mountainous dwarf.

"Now we're talkin'," the former ranger bayed like a hound on the hunt.

Tomza's attention was divided as she quickly scooped the sprigs she'd just collected into a bowl with some mushrooms, then ground them. When she could look up, she saw Waelon had not just grappled with the injured tweldwan but was slamming blows into Okmur's face.

"Commander wants him alive!" she shouted, doing her best to ignore a battle barber to her left when he voiced his anger at the state of his operating station, into which a dwan had crashed. "If you beat his head in, you'll have Torbjorn to answer to."

The red-headed dwarf stopped, but Gromic, eyes alight with wrath, attacked. Okmur had been trying to ward off Waelon's blows with one hand. The other kept his insides from relocating, so he was ill-prepared. Gromic's powerful cross, thrown with skill and his considerable weight behind it, landed with a distinct smack and sent Okmur stumbling back. He struck the edge of the operating table he'd been on, and with a grunt, he crumpled to the floor.

"Quick, grab 'im," Waelon shouted, hands extended. "I don't want to have to haul his arse back onto the table."

Together, Gromic and Waelon managed to prop up the half-conscious tweldwan, but it took the help of more dwans to get the colossus back on the table. Panting and sweating, Waelon scowled at the big nearly-unconscious dwarf, looking ready to spit.

"Don't see why Torbjorn wants this one alive," he growled, swiping sweat from his eyes. "We know he wouldn't return the favor."

Gromic wheezed, leaning back with his hands on his head, "Maybe that's the point."

Okmur rallied once more and executed a dismount from the table.

In answer, the two burly dwarfs sprang on top of the tweldwan's chest while shouting for the other dwans to secure the legs that kicked and flailed.

"What is that supposed to mean?" Waelon demanded as he fought to stay atop the struggling dwarf. "This aurochs must've hit you harder than it looked."

Gromic was ready to defend himself when Tomza's voice sheared through the din.

"Both of you shut it and get out of my way!" she cried as she moved to the operating table. The dwarfs obliged, but Okmur's struggles were intensifying, along with the curses emerging from between his clenched teeth. In answer, Tomza ladled a handful of the mixture she'd mashed together in her mortar into his face.

The eye-watering concoction covered Okmur's face and beard and created the visual and olfactory impression that the tweldwan of the 6th had very recently lunched at a particularly odious dung heap. That could have prompted a laugh from Tomza and company if Okmur hadn't tried to bite off her fingers. The dwarfess got her hand clear just in time.

In answer, Tomza thrust the mortar and its remaining contents into her patient's face. Gromic and Waelon winced as the bowl jammed between the snapping jaws, depositing more of its contents. One choked breath later, Okmur's resistance was fitful.

"What is that stuff?" Gromic asked, blinking back tears after he leaned too close.

"Soporific mushrooms and a lot of Denia's sprig. Made it strong enough to flatten a whole forme. Seems like that was just enough, but—"

A burp heaved up and out of Okmur and made both veteran dwarfs duck. The dwans who'd been part of the effort to pin the tweldwan down were not as lucky. A cascade of vomit splattered their chests and shocked faces, then Okmur collapsed, finally limp.

"Don't breathe in, and don't swallow if it's in your mouth," Tomza cried, hands held up in warning. "You do that, and you're likely to—"

Her warning came too late. The young dwarfs gave her glassy stares as they sank to the floor of the tent.

Gromic observed, "Might need to work on your timing, lass."

Waelon's nose crinkled at the stink as he surveyed the stricken dwarfs. "That or talk faster."

Tomza threw a scowl over her shoulder at both dwans as she picked her away among the downed dwarfs. "Everyone's a smith until you stick 'em at the anvil," she groused as she retrieved her battle-barber kit. Though the worst hadn't happened, she had her work cut out for her, mending the sizable wound opened in the tweldwan's belly by a former subordinate's vengeful magsax.

"All right, the two of you can drag this lot outside," the young ascedwan declared as she checked to make sure she had everything she needed. "They should wake up before long, though they're going to be unsteady on their feet for a bit. One of you might need to watch 'em."

Waelon and Gromic shared a frown, wondering when they'd agreed to the current command structure.

Tomza didn't bother to comment, just crisply gave further instructions. "The one who isn't watching 'em needs to come back in here," she continued, hoisting a gleaming needle strung with a matte-black fiber. "I'm going to need one of you to help shift him at some point so I can check him for other wounds, though Shaper knows how he's survived this long with the one he has."

Tomza paused as she loomed over Okmur's body and saw the pair of veteran dwarfs staring at her in bemusement.

"Enough gawking," the dwarfess scolded in a sharp matriarchal tone. "We've got work to do. His Majesty's orders."

"Again."

The *swish-smack* of rods on bare backs was a sound Torbjorn could have done without hearing for the rest of his life. The leather-muffled cries of the dwans were unpleasant too, but for whatever reason, they didn't reach him the same way.

Perhaps it was particularly noticeable because of who was being punished. Perhaps not.

"Again."

Swish-smack.

Each time it happened, his skin itched, and he fought the urge to curl in on himself, forcing himself to stand straight and stiff, face impassive. Others were watching, either finding an excuse to come to the edge of the camp or coming without bothering to make up a reason. Torbjorn ignored them and let his gaze rest on the bowed backs of the dwarfs being whipped.

The welts on their bodies were a testament to his displeasure, a reminder written in flesh. If this rebellion was to have a chance to be more than a waste of dwarvish lives, everyone had to learn that lesson.

"Again."

Swish-smack.

Someone groaned, and not one of the dwarfs being chastised. After the first few blows, they'd lost the heart to make a sound except when the rod drug it out of them. The weary groan rose from the dwarfs bearing the rods, a stout batch gathered by Mordah at his instruction after they'd managed to drag the surviving loyalist command staff from the grips of the vengeful mob. Hardened dwans had gone through the ranks, selecting those with blood on their weapons.

They'd had to look into the terrified eyes of the dwarfs they were now punishing. It wasn't something he was proud of, but down to his bones, Torbjorn believed it was necessary. It wasn't just the new recruits who were going to learn a lesson from this.

"Again."

Swish-smack.

It was Torbjorn's turn to groan, his stomach turning inside him. He refused to let it show, refused to bend, but the tortured sound slipped out through his set jaw. It was inaudible to anyone but him, but that only made it worse.

He reminded himself of what he'd seen when he'd waded in to drive back the mob. The screams of glee as magsaxes rose and fell again and again. Dwans laughing as they stomped and kicked the dead and dying. The sight of Okmur, bloody and battered, fighting like a bull surrounded by a dozen yammering bulldogs.

The shame still burned in his mind, seeing tweldwans and dwans reduced to such a state. It couldn't happen again. He would make certain it didn't.

"Again."

"Your Majesty," Mordah called before the rods could descend. The punishment squad stood, arms raised and trembling as they waited. Something in Torbjorn bristled that they'd failed to obey, but he buried that part of him. It was understandable, and given their hearts were sick at the task they'd been set to, it was expected.

Having held his position so stiffly for so long, Torbjorn shuffled about to face the fordwan. "Yes, Fordwan?" He was careful to keep his emotions out of his voice and expression. This was a punishment administered by a fair and impartial leader. He neither enjoyed nor balked at what he must do.

This was made even harder when he saw the tears glistening in the dwarfess' eyes. When he heard the tremble in her voice, it was agonizing.

"With all respect, Your Majesty," she began, swallowing hard, "do you know how many stripes are going to be doled out? In total, that is?"

Torbjorn searched her face.

She's making sure you haven't lost yourself in the punishment. Wants to know you're not just fumbling and flailing. Good lass.

"Yes," Torbjorn lied, then called over his shoulder without breaking eye contact with Mordah, "Again."

It was small comfort that Mordah winced at the pronouncement. He hoped she could tell this was gnawing at him too. It was hard to tell since her eyes had sunk to the ground, and she was contemplating the earth between her boots like it might hold the answers.

"May I know how many more, Your Majesty?" she asked, her voice hoarse.

To defend his first lie, he thought about creating a number, but Torbjorn's knotted guts told him he couldn't stake this on a guess. He stared at the dwarfess for a handful of seconds and ran through a half-dozen bad options. In retrospect, he wondered why he hadn't just determined a number and stuck with that. He stared at Mordah's downcast face for another heartbeat, cursing himself for being so angry and determined to make things right that he hadn't stopped to think about the basics.

"Three more," Torbjorn stated flatly with the barest of nods, a lie of the body to go with the mouth. Mordah answered with a nod and looked at the rod-wielders. She now had a destination, a goal, an objective. Like any dwan, she could march toward that through even the worst of terrain.

He couldn't afford to think about what that implied about him. Not now.

"If that is the case, perhaps I should finish this," the fordwan offered. Her face paled as she said the words, but her gaze remained steady. "Haeda informed me that you have not slept, and there is still much that needs to be done."

Torbjorn wanted to reject the proposition, but he wasn't sure how to do it. Should he tell her that the damage was done or that he needed to be here, both for himself and for those he was leading? Should he—

"Torbjorn. *Torbjorn!*" He saw Haeda coming through the outskirts of the camp.

"We've got visitors," she shouted, and every dwarf looked back the way she'd come as though expecting to see an invading horde hot on her heels, shrouded in a cloud of dust.

"Visitors?" Torbjorn asked. "Have the 9th and 11th come back to play?"

Haeda's eyes flashed as she shot him a mischievous wink.

"Even worse, Yer Majesty. Svartalfs. Utyrvaul's back, and he's brought friends."

CHAPTER FIVE

Torbjorn smirked. "Well, you've been busy."

Sir Utyrvaul Urivianoc chuckled as he executed an elaborate bow that managed to encompass the host arrayed behind him, a few dozen svartalfs in the full regalia of war mounted on the sharp-snouted theropods called adyrclafs by the dwarfs. The closest svartalf encampment was three days' ride, located near Lake Blacemere, but none of the elves bore the stains and smudges of hard travel.

From their tall helms to their boots and sabatons, each myrkling was gleaming and polished. Even the adyrclafs' scales shone, and the plumage on their necks and heads didn't have a quill out of place.

Did they stop a quarter mile out to polish up? the dwarf wondered, hoping his face didn't show his incredulity.

"From the looks of things, I could say the same of you." Utyrvaul chortled as he sank back into his saddle and swept his gaze over the dwarvish camp. "It hardly seems possible, but I'd say that you've nearly doubled your forces since we parted ways."

Torbjorn looked over his shoulder as though just noticing the sprawling encampment.

"I suppose." He shrugged, affecting nonchalance. "We haven't had time to take a count."

Utyrvaul looked at the mounted elves and winked. "'Tis quite a thing, isn't it?" he asked with a jerk of his pointed chin at the dwarfs. "How many forces grow larger after they face an enemy in the field? Excluding the Dirgespawn, but from what I can tell, those are all living dwarfs shuffling about, though you'd be forgiven for thinking it was otherwise."

Several of the svartalfs laughed at the jab, but Torbjorn didn't show offense. He was too busy studying the myrklings. He saw their slanted eyes widen and the quickness in their smiles and heard the nervous insistence in their laughs.

Wasn't quite what you were expecting, was it, my good lords? Torbjorn thought, endeavoring to keep his expression blank. *I can hear the wheels turning between those pointed ears.*

One look at Utyrvaul, who gave the barest twitch of a smile beneath the toothy show he was putting on, confirmed that the canny elf had made a similar assessment.

"I assume that such esteemed guests didn't come just to gawk," Torbjorn called in a strong, clear voice as he met the eyes of each svartalf. "If you'll do me the honor, I'd like to welcome you all to my tent. Our fare isn't as fine as you are accustomed to, but it's hearty, and there is plenty."

And it's probably tastier than the scraps you've been living on since we stopped the Holt'Dwan's supply runs to you mercenaries.

The svartalfs were slow to acquiesce, but eventually, they nodded or murmured their acceptance, though more than one whispered a snide remark a little too loud.

The dwarf commander took it all with a grin, yet none moved forward, nor did Utyrvaul lead them into the camp.

Torbjorn's brow furrowed as he looked at them, wondering if he'd missed something. It took a moment more scanning for him to realize that all of the elves were trying and failing to hide the fact that they were all looking at one member of their coterie.

Torbjorn spotted the svartalf a heartbeat before she nudged her mount forward.

She was astride a massive albino adyrclaf, ghostly pale except for the gory eyes that matched its rider's, and watched the world from within a tall helm that spilled opalescent plumage down her back. The she-elf was bedecked in fluted plate of alabaster framed in silver, fitted so perfectly that it provided protection while hinting at the supple feminine form beneath. One ornate gauntlet held her mount's reins, while the other rested upon the only thing that clashed with her ensemble—a battered longsword whose matte-black blade had been slid through a baldric, bare to all. The svartalfess' silver-nailed gauntlets played on the rough hilt, almost caressing the thing as though to soothe it.

The striking myrkling came to stand beside Utyrvaul, whose mount stalked back with a thin hiss before its far larger mutant kin.

"May I present the Lady Marshal Annuvel Arouveth?" Utyrvaul intoned with a sincerity that Torbjorn might call reverence. "Lady Marshal, this is Prince Torbjorn Hralson of Clan Cyniburg."

Torbjorn peered around the toothy head of her enormous mount and gave the she-elf a nod. "Lady Marshal, welcome."

The red eyes stared at him for a moment before the svartalfess left off tickling her sword hilt to doff her helmet.

Torbjorn had seen many myrklings, but he was ill-prepared to hide his surprise when Lady Marshal Arouveth revealed herself. Svartalfs' skin tones ranged from light violet to the inky blue-blacks of a deep bruise, with a dizzying number of subtle yet distinct variations between. Paying attention to these differences in hue was the only way Torbjorn could differentiate svartalfs since their features were a generic blend of elegant and predatory.

He had never met a svartalf with skin the color of the Lady Marshal's.

Perhaps it would be better to say a lack of color since, like her mount and war gear except for her sword, Annuvel Arouveth was ghostly pale. Skin as pale as fresh snow covered her sharp, angular features, the wintry perfection only interrupted by lips and eyelids the shade of frost-kissed mulberries. Her eyes were the crimson pools of her kind, but hers seemed to have a silver sheen.

"Prince Torbjorn," the svartalfess replied, her voice like wisps of smoke curling off seared honey. "It seems we have much to discuss, you and I."

Torbjorn again nodded, unwilling to betray his amazement.

"Aye, I suppose we do," he stated matter-of-factly. "I imagine that would be best done in comfier places. We are not very far from where they're going to be digging fresh latrines."

Some of the svartalfs give sharp sniffs and a few hissed words in their tongue, but the lady marshal inclined her head. "Fair enough," she murmured, and her words made his skin prickle. "Lead on."

Torbjorn turned, glad to have an excuse not to stare at her.

"No need to nibble on my account. There's plenty here, so please, dig in, as we'd say."

When the gathering of svartalfs fell like wolves upon the hastily prepared seared pork, Torbjorn wasn't sure if he'd spoken too soon. The needle-like teeth of the myrklings sank into the meat with an eager relish that a dwarf with a very healthy appetite would have found disturbing.

Annuvel was sitting at his side. "As you can see, Prince Torbjorn, even the lords and ladies of our host have been obliged to tighten their belts these past few months."

Torbjorn nodded, fighting the instinct to state that that had been the point. "Yet I don't see your ladyship availing yourself of our hospitality," he replied, settling a hand on a plate on which seasoned skewers of meat were steaming. "I wasn't lying about our fare being simple but plentiful. We've secured ample stores in our march across the valley, and Tuvaloth does its part to supply us."

Annuvel Arouveth's eyes, which were on the proffered meat, snapped up and narrowed at the mention of the woselaf city. Her unarmored hand reached over her gauntlet to take up a goblet brimming with wine while her other hand tenderly traced the black blade on her lap.

"Your conquest of the savagelings is a tale I am keen to hear," the lady marshal declared, her voice just enough that the ravening elves around her quieted. "Would you perhaps regale me with the tale?"

Torbjorn, hardly adept at such games, sank back into his chair and shrugged.

"String of coincidences, really," he replied, flapping one hand as though to dismiss the situation. "Things were already in motion, and I was there to take advantage."

It was a gross oversimplification that would have earned

the wosealfs' ire had they heard it, but it had the effect he'd hoped for on the svartalfess.

"Oh, really?" the lady marshal purred, eyes twinkling above her glass as she gave Torbjorn a measuring glance. "Do you often find yourself in such fortuitous situations, just happening to defeat your enemy with hardly a drop of blood spilled?"

A shudder crawled up his spine as he remembered how "bloodless" the winning of Tuvaloth had been. The frantic battle against the Witches atop the Tower of Princes, the plummet to the earth, and then nearly drowning in the thing's pooled offal. Then there'd been her stupid champion. What had his name been? Torbjorn almost laughed when he realized he couldn't remember the name of the individual who had been responsible for him becoming master over the savagelings and sparking his rebellion.

"More than a few drops." Torbjorn frowned as he ran a thumb across his cheek. "But if you've had any time to speak with Utyrvaul, you know that most of the time, fortune has not favored my endeavors or me."

The pale elf's chortle was as soft as summer rain, and Torbjorn cursed internally.

That'll win her over, he scolded himself. *Most of the time, we bounced from one failure to the next. Do you want me to lead your people in a war that is of no significance to you and yours?*

Torbjorn was certain he was not the right dwarf for the job.

"Well, whatever your past exploits, your fortunes seem to have changed," Annuvel cooed after taking a slow draught from her goblet. "First, you tame the wild elves of the West. Then you convert the hosts sent against you when you meet them. In less than a full campaigning season, you have assembled a force to rival the one that initially conquered this valley."

Utyrvaul had coached Torbjorn on what to expect, and flattery had been a point to consider, but this felt different. He wasn't certain if it was her striking appearance or the way she looked at him as she rolled her goblet pensively. Was it odd that he thought he heard genuine admiration in her tone?

"Things are different, that's for sure," the dwarf replied, wishing, not for the first time, that he'd asked for something stronger than water in his glass. "I'm not sure this means they are any better. I don't imagine Ashfer will show me much respect if he gets his hands on me."

The lady marshal sniffed. "So, your primary concern is winning this little squabble. That is perhaps why you've dangled food in front of starving svartalfs—in the hope of winning our support."

It was said without malice or anger, but Torbjorn couldn't help noting that her smile seemed sharper than before.

"As you said yourself, your people could do with more provisions," Torbjorn began, gesturing at the food. "I didn't think there was any harm in offering you all an opportunity to enjoy my hospitality and possibly negotiate your resupply."

The smile didn't widen so much as lengthen as her lips peeled away from her teeth. "Do you often give supplies to your enemies?" she asked. Her goblet settled on the table, and her bare fingers traced the filigree knuckles of her gauntlet. Her eyes rested on him, trying to plumb his depths.

Torbjorn forced a low chuckle and thrust his chin at the entrance to his tent. "Head on out there and tell me what you think," he suggested with a hard edge in his voice. "Go look at my forces, and you will see former enemies. Whether elf or dwarf, many would have been all too happy to slit my throat not long ago. Now they are ready to fight and die at my command."

Her eyes narrowed, but if Torbjorn was any judge, she was interested rather than angry or irritated.

"You must be a powerful prince to compel such changes." She leaned close enough that Torbjorn could make out the spidery blue veins at the corners of her eyes. "Tell me, Torbjorn Hralson…what is your secret?"

Torbjorn's dark eyes bored into her red ones. "Bad luck. From beginning to end, I've been tossed one way or another, shoved from bad to worse, and I've not had enough luck to just die. I absorbed the lessons learned from those misfortunes, and I'm using them to pull the strings that had me dancing for so long.

"I think that those poor bastards out there know that and feel the same, which is why they left off trying to kill me and each other and we are now working together to change things. And by the Shaper, Erduna, Grimmoth, and every heathen god of the savagelings, I intend to make sure this insane confluence means something for once, and that's why they follow me. They follow me because break or bend, maim or mend, the hammer's in *my* hand now, and I'm goin' to start swingin'!"

His rant finished, Torbjorn sank back into his chair, bones aching and head throbbing. His tongue was thick and his spittle tacky as he groped for the tankard, which remained disappointingly full of water. Clearing his raw throat, he took a few deep swallows, thankful it helped his throat, though he wondered at the fatigue and bone-deep weariness that came over him.

His gaze sank to the table, and he saw the untouched skewers of spitted meat. He wondered if food might set him right. "Well, if you're not going to eat them," he growled and reached for the nearest skewer. He'd just recalled his lack of sleep as an explanation for his condition when a pale elvish hand darted forward.

Stricken as he was, Torbjorn could only sink back with a groan as he watched the lady marshal nip off a bit of skewered pork. Her eyes were hooded beneath her dark lids, and her movements precise, but there was little she could do to hide her appreciation at the first taste.

"Some of my peers, of which there are few, don't take revenge work," the white elf began before taking another bite. "A client out for revenge will promise you anything and everything if they think it will get them what they want, even when it isn't theirs to give. Even when it never could be."

The svartalfess nipped a large chunk off, and she was obliged to pause and chew it. As she attended to that, Torbjorn scanned the table. His guests muttered, the sounds sibilant as they slid between their sharp teeth. They were enjoying feasting, seeming engrossed in the food even as they listened.

"This isn't about revenge," Torbjorn stated, turning back. "This is about change and fixing things. I'm not going after a person. I'm defying a system."

Annuvel set her skewer down, ready to say something in reply, only to smile and reach for her goblet.

"You don't believe me," Torbjorn stated, his tired mind refusing to produce more vigorous arguments. "You don't... well, you just don't believe me."

The murmurs took on a serpentine hiss as the svartalfs about the table tittered. The lady marshal stared at him, then shot a look across the table that silenced her subordinates.

"Prince Torbjorn, it doesn't matter what I believe," Annuvel explained, meeting the dwarf's eyes. "What matters is that you understand. We are here because our paymasters, your enemies, can no longer supply us with food, much less pay our considerable fees. Your vengeance, your change, and your grand quest will only be my concern if our terms are met and your commitments are kept. Do you understand?"

Torbjorn forced himself to sit upright and meet the elf's gaze, mustering a strength he knew he did not have. "Aye," he drawled, holding her gaze. "I understand how mercenaries work."

The lady marshal smiled, an icy thing that matched her purple lips. "I hope so. Otherwise, you can expect as much loyalty from me as your enemy now receives."

Torbjorn nodded as he scooped up his cup and drained the last of the lukewarm water. "Duly noted," the dwarf rumbled and swiped his hand across his mouth. "I suppose the next question is, what do you expect in return for your assistance? I don't imagine you'll commit just for food in your bellies."

Annuvel Arouveth's red eyes shone. Torbjorn felt like a piece of meat under her gaze.

"Oh, don't you worry, my prince. Our demands will be made soon enough. Let us simply enjoy this feast you've so kindly set before us."

Torbjorn frowned and leaned toward the predatory creature. "No offense intended, Lady Marshal, but I've got an army to prepare and a fortress to capture. I don't have time to be coy."

Annuvel's eyes darted meaningfully to her compatriots across the table, but Torbjorn wasn't sure what he glimpsed in her expression. It surely couldn't be fear.

"All things in good time, my prince."

CHAPTER SIX

"Grimmoth's smoldering prick!"

Tomza chuckled at the profane exclamation as she moved to her patient's bedside.

"That's a new one for me, Tweldwan," she remarked as she squatted near the cot that was straining to support Okmur's massive frame. "That takes some doing after a year with Waelon and Gromic."

"Where am I?" the hulking dwarf asked hoarsely. "What's going on?"

"Steady, now," Tomza cooed, shuffling closer. "You're mostly held together with string and wishful thinking at this point. You don't want to ruin my good needlework."

The Peak-Breaker stared at her for a moment, then swept his gaze from left to right and back, his brain slow to comprehend what he saw. The dwarfess' face seemed familiar, her gray eyes like something he'd seen in a dream. However, his thoughts were not distinct, only murky scraps, along with his fuddled memories.

Where was he? Had she answered that? Little by little, the

pieces congealed in his mind as Tomza patiently waited. When the answer finally came, he frowned and looked around again. As he took in the interior of the canvas tent and the smells of alchemical antiseptics underlaid with blood and ash, his pale eyes kindled with rage.

He thrust his hands toward her, fingers curved like blunt claws, but Tomza neither lurched back nor flinched. Before the grasping mitts came close to her, chains clanged against the iron rail of the cot, each terminating in a manacle around Okmur's wrist. Tomza remained where she knelt as Okmur continued to strain, her expression flat as she watched him closely.

Okmur continued to strain for a few heartbeats more before collapsing on his cot. As he sagged into fabric suspended between the poles, his grunts and gasps were combined with plaintive wheezes and hisses of pain. The tweldwan's hands wandered over his belly, pressing and scratching at the bandages that swaddled it. Beneath those probing fingers, splotches of red filtered through in darkening stains.

"Now look at what you've done to yourself," the young dwarfess cried, exasperated. "Leave off it, and let me see what mess you've made of my hard work."

Okmur was slow to respond. His thick fingers kept shredding the bandages, but Tomza had a remedy for that. She rapped a small file across the dwarf's knuckles.

"Owww!" Okmur cried and lunged at Tomza's instrument. He only managed to earn another sharp rap.

"Loveless needle-harpy!" Okmur growled, raising his head to glare at her before sinking back down from the effort of supporting his heavy head.

"Hardly the sort of gratitude I'd expect from someone who

saved *my* life," the dwarfess chided as she cheerfully organized more items in her apron. "I'm not saying I wouldn't do it again for Torbjorn, but I don't think you want to test those tunnels for trolls if you're already clutching your belly like that. It might not work out.."

Okmur watched her for a moment, then settled back to stare at the ceiling, jaw working against the words that wanted to slip between his lips. "What is all this about then?" he finally demanded. "The traitor wants to keep me recognizable for a public execution? Going to use me for a spectacle? Is that it?"

Tomza sized up her patient. "No, you rock-headed fool." She snorted as she took out a small but sharp knife. Its blade was unlike many others, which were sturdy, well-forged dwarven steel. This one was stone from the sunken base of Mount Smarthdun. The black glass-stone had been knapped to a fearsome edge, and she favored it when quick, precise cuts were required. The black edge glinted hungrily in the light of the lantern and what came through the flap.

Okmur saw the merciless edge approaching and suddenly didn't want to be close to the ascedwan. "What are you doing?" he growled, his bound hands attempting to protect his wounded stomach. "I thought you said you were just checking!"

Tomza rolled her eyes, then brandished the blade with a maniacal grin. "Yes, I did all that work to shove your entrails back in just so I can cut on you some more. Do shut up and move your hands. Otherwise, I'll end up cutting you for being an idiot."

The stains on the tweldwan's belly were now darker. Reluctantly, Okmur did as he was bid. His hands settled fretfully on either side of him. Seizing her opportunity, Tomza worked one handed to peel away layers of bandage.

"This probably doesn't surprise you, great big strapping fellow that you are, but when you move just about any muscle, you pull on others. You keep on with this business, and every stitch I put in will rip out. Then you might as well say your goodbyes."

As she spoke, one hand held the knife while the other deftly flitted through the layers of fabric. Finally, the bandages came away with a sticky sound that made Okmur wince. Then she searched his belly, pausing occasionally to daub off fresh blood. The ascedwan chewed her lip, eyes narrowed as she worked, but a moment later, she nodded and reached for clean fabric to pack the wound.

"You've managed to rip the flesh around some of the stitches," she explained as she plunged back into the gory task. "Still, they're holding, and none of the tearing is that bad, but please stop trying to choke the life out of me while I take care of you."

Okmur just watched her through narrowed eyes as she bent to her work. As before, her movements were swift and sure, with no indecision. Some of the bandages were fine. Other bits were removed easily, but some required more effort. They were stuck in some places, and on those, it was necessary to employ the fearsome razor.

The tweldwan supposed that it was a testament to the sharpness of the edge that he didn't feel anything as the blade parted cloth, blood, and sometimes flesh. That did little to assuage his concerns, and he didn't relinquish his vigil until the last of the bandages were all replaced and the small blade had been cleaned and had vanished into her kit.

"That'll do." She sighed. "Not sure if this is me saving your life again, but it's close, so I'm going to say that's two you owe me."

The hulking tweldwan growled, then winced. The growl turned into a wheeze. As Okmur recovered, Tomza collected the soaked bandages for disposal. The silence stretched as she worked at a basin that fumed with an alchemical antiseptic.

Okmur staring at the ceiling. Eventually, his eyes closed, and if not for the occasional grinding sound from his clenched jaw, one would think he had swooned.

Tomza applied a pestle to a selection of herbs in a small mortar. Her movements were sure and her rhythm was even, but her eyes were distant. Her body moved with purpose, but her mind went back in time. She recalled the sensation of a different edge parting the skin on her scarred thumb.

She'd shaken the memory off, but as the earthy scent of the herbs she was grinding wafted up, it reminded her of what had come after that. With several drops of blood and a few jagged words, these herbs would kindle on their own and wither into sweet-smelling smoke. In the wake of the transformation, flesh would knit, vitality would be restored, and the patient would be hale once more.

She'd once wielded such power and could wield it again. She could make Okmur Peak-Breaker whole in one minute with no concern about the wound going foul. No days of waiting and examining, and no possibility that the stitches would be torn since there would be no need for them. No need to waste resources or hours or concern. No—

"No."

Tomza didn't think she'd spoken out loud until she heard the patient's rasping question. "No, what?"

The dwarfess cursed internally, releasing her death grip on mortar and pestle as she tried to clear her head. Her chest tightened with every breath, and her breath tasted foul on her tongue. Paranoia gripped her; she was sure her sins would finally be judged. She couldn't bring herself to look at Okmur. How could he know what she'd done?

Yes, how could he?

Like a nightmare, the paranoia dissipated. She twisted around and saw that Okmur still lay upon his cot, staring at the ceiling. His big chest rose and fell steadily, his breathing unhurried, while he gazed at the ceiling, not the posture of an accuser leveling a damning inquiry.

As she watched, a frown crossed his face, and his eyes focused a little more. "No, what?"

Her silence had drawn his curiosity, nothing more. He did not know, and her memories, though loud in her mind, were still inaccessible.

The last of the terror's icy grip upon her heart melted, and she found her tongue once more. "What's that?" she asked as she scooped up the mortar and brought it over to a small kettle dangling over a smoldering brazier.

"I said, 'No, what?'" Okmur growled, not yet irritated enough to raise his heavy head to glare at her. "I heard you say 'no' as clear as a cave river, and I asked what you were saying no to."

"Oh, you know how it is," Tomza answered with a forced chuckle. "You start having a conversation with yourself as you're doing something, and you end up answering yourself. I hope that doesn't sound mad, but we've all got our little quirks, don't we?"

His head rose from his cot. She wasn't sure if her attempt

at friendly chatter had served its purpose. Fetching a handy square of patched fabric, Tomza took the kettle from its hook and dribbled hot water into the mortar, then looked at her scowling patient.

"What were you talking to yourself about?" the tweldwan asked with a suspicious glower. "Something about me?"

If only, she thought as she scrambled for a suitable lie. "Well, to an extent, I suppose so," she lied as a recollection struck her. "I just realized that you're the tweldwan of the 6th Division, right?"

Okmur's pale gaze clouded with confusion, and a shudder traveled up and down his body. A wince twisted his features, and he sank back with a hiss. One hand rested against the side of his belly.

"Easy now," Tomza muttered, turning her head away from the fragrant steam rising from the mortar. "You'd be surprised how much belly wounds affect everything else. Like most things on a dwarf, we don't give it much thought until it stops doing its job."

She didn't need the vapors of the solution she was making to spark another memory. This one would be more awkward to explain, and she wondered why she felt she needed to.

As though to reinforce the point, Okmur's manacles rattled as he shifted to a more comfortable position.

"So?" he growled, returning to angrily contemplating the tent's ceiling.

"What's that?" Tomza asked as she replaced the kettle and went to a nearby table. She shuffled vessels around until she found a high-lipped bowl and slowly poured the contents of the mortar into it.

"What does me being the tweldwan of the 6th have to do

with anything?" Okmur asked, brushing a hand over his bandaged abdomen.

"Oh, that," Tomza chirped to buy herself some time. She stirred the steeping herbs. "My brother and I were members of the 6th before...well, before we joined up with Torbjorn. I don't imagine that you remember us or anything. We were fresh recruits, after all, but I remember you delivering an address to our divi—"

"Ascedwan Tomza Drauldottr of Clan Jaln," Okmur interjected, his gaze sharpening as his expression hardened. "Your brother is Dwan Ober Draulson, also of Clan Jaln. Of course I remember you."

Tomza stopped stirring and looked at him, unable to keep the surprise out of her voice when she spoke. "Oh. I didn't realize. I guess whatever else anyone says, you cared enough about your dwans to know the names of even the new recru—"

"I remember you," Okmur cut in again, his voice flinty, "because I was the one who wrote the letter to your clan to tell them to strike your name from the Clan Stone when you were both found guilty of cowardice in combat. Cowardice that resulted in the deaths of your entire forme during a savageling attack."

Tomza hadn't expected the old charge to have such weight and bite, so it was a long moment before she dragged her gaze back to her former Tweldwan.

"That was the charge," she agreed, unsure of why her voice quavered but unable to still it. "I suppose you weren't there outside Greyshelf, and after you saw what Ober did last night, you understand that wasn't really the case."

Okmur's sharp glare met her gaze. "What are you talking…" His voice trailed off, and his eyebrows rose. With a long groan, he relaxed on the cot.

"We thought the savagelings had desecrated the bodies," he muttered, eyes unfocused as he probed his memories of the battle. "Torn to pieces to the last dwarf, but we couldn't understand why the savagelings had done the same thing to their own. In the end, we shrugged and muttered about cannibal heathens while we sent you two off to Arbefast."

Okmur's head swung slowly from side to side, chest rising and falling faster and fingers twitching as they tried to grip something that wasn't there. When he spoke again, his voice was soft, almost gentle. "It wasn't the savagelings though, was it?"

"No." Tomza sighed, and tears welled in her eyes. "It wasn't. They ambushed us, but we were wary and on patrol, so we formed up in good order. Would've done any division proud when the fighting started."

The young dwarfess watched her concoction cool as Okmur made several attempts to form words.

On the fifth attempt, he managed to ask a coherent question. "Which one of you is the wolf thing, and which one of you is the bear demon?"

The sincerity and ignorance of the question struck Tomza like a thunderbolt, and she couldn't keep a belly laugh from escaping. "As flattering as that is, I'm neither." She chuckled as she scooped up the bowl and made her way toward the cot. "Those wolf *things*—and there are two, mind you—aren't dwarfs but elves who are cursed like Ober, though their kind calls it a blessing. Ober is the bear demon."

Despite her assurance, the massive dwarf scooted to the far edge of the cot as she knelt beside him. "He wasn't always… I mean, something happened to him, didn't it?

Something like that can't live among dwarfs once it's become…*a demon.*"

"Something *did* happen to him." She frowned thoughtfully. "And it wasn't easy keeping things under control, and obviously, we didn't always, but Ober has come to an understanding with the thing inside his skin."

Shaking her head to dismiss the confounding mixture of emotions threatening to distract her, the dwarfess cradled Okmur's head as she raised the bowl. Flinching back, the dwan twisted to one side, shifting the cot an inch as he looked up at her with wide eyes.

"Don't be stupid if you can help it," Tomza chided. "I told you I don't have Ober's…uh, condition. I'm just trying to keep that nasty belly wound of yours from souring. Gut wounds are the worst for fouling, and as bad as you think dying by fangs or claws is, dying from an infected wound is far worse because you linger."

Okmur's hands flitted to the bandages again and trailed over the fabric.

"So, he killed them all? His entire forme?" the tweldwan whispered as he stared at her face. "All except you, and you didn't kill him?"

Tomza shot him a wry glance as she shook her head. "You did see what happened last night, didn't you? What makes you think little ol' me could've done that? Hundreds of your best dwan on an open battlefield couldn't put a mark that mattered on him. No, whatever that thing in Ober is, it doesn't know how to die, and it won't let Ober do it either, despite his best efforts."

Tomza met Okmur's eyes, and as she stared into them, she saw that he understood what she was saying. What was more, he believed her.

The dwarfess reached out to cup the back of his head, and he didn't recoil this time. He shuddered at her touch, and the silliness of the brute reacting that way, even chained as he was, forced her to stuff down a chuckle that bubbled up inside her. She did smile, but it was a warm one without mocking or malice.

"Small sips," she instructed, bringing the bowl to his lips. "Should be cool enough, but it's got a tickle to it that makes it hard to swallow in gulps."

Okmur took his medicine without complaint or incident, and after the bowl was empty, he sank limply onto the cot. His eyes unfocused as Tomza rose to take the bowl back to the table for cleaning, and her training told her to examine him for further ailments or injuries to explain his listlessness. The dwarfess stood over him for a moment, cataloging possible physical ailments, but in the back of her mind, she knew what was occurring.

"World's changing shape on you, eh?" she asked. Okmur gave a slow nod. Tomza sighed again, and for all the harshness that had been in the tweldwan's voice before, she pitied him. Her family's unorthodox history had prepared her and Ober better than most, and the Bad Badgers had experienced all manner of peculiar things. A dwarf of the line, a staunch and stoic dwan, was going to have a hard time with all this.

Tomza found herself at the table. Her mind had wandered, so she couldn't remember walking over, but she cleaned and scoured the bowl in the basin set aside for that. Her mind was tempted to wander again until a hoarse call came from the cot behind her.

"What does the Kinslayer want with me, then?"

Tomza froze, holding a rag dipped in a diluted antiseptic solution. Its sharp smell stung her nose and helped to clear away the trailing vapors of thought that threatened to distract her.

"To be honest, I don't know," the dwarfess admitted. "I *am* one of the Bad Badgers, but he doesn't tell us everything. He insisted I keep you alive, so your life means something to him. That is more than you'd expect, considering how you behaved the last time you two met."

The tweldwan didn't defend himself. Tomza wondered if he felt guilty. Her limited memories of the stern and ferocious officer, combined with the recent revelation of his duplicitous attack, made that seem unlikely, but she knew how the world changing shape could change a person. Her eyes strayed to her scarred thumb, and she shook her head sharply.

"What happened to the others?"

Tomza kept scrubbing, but the cadence of her efforts became more insistent and determined.

"Not many of them made it," she called over her shoulder. "After we finally got you settled, I helped the other ascedwans care for the few who made it out of the carnage that was supposed to be handing you over.

"There were five, maybe six, who had a chance of making it when I joined in. Two of those died, and two more are so broken that they'll be lucky if they can sit up and feed themselves. The other two are on the mend in body, but the heart's gone out 'em. The impossible happened when their brothers forsook the Holt'Dwan, and then those same brothers tried to kill 'em."

Okmur was silent. Tomza eventually realized that she was beyond cleaning to the point of wearing a hole in the bowl. She finally forced herself to look at the tweldwan. "So, are you going to go the way of the others? Are you broken in more than just your meat, or is Okmur Peak-Breaker made of sterner stuff?"

She told herself she was trying to inspire the dwarf, but the explanation sounded hollow in her own mind. Was she asking him because she wanted to know the answer, or was it just her way of asking a question she was scared to think about?

"I guess we'll have to wait and see," Tomza grumbled as she went in search of something else to clean.

CHAPTER SEVEN

"That's the last of 'em."

Torbjorn groaned as he sank back to watch Mordah gather the final pile of the signed and sealed orders. They'd spent the better part of the evening sorting out the new dwans, accounting for losses, leadership realities, and logistical problems. It had been a mind-numbing, spirit-sapping exercise in frustration, but they'd managed to make all the puzzle pieces fit, more or less—until something went wrong, and they had to come up with a new plan.

"That's the best news I've heard today," Torbjorn rumbled as he stretched to retrieve a bottle of schnapps he'd refused to drink until they finished work. The cork came free with a satisfying squeak, and he let the smell of the liquor drift to his nostrils. The burn of alcohol was mixed with warm, peppery spices that drew an appreciative sigh.

"That's the best thing I've smelled in this sweat-sodden camp." He chuckled, then saw that the fordwan was watching him. "Not that you smell bad, Mordah, but I don't make a habit of sniffing my subordinates."

"Something for which we all can be very thankful, Your Majesty," the dwarfess replied, color rising in her cheeks. "If you'll excuse me, I'll get these to our runners so everyone sees them before dawn."

"Hold on," Torbjorn called and motioned the fordwan over as he fetched a pair of glasses from a collection beside the bottle. "There's no reason to run off just yet. I've got a bottle open, and we've both worked hard enough tonight to enjoy it without feeling guilty. Why not stay and have a drink before you run off to make the dwans miserable delivering orders to sleeping officers?"

The rosy glow became a blaze on Mordah's cheeks as she stood, her arms full of missives. She alternated between staring at the floor of the command tent and looking pleadingly at Torbjorn.

"Is this an order? I mean, is that your will, Majesty?"

Torbjorn glanced up to see the fraught look on the dwarfess' face.

"Only if you want to be," Torbjorn answered, bemused. "It's not the best liquor, but it's guaranteed to be better than anything else you can get out here, so I didn't want to be greedy. Without your help, those orders never would've been sorted, and—"

"Working with you is honor enough, Your Majesty," Mordah assured him too quickly for Torbjorn to believe her words were genuine. "I would be just as happy knowing you could enjoy your drink without feeling you must share it with the likes of me."

The likes of you. Torbjorn grunted. *Shaper have mercy. This lass knows I'm a stumbling, snoring, farting lump of dwarvish flesh like any other.*

"Come on, Mordah," Torbjorn drawled as he hefted a

brimming glass. "You're telling me you don't want to help yourself to a bit of this?"

Mordah's eyes locked on the glass of schnapps like it was an enemy fortification she was about to assault. Torbjorn saw determination, fear, and bloody-mindedness in her eyes. As he watched her gaze harden, he became concerned that he might lose his other hand when she stormed Fort Schnapps.

"Mordah," he called, drawing her attention away from the proffered glass. "You don't have to drink if you don't want to. It was just an offer."

A heartbreaking mixture of confusion and relief took over the lass' face as her shoulders sagged. "So, you *don't* want me to stay and drink with you?" she asked, eyebrows rising.

Torbjorn lowered the glasses to the table carelessly enough to spill a bit of the precious liquor, then muttered an oath. He swiped the droplets off the table and forced himself to make his voice sound friendly and sincere. "Mordah, only stay and drink if you want to. I will be neither disappointed nor upset with you if you refuse, and I would never command a dwan to drink with me. This liquor is to be shared by friends, not superiors and subordinates. Does that make sense?"

Mordah nodded, again with disconcerting speed, but when she met his eyes, the confusion had been replaced with a stern strength Torbjorn couldn't help but admire.

"Then I would rather see to my duty, Your Majesty," she stated with a firm nod. "It's been a busy day, and I'd like nothing more than to see these distributed and then get a few hours' rest before ensuring things are running smoothly in the morning. Please, enjoy my share of the drink."

Torbjorn bobbed his head and picked up both glasses. "As you wish, my good lass." He raised them in salute. "As you wish."

The first round slid smoothly down his gullet, the liquor blended with saffron, anise, and ginger. When he downed the second, the burn was deeper, but he took it in stride. In the time it took Torbjorn to smack his lips appreciatively and return both glasses to the table, Mordah left.

Torbjorn's eyes swept from one end of the now-empty command tent to the other, and a crevice widened inside him. His mind tumbled into the gap to examine memories long put aside.

When he was very young, he'd snuck out one night and found his father in his study, head in his hands. At first he'd been afraid to say anything, but seeing his stoic, powerful father in such a state had transfixed him. When his father raised his head and there were tears in his eyes, it was too much for young Torbjorn.

Certain his father was mortally wounded, he'd rushed over and asked his father what was wrong. Caught unawares in a vulnerable state, his father was ready to rebuke him as he always did, but this one time, Hral, sovereign of the dwarvish empire, had chosen differently. He'd allayed his son's fears of both injury and chastisement and then endeavored to teach him something.

Taking young Torbjorn by the hand, he'd led him through the winding, austere halls of Airur's Palace on Mount Smarthdun. Torbjorn remembered how quiet and empty the corridors had felt that night. Then they'd entered the Grand Hall, and it had been like plunging into a void. The only things that provided any sense of proportion were Glave's bones mounted overhead like some grisly constellation, the Jotun's malformed skull leering down. Torbjorn had clung to his father's calloused hand until they came to the dais and the throne, which thrust like a metallic mountain out of a sea of stone.

Without a word, Hral had scooped up young Torbjorn and placed him on the broad seat of the throne. That was a shock. Torbjorn had always understood that the throne was forbidden territory, even if he couldn't remember who had told him. Yet, the emperor had placed him on it, so who would gainsay that?

Torbjorn had looked out across the Grand Hall, excitement and awe setting him abuzz, and his father had told him to close his eyes. Torbjorn obliged, and Hral, who'd always had a way with words, wove an image of the Grand Hall filled to the brim with courtiers, attendants, supplicants, and all manner of hangers-on.

With his deep, stirring voice, the emperor raised scrutinizing gazes, straining ears, and demanding mouths from every flagstone until Torbjorn's head swam. Then Hral had commanded him to open his eyes, and when he did, his youthful imaginings were overlaid on the vast chamber. The feeling had been so acute and terrifying he'd shrieked and reached out for his father, but Emperor Hral wasn't there. With a betrayed wail, Torbjorn had tumbled from the throne and down the hard steps of the dais.

Winded and shivering with fright, Torbjorn had lain on the floor, staring up into Glava's mocking sockets. Then Emperor Hral had come around the dais to kneel beside his son.

"Da!" Torbjorn had squeaked, reaching out. He stopped short when he saw his father's grim expression.

"Why are you on the floor?" Emperor Hral asked, his voice echoing. Torbjorn felt like he'd failed. That the aloof stance was because he'd somehow shamed his father. It wasn't the first time, and even then, the child had known it wouldn't be the last.

"I was scared," the wee dwarfling had confessed, tears running down his cheeks. "I'm sorry."

He reached for his father again, but the emperor stopped him again.

"Why were you afraid?"

Torbjorn's hands sank back down as he considered the question. If he answered correctly, would his father hold him? What did that mean? Was the truth the same as the right thing?

"I-I… It…it w-was," he began, his breath hitching and sobs wracking his small frame. "I-I w-was *alone*!"

The last word came out as a wail, and for the first and only time, Torbjorn's unyielding father succumbed. Emperor Hral scooped his son up and held him, shuddering and weeping, to his chest. Arms strong and secure, hands gentle and soothing, the sovereign of the dwarvish empire, the head of the Cyniburg dynasty, cradled his son to his breast and listened as broken, tearful words tumbled out, half of them nonsensical.

Torbjorn had felt the demand, the pressure, and the weight of so many eyes on him and had seen that he was alone without help or friend. Worst of all, when he'd reached out for the support that was supposed to be there, his father wasn't.

He'd fallen then since the world neither knew nor cared for him.

The emperor had listened, picking out the meaning of Torbjorn's broken words, and after the young dwarf had stopped crying, he'd held him at arm's length. Torbjorn could see those tears again, the sight as alien now as it had been at the time, and heard Hral tell him that what Torbjorn had seen and felt was what being the king was like every single day.

Torbjorn had cried again, unashamed of his tears since they bound him and his father together at that moment. They'd clung to each other, and Torbjorn had sworn to always be there for his father. To be with him so he would not be so alone. Emperor Hral had not answered, only held him tightly, then carried his son to his room and laid next to him until he was asleep.

Torbjorn had awakened the next morning shaken but eager to be with his father, but he learned that his father had left to inspect the Norstan Holt'Dwan. Torbjorn was sent to study in Torvgrud. From then on, Emperor Hral was absent when Torbjorn was home, or Torbjorn was sent away when his father was about to return. In the few moments they'd spent together in the years before he left home, Torbjorn could feel the tension, as though the emperor was embarrassed and desperate that Torbjorn not mention the moment they'd shared in the Grand Hall. In time, he had wondered if his father resented him for drawing that moment of vulnerability out of him.

Torbjorn had never spoken of it. Not to his tutors or his confidante Klaus. Not even to his Bad Badgers. He had begun to believe he'd made it up, the pathetic fabrication of an abandoned youth, but sitting in the empty command tent now, he remembered every detail and felt every jagged edge in the memory.

"Here's to you, Da," Torbjorn rumbled as he refilled a glass. "I'm pretty sure this wasn't where you thought I'd use that lesson, but I'm here all the same."

The liquor went down smoothly. The empty glass had hardly hit the table before someone called from the tent door,

"Drinking alone is bad enough," Utyrvaul purred as he slid through the flap. "But talking to yourself as you do so is a sign that something is very much amiss."

Torbjorn scowled at the elf. Half a dozen retorts came to mind, but he settled for filling the second glass and scooting it across the table. "Well, sit down, and we can take care of both those problems."

The svartalf eyed the drink and the dwarf, thoughts inscrutable behind his crimson eyes. With an infuriating grin, the myrkling crossed the command tent to take up the glass and down it in one quick pull.

"Refreshing." Utyrvaul smirked, rolling the glass between his long fingers just beneath his nose. "Of all the things you dwarfs guzzle, that is the least repellant I've had in some time."

Torbjorn grunted as he refilled his own glass. "Your friends seemed to enjoy the wine during that dinner theater earlier today," the commander observed. "Not a drop left when they finally tottered off."

The svartalf smiled sardonically, gave the glass a final sniff, and placed it back on the table. "We both know that was because it was a human vintage no dwarf would touch, much less make. Also, they've had to slurp up whatever boot-brewed swill they can make these past few months. Their standards have dropped as a result."

Torbjorn agreed to both points with a nod before downing his glass with a backward snap of his head. He raised it to see Utyrvaul staring at him, the empty glass still in front of him.

"You better scoot that over here," Torbjorn muttered as he filled his glass again. "Or else I'll keep this for myself."

Torbjorn looked up to see the svartalf still studying him. "What?"

The elf's eyes narrowed, and his lips peeled back. "As fun as this is, I didn't come here to climb inside a bottle with you, Torbjorn. Lady Marshal Annuvel Arouveth decided that now is the time to reveal her demands for the assistance of the mercenary companies under her banner."

Torbjorn had raised the glass to his lips but paused as he absorbed the news. He frowned, feeling the warm call of the alcohol tickling his lips beneath his mustache. "Is it a rule that your kind waits for the most inopportune time?" Torbjorn asked over the brimming cup. "That is a serious question, by the way, not a rhetorical one."

Utyrvaul tittered as he ran a finger over the interior of his glass. "An argument could be made that our opportunistic nature lends itself to that," the svartalf acknowledged and raised his finger for a contemplative sniff. "But it must be remembered that our *kind* has had mixed results in dealing with the supposedly impeccable honor of the dwarfs. Those responsible for many of our kin have learned it is unwise ever to tell a dwarf anything they don't need to know, whether or not they think they do."

Torbjorn snorted and set his glass down, careful not to spill the precious contents. "And it's left for us to hop to when they decide that we need to know." The dwarf huffed and shook his head, then kneaded his temples. "I sent out orders for reorganization and mobilization. What are the odds that she's not going to demand something that will kak all over my hard work?"

"Very slim," Utyrvaul offered, then ran his tongue across his finger and gave an appreciative nod. "But as we discussed at the outset of this escapade, we need her companies' reinforcement, both to dissuade the remaining mercenaries in the Vale and to assure a swift resolution at Greyshelf and open the way to Heimgrud so we can depose Assface and finally acquire your father's attention."

Torbjorn flinched to hear the matter laid out in bare terms, even though he could not argue with what the svartalf had said. "Why does it sound so petty when you talk about it?" He groaned. "Would it kill you to apply your wit to making it sound less like a sordid family affair?"

The svartalf turned on his heel and made for the door, chortling. "Oh, Torbjorn. You can't afford to be so naïve! Matters and machinations of state are always petty, always sordid, and always a family affair. It is just a question of who understands it and who is still pretending it is otherwise."

Torbjorn wasn't sure if he wanted to down the schnapps or hurl the bottle at the elf. He settled for crossing his arms and glaring. "I'll keep that in mind. Now, go get the lady marshal so we can get this business sorted."

Utyrvaul paused at the tent flap, eyes sparkling with mischief.

"The lady marshal is indisposed at the moment," the myrkling explained. "So her terms—her non-negotiable terms—will be presented by her lieutenant, Lord Banneret Gwyllethon Gwydarioc."

"Gwydarioc," Torbjorn repeated, his tongue moving gingerly around the unfamiliar name. "Haven't we already had dealings with that one?"

The breadth of Utyrvaul's smile was ambitious for his narrow face and all the more unnerving for it. "That would be Lord Gwenmaelon Gwydarioc, the Banneret's late uncle. He was the former commander of the greater contingent of svartalfs serving in the Vale via the svartalf princep's official approval. He was also Lady Marshal Arouveth's paramour."

Torbjorn's eyes narrowed, and he felt a prickle of suspicion. "That sounds like a complicated situation."

Utyrvaul threw his head back and laughed as he ducked out of the tent to fetch the Banneret.

"Petty, sordid family affairs, my dear dwarf. Never forget it."

CHAPTER EIGHT

"I don't like it."

Not a single dwarf was surprised by Waelon's declaration. The assembled Bad Badgers' responses ranged from rolled eyes to scoffs and mutters.

"Who would have thought?" Haeda grumbled.

"You don't say," Clahdi remarked.

"Wait, let me guess." Ober chuckled. "Does it have something to do with how you don't trust elves?"

The former ranger's glare swept over the group. He'd been unable to keep track of who'd said what other than the final statement. Dark eyes met gray, and neither gave an inch.

"That's just the tip of it," Waelon growled. "We're not just going after elvish witch scribbles while the entire army is heading to Greyshelf. Doing it means we're going to be stuck in the middle of more blade-ear politics."

"And?" Ober retorted with a shrug. "You heard Torbjorn. We need the myrklings on our side, and this is the way we get it."

"My ears work as good as yours, lad," the red-haired dwarf

rumbled. "I'm not saying we're not going to do it. I'm just saying I don't like it, and only a fool could imagine that this isn't going to go sideways quicker than a scared grem."

"Well, then it's good that I'll have you there to watch my back," Torbjorn interjected, drawing every eye with the declaration.

"Y-you're going?" Haeda stammered. "What? Torbjorn! *No!*"

"You're too important to risk that," Clahdi insisted. "Sending us is one thing, but you coming is just, well, *stupid*."

Gromic shot the young dwarfess a disapproving scowl, but when he turned to Torbjorn, his expression was grave.

"The lass needs to mind her tongue," the stout dwarf began. "But she's not wrong. Fact is, you are too important for this sort of thing. You can't put everything at risk like this, my tweldwan. Not for all the myrkling mercenaries from here to the Caged Sea."

Torbjorn faced the combined weight of the Bad Badgers sans Tomza, who was still attending to the tweldwan of the former 6th Division. Their concern pressed on him like a soft weight, gentle yet inexorable.

"Now see here," he replied, locking eyes with each in turn. "This isn't because I've got a death wish or even because I think the job won't get done without me. This has everything to do with how we're going to get the 'witch scribbles' intact so the elves are happy and we can get on with things."

"You said the scroll the elf-bitch wants is being carried upstream from Longsnout," Haeda stated, brow furrowing. "What's so hard about taking that off whatever tub is hauling it?"

"It's chained and rune-stamped," Torbjorn explained, struggling to keep the irritation out of his voice. After the meeting with the Banneret, he'd managed to grab a handful of hours of sleep before he'd risen to deliver the latest news to his Bad Badgers. The few hours he'd gotten had been solid and mercifully uninterrupted, but not nearly enough.

Once we get to Heimgrud, he promised himself, *I'm going to sleep for a week.*

"That's easy to get around." Waelon scoffed. "We just find whoever in the guards can clear the stamp. A hand will open it, whether or not it's attached. I can tell you that for certain."

Torbjorn flexed his wooden fingers at the thought, then shook his shaggy head. "Except that none of the guards can clear the stamp." He sighed. The explanation was necessary, even if he was weary of giving it. "The scroll isn't supposed to be accessed until it reaches Heimgrud. There, both a member of the princep's house and the Cyniburg royal family will meet to clear the rune stamp so the scroll can be accessed."

Grim nods met Torbjorn's eyes as he glanced around the room.

"So, you need Lord Gwyllethon and me on that ship to clear the stamp," Torbjorn continued. "Once that's done, we can take the scroll and get back to the lady marshal."

If Torbjorn had to put what each expression told him into words, he'd say the rest would be hard-pressed to put it more succinctly than Waelon had. They didn't like it.

"What's so special about this scribble, anyway?" Gromic asked. His question drew encouraging nods.

Torbjorn paused, trying to recall what the elves had said last night. Before he could answer, a lilting voice rose behind him.

"An Adamant Scroll is a potent magical artifact that dates from millennia ago," Utyrvaul declared as he slid into the Bad Badgers' communal tent with a flourish. "They are from the pinnacle of my people's civilization when we could fashion miraculous objects as readily as dwarvish smiths hammer out nails from pig iron."

"Yes, yes. You were very impressive once upon a time," Haeda snapped with a scowl. "Does the damned thing do anything besides be old and very obnoxious?"

"Oh, how I've missed this coarse discourse these past few months." Utyrvaul tittered as he moved into their midst and sat on an empty cot. "Only statements of truth can be transcribed upon Adamant Scrolls. The material will refuse to accept any inscription that is false. This obviously is incredibly valuable for a people such as mine, where the veracity of any given claim is a slippery thing."

Most of the dwarfs in the tent uttered affirming grunts, but Gromic shook his head. "So, you lot are such liars that you had to turn to witchery to know what's true?" the stout dwarf asked. "That's just sad."

"Quite," Utyrvaul replied curtly, put out at being interrupted. "An additional effect is that when a member of royal blood inscribes a matter of charter and royal writ, that statement is fact until the royal rescinds it. That almost never happens, or the functionary is eliminated."

"Which I imagine happens frequently," Torbjorn remarked, meeting Utyrvaul's sharp glare. "As we've seen more than once."

Torbjorn wasn't sure if he'd expected Utyrvaul to blush or splutter indignantly, but the svartalf's smile was anything but subdued. "Yes, dear old Tegwylivere Tivalino," the elf mused. "A shame I lost all her assets when I was captured by the wosealfs, but that placed me in your good company."

The dwarfs' groans were more forced than any of them would admit.

Torbjorn waved them to silence. "Anyways, the lady marshal wants her name inscribed as commander of the myrkling forces in the Vale. She has the bulk of the forces, but to cement her position beyond question or challenge, she needs the Adamant Scroll."

"Our young friend Gwyllethon is keenly aware of that," Utyrvaul explained. "To the extent that he's willing to hire someone to assassinate his previous superior when he uses the Adamant Scroll to install himself in her place. He claims his uncle declared it should be thus before his death at the hands of wosealfs last year. He's convinced that once Annuvel is removed and his name is inscribed on the scroll, the others will fall in line."

"How do you know?" Haeda asked skeptically.

In answer, Utyrvaul smiled and waggled his arched brows.

"Because you're the one he hired to kill the lady marshal," Waelon growled, and the group emitted a chorus of curses. "I might've known."

"Oh, it gets better." Torbjorn sighed and shot the svartalf a sidelong glance before nodding his assent. "Go on."

Utyrvaul's tongue darted across his lips in anticipation. Then he launched into the full explanation. "It seems the lady marshal is not convinced of her subordinates' loyalty, which is obviously prudent. As a result, she's formulated a plan that once the rune stamp is removed, someone will kill the ambitious little upstart. She believes she possesses a means to inscribe her name upon the Adamant Scroll as long as she has some of the young noble's blood, which should be easy for an assassin to acquire after the lad is dead."

"Let me guess," Haeda interjected before Utyrvaul could continue. "You know all this because you're the one the lady marshal hired to dispose of young Gwyllethon?"

Utyrvaul chuckled. "'You'd think so, wouldn't you? But as it happens, she's found someone even closer to the Banneret—a retainer with whom he is currently engaging in a torrid love affair. The poor idiot believes that she not only sees his potential, but she actually loves him."

Dwarven heads bobbed as the svartalf guffawed, though perhaps not for the same reason.

Gromic crossed his arms. "Then how do you know all this?"

Utyrvaul paused to give the dwarf a look that suggested he believed Gromic had missed something obvious, only to realize that the other Bad Badgers had the same question. That caught the elf off-guard, but after a few false starts, he managed to blurt an explanation.

"Well, obviously, I've been wooing the retainer as well," the myrkling stated. "The wench is a greedy little leech, and she knows that for all his pedigree and promises, Gwyllethon is not going to last long, even if he does manage to seize power from Annuvel. She's looking for her next meal ticket after she is cleared of killing her former lover."

The Bad Badgers muttered oaths and the usual warnings about trusting elves. Torbjorn nodded at Utyrvaul and said he would take it from there. The svartalf produced another flourishing bow and settled into watchful silence, drinking in dark looks from Waelon. Most of the dwarfs just rolled their eyes and gazed at Torbjorn.

"So, yet again, we are in a situation where different folk want different things, to say the least." The dwarf sighed as he met the eyes of his faithful company. "There's no way to make everyone happy, but I don't much fancy being used to sort out myrkling power disputes via murder."

"Could just kill them both," Waelon put in, earning scowls

from the group. That prompted him to explain. "No, why not? If they're too busy killing each other to pay attention to what is at stake, I say give 'em all what they want. Then have Utyrvaul do the witchy thing on the Scroll and have our blade ear sign his name."

Torbjorn was about to object, but the thought struck him. He and the other dwarfs turned as one to the elf in question.

Never one to shy from the spotlight, Utyrvaul straightened and looked down his nose at Waelon. "While I'm sure it was meant as a term of endearment, this blade ear does not belong to anyone," the svartalf began.

He was interrupted by wry snorts.

"You mean, not since you killed your last liege," Ober muttered, drawing nods from the others.

"Then I am in fit company." Utyrvaul sniffed. "But we are getting off-track. The matter at hand is whether I would have a qualified candidate to use Annuvel's methods to sign my name. While I believe I'd be more than qualified for the job, I've no idea of the process she'd use, and I'm unlikely to uncover it any time soon. Therefore, while I hope to attain that station someday, I can't use that method to achieve it. Still, I'm flattered that you all think so highly of me."

The red-bearded dwarf could not let the matter lie. "We already know what sort of sneaking—"

"Waelon," Torbjorn chided.

"Slithering—"

"Waelon."

"Slimy—"

"Waelon!"

The former ranger's mouth shut with a click of teeth, which he bared in a mirthless grin. Utyrvaul stared at Waelon, a smile tugging at the corners of his mouth. Looking at the two, Torbjorn could swear he felt the air churning with the promise of violence.

As usual, the moment stretched, neither elf nor dwarf making a move. Thankful for that, Torbjorn heaved a sigh and addressed the crew of dwarfs.

"So with that not an option, we're taking a managed neutrality position on this one," the commander explained. "We execute the raid on the tub traveling upriver, making sure Gwyllethon gets there and helps us take care of the rune stamp. From there, we keep the retainer from killing him while also not letting him sign his name on the Scroll. Then we hoof it back to the main force, which will be heading to Greyshelf. Then we can let the Banneret and the lady marshal sort out their differences."

"My money's on the lady marshal," Haeda called, looking for takers. "That one's as cold as any pale eel I've ever seen, and she'll drop that princeling sure as stones roll downhill."

Several of the other dwarfs put in their opinions and bids, but Torbjorn waved them down before things got unmanageable. The Bad Badgers lapsed into silence and watched their leader with appropriately chastened expressions…except Waelon, who still looked sour about the idea of working with elves again.

"Right, well, that's done. We need to talk about who's going," he began, and a sharp look from under a raised brow stilled potential arguments. "I have to, which doesn't mean you all do. In truth, I need some of you to stay. This will be the first time the army's operated without me here, and while I'm fairly certain every dwan out there has fully bought in, whether they like it or not, I don't know for sure.

"I need a few of you to stay behind to make sure no one gets any bright ideas that result in usurping my command or changing course. I've plotted a route that will take them to Greyshelf without going through lootable towns. I want this to remain so."

The Bad Badgers nodded their understanding, though their expressions said they recognized the monumental task he was suggesting. A dwan's right to plunder on the campaign trail, much less a mercenary's, was a time-honored if unspoken certainty. It was clear why Torbjorn didn't want his forces engaging in that, but it wasn't hard to see that many within the newly united army might not be so enlightened.

"We might not be Shabr'Dwan anymore, but who would listen to us?" Haeda asked, speaking for the rest of the company. "We're not held in high regard even now."

"Don't sell yourselves short," Torbjorn countered with an infectious grin. "You are the right-hand dwans of Prince Torbjorn, the Champion of Greyshelf, Chosen of the Shaper. If that isn't enough, I'm going to elevate Mordah Jorridottr to be the lardwan and her tweldwan Korm Dramson to be the vindwan."

"Tweldwan Korm as the vindwan?" Waelon spat. "The fool who marched into Tuvaloth like he'd been invited, who the savagelings had surrounded every step of the way?"

"Korm's not the canniest dwan. I'll give you that," Torbjorn admitted. "But he was the first one to have his forces join us, and many of the other tweldwans we've brought in look up to him for some reason. Besides, how would it look to all the other tweldwans who have joined us if I elevated one of his fordwans above him? I don't imagine any of them would like the idea of a subordinate ordering them about."

The former ranger crossed his arms and lapsed into silence.

"So, they'll do the bulk of the official ordering about, while those of you left behind will act as my eyes and ears," Torbjorn continued. "For keeping an eye on the army's course to Greyshelf, I'm leaving you, Haeda. I'd recommend that you keep track of our supplies as well. I don't want someone getting creative, so they have to make a detour to one of the smaller hamlets to acquire supplies."

The driver opened her mouth but paused when the eyes of the others turned to her. Then she saw Torbjorn's pleading glance.

"Yes, sir," she agreed, head bobbing even as her shoulders bowed under the weight of her acceptance.

"Good lass. I knew I could count on you." Torbjorn turned to Ober. "Your sister needs to stay here to tend the wounded, and I'm not just talking about Okmur. I'm going to have you hang around as well. After seeing you in action, even the most disgruntled dwarf will think twice about discussing dissension while I'm away. I'd rather they all follow out of loyalty, but for the moment, fear will do."

Ober's mouth compressed into a line as he fought to swallow every objection that sprang to mind. A quick glance at Haeda, who gave him an encouraging nod, sealed the deal, and with a deep sigh, he bowed his head.

"Yes, sir," the young dwarf replied, looking up when he felt a hand on his shoulder. His eyes rose to meet Torbjorn's, who grinned reassuringly.

"Don't worry. There's plenty of excitement to come, so you'll have more than one chance to die heroically. You can bet your life on it."

CHAPTER NINE

"Why am I still here?"

Tomza didn't have a good answer to that question, and the situation was unlikely to change anytime soon. Her charge asked every time she came to tend to him.

"I don't know." It was the same weary answer she always gave. "It's not my business to know. It's my business to make sure you get healthier while you wait."

As he'd done over the past several days since they'd set out for Greyshelf, Okmur nodded, then let her minister to the slowly healing wound on his belly. She would probe the wound and test the stitches to see if they were holding. She would then tell him it would be a few days more until she'd think about removing them, administer an herbal salve, and redress the wound.

The big dwarf was quiet and compliant throughout the process, only speaking when asked a question and only producing a nod or shake of his head or a grunt or a sigh if he could get away with it.

Sometimes the young dwarfess wondered if something

had broken in the former tweldwan, but each time, she dismissed that thought when he met her eyes. In those pale depths, Tomza found a will she couldn't deny. He was still and silent, not because he'd given up but because he was waiting.

When she thought about it, she felt a prickle of fear, but peering into his eyes affirmed that it was not a predatory patience. He was not watching her or waiting for a chance to strike. Yet, he still waited and she didn't know why.

She climbed out of the iron-barred wagon that had become Okmur's prison while they were on the move. "Why is he still here?"

Tomza swore. She'd nearly lost the wad of old bandages and her herbal satchel when she started. The dwarfess had been so wrapped up in her thoughts that she hadn't noticed her brother's approach. She turned a baleful eye on him, but he was staring after Okmur's wagon and didn't notice.

"Could it be for information?" the young dwarf asked, scratching his chin. "Maybe something to do with the defenses at Greyshelf?"

Tomza gave up on trying to get her brother to notice her glare and scoffed as she set off down a line of wagons framed by ranks of resting dwarfs. She always timed her visits to Okmur for the stops made along their march, determining that it was safer that way for all involved. That and when the time finally came for her to remove the dwarf's stitches, it would be far easier without the wagon swaying under her and her patient.

It was a short walk to the trio of wagons that operated as mobile infirmaries for the force. When she reached them, she would deposit the bandages in a cleansing mixture. Its scent would make the eyes of a drake water, but it did a fantastic job of expunging the lingering soil from the fabric so that, once dried, the bandages could be reused.

Ober had followed her.

"I've already told you I don't know, and seeing as Torbjorn's a good few days' ride away, it's unlikely that I've suddenly got the answer. Now, don't you have something else to do besides pester me?"

Ober did *not* have anything else to do, which was why he kept asking questions about Torbjorn's plans for their stricken former commander. It turned out that being a fearful symbol of an absent leader's power and authority was not hard, and as long as everyone remained cowed, it was boring.

"Maybe he plans to use him as a hostage in negotiations with those idiots in the fortress," Ober mused, not seeming to notice his sister's irritation. "Though, given what little I've heard about Peak-Breaker's reputation, I'm not sure how much leverage his life will give us. The dwarf's a terror on the battlefield and not a bad tactician when he's trying, but he's pricklier than a blotferow's bum at the best of times."

An ascedwan at the nearest infirmary wagon saw Tomza coming and removed the lid on the pitted cauldron hanging from the back of the large wooden vehicle. Looking away at the last second to shield her eyes from splash-back, Tomza deposited the bandages in the slurry.

"Erduna's dugs," Ober swore as he held up a hand to ward off the potent fumes. "Are you sure there will be anything left of those rags after they soak in that stuff?"

It was Tomza's turn to ignore the question. She asked the attending to ask for a restock of the herbs she'd used throughout the day. By now, the ascedwans working in the infirmary didn't scrunch their noises or frown at the list of herbs. They'd learned that while Tomza's applications were sometimes unorthodox, they were effective.

It could be so much more, said the voice that represented the worst part of her. *You could cure an entire camp full of maladies if you really wanted to. If you cared.*

The young dwarfess drove it back into the murky depths of her mind and forced a smile of gratitude for the ascedwan who handed her the herbs she'd asked for.

"We've got a handful of cases of nasty scalding," the ascedwan said as Tomza tucked the last of the herbs into her satchel. "Perhaps you could put some of those to use up there, as only you seem to know how."

Tomza frowned as she met the dwarf's eyes, pleasantly surprised to see sincerity, not mockery, in them.

"Seems some of the new lads are still tender-skinned," the ascedwan stated with a long-suffering sigh. "Though that's no reason to go easy on them. If they'd done as they'd been trained, we wouldn't have a bunch of chapped dwarfs taking up space in the medical wagons, complaining about their scruffy danglers."

Tomza forced a chuckle, knowing that if the situation was different, she would have enjoyed the repartee with fellow professionals. As it was, she thought it would be a poor escape route from her brother's questions to tend to a collection of chafed groins.

"I'll see what I can do," Tomza stated and gave a half-hearted smile. "And I'll try not to go too easy on them."

"'Once in the morning and once at night, a wire brush will this put right,'" the ascedwan in the wagon recited as he brandished an imaginary one. "That's what me ol' battle barber used to say to get 'em to straighten up. If nothing else, you can try that one."

Tomza saluted and headed toward the infirmary wagon he'd indicated. Behind her, Ober stared in mute horror at the grinning ascedwan before scurrying to catch up.

"He didn't mean that about the stiff wire brush, did he?" Ober asked in an urgent whisper. "That was just a joke, right?"

Tomza glanced at her brother. Just as she feared, Ober's face was thrust forward, eyes big and pleading for an answer to his question. It was moments like these when she could forget everything that had happened to them over the last few years and that her brother was a full-grown dwarf who'd waded through hell and back. As she stared into his big gray eyes, she could almost forget about the thing lurking behind them. He would slumber until the pulse of drums and the scent of blood drew him forth again.

"Why do you look so nervous, brother?" the dwarfess teased, one hand snaking out to tug on the hide armor he wore. "Things rubbed raw down there, Obie?"

Ober made to swat her hand away, but Tomza was quicker. Her brother staggered forward.

"I didn't say that," Ober retorted. "And I don't intend to, but that doesn't mean I can't feel bad for the poor bastards who are about to have their family jewels rough-polished."

"'Once in the morning, and once at night,'" Tomza intoned with mock sincerity. "Don't disdain the wire brush until you've felt its power."

"I'd very much rather not." Her brother chuckled, and the pair shared an honest laugh for the first time in a long while. Tomza felt the pressures within her slacken, and the irritated melancholy that hung over her while tending Okmur came apart.

Then two unmistakable four-legged heralds loped forward bearing bad news. The columns of dwarfs on either side of the wagon shuffled as one to give the creatures a wide berth, hands instinctively groping for the stocks of the duabuws slung over their shoulders.

"What are you two doing here?" Tomza demanded, resting her knuckles on her hips. "And wearing your wolf shapes, no less."

Tomza looked to her brother for support in chastising the pair, but Ober's eyes slid from one to the other, looking impressed as they advanced with sure strides. Tomza wondered if he admired them for the control they had over their forms, or was it an un-dwarvish appreciation for elvish grace that shone through even in their quadrupedal shapes.

Tomza shook her head in irritation and watched them shed their bestial shapes.

"You need to come," Bella declared, pointing to the east. They'd been with the bulk of the wosealf forces. Their fieldcraft was such that the only reminder of the savagelings being out ahead of the army were the occasional reports that filtered in.

"There is something your prince would want you to see," Hukka declared, craning his neck in the direction his sister pointed. "We've told the scouts not to report it to your officers yet, but it will only be a matter of time before your rangers stumble on it. Even *they* cannot miss this."

Ober looked at Tomza, who gave a weary nod after peering closely at the inscrutable pair.

"Go ahead," she muttered, nodding at the infirmary wagon ahead. "I'll just have to apply the stiff wire brush on my lonesome."

To the dwarfess' surprise, both elvish skinchangers shook their heads vigorously.

"No, you must both see," Bella stated matter-of-factly. Hukka added, "And quickly."

Ober and Tomza raised their eyebrows but assented. "Fine," Ober said, squinting to the east. "How far do we have to leg it?"

"No time," Bella growled. Her body twisted back into wolf shape. "Climb up. We don't have any more time to waste."

CHAPTER TEN

"That's more than I bargained for."

Torbjorn watched the perpetually chilly Heimwash snake its way over the earth like a dark vein winding through flesh. Its waters were fed by the Heimlagu just beyond Greyshelf, which lay like an icy heart within the stony ribs of the jutting crest of the Central Wyrmspine Mountains and wound its way toward Lake Blacemere in the south.

Only in the depths of winter did the Heimwash freeze, the ice typically ascending from the edge of the lake until its frosty grip encrusted everything up to the cataracts within Greyshelf. Something as natural as ice could not find its way up to Heimlagu, though. It was ruled by the things that swam beneath its surface.

Here on the Heimwash, the waterway was currently obstructed by a tangled collection of wood being drawn upstream. In the center was a wide-bellied barge with a broad sail and teams of worcsvine pulling it along the shore. Around it were smaller skiffs with rowers who labored against the current, forming a drifting escort.

On each skiff was a team of svartalf irregulars armed with bows and javelins, and a dozen svartalf knights bedecked in fine plate armor guarded the barge. Attending the teams of worcsvine on either side of the river were goblin handlers watched by more irregulars. They were the least well-equipped of the myrklings present.

"Given everything I've heard about you, this won't be a challenge," Gwyllethon declared, handing off his adyrclaf's reins. "Those guards down there haven't been paid by your ondwan in months, like the rest of us."

Waelon growled in irritation, and Torbjorn silenced him with a sharp look.

"Of course, if that's just camp prattle, I don't see our alliance lasting very long," the svartalf continued, not oblivious to his audience's mood but disdainful of them. "More disappointments from your kind won't surprise me, though I'm sure they will disappoint my dear auntie."

Torbjorn eyed the young svartalf and, not for the first time, fought the urge to plant his ensorcelled fist in the elf's guts. Slight even for an elf, as well as being a head shorter than any of his kin, the myrkling carried himself with a presumption and arrogance that would've been overblown for an emperor. He managed to look down his nose at every elf around him despite his diminutive stature, and when he addressed a dwarf, usually Torbjorn, a sneer was present in every word.

If your uncle really wanted you to be the commander of the mercenary companies, he was a fool, Torbjorn thought, though he knew that did little to help him compose himself to reply to the elf. "I'm not certain what alliance of 'ours' you are referring to," Torbjorn replied with a glance to make certain his dwarfs contained themselves. "I was only noting that the escort is more extensive than the lady marshal led me to believe. No one was talking about not going through with this."

"I'm glad to hear that." Gwyllethon chuckled, the sound and toss of the elf's head suggesting he truly believed Torbjorn's commitment was a result of his words and nothing else. Torbjorn bit back the urge to disabuse the snooty little blade ear of the notion.

A dwarf spoke at his shoulder. "The real issue will be beaching the barge, if that's where they're keeping it," Gromic observed, still squinting at the water-borne procession. "Though I can't for the life of me think why they'd go about it this way. You'd think a few swift riders with spare mounts would be the way to do it."

In answer, a tall and imposing svartalfess stepped forward, still holding her liege's adyrclaf's reins.

"They're coming up from Blacemere," Gwyllethon's retainer Lorellieth stated in a clipped voice. "Scroll was lost when Lord Gwydarioc's forces were overrun last autumn. Now that it's back, they're not taking any chances."

Gwyllethon projected an exaggerated yawn that had every dwarf scowling at him.

The she-elf bowed her head. "Apologies, my Lord," she muttered, stepping back to stand with the mounts and the other two retainers Gwyllethon had brought with him.

"What was that? Oh, not to worry, my dear Lorellieth," the Banneret drawled, his knowing grin in desperate need of being rearranged by a dwarvish boot. "I was just stretching while I waited for word that we would go liberate our objective."

"Perhaps you'd like to lead the way, good Bannaret," Utyrvaul offered, his fingers playing over the hilt of the heirloom blade. "Should you issue forth, we will all be right behind you, though I'm not sure how you plan to cross the river to reach the barge. Do you think your adyrclaf would mind the chilly water?"

Torbjorn couldn't find it in him to chastise or even discourage the elf for his rejoinder. He stood with bated breath as the younger svartalf leveled a long look at Utyrvaul. "Perhaps I should order you forward," Gwyllethon stated, his stare icy but his teeth flashing in a smile. "It seems like the perfect opportunity for a disgraced cavalier to prove his value to his betters. Perhaps, you could test the water, and if you manage to stay afloat, we could use you as a stepping stone to leap onto the nearest skiff."

Utyrvaul's laugh was as clear and sharp as a glass blade.

"Oh, Gwyllie, you really are too much." The svartalf met the Banneret's stare. "While I appreciate your inventive strategies, I'd be remiss if I didn't tell you that since both my immediate liege and *her* liege, your dear uncle, are dead, I'm unaffiliated. My contract was elf to elf, not house to house, so Urivianoc owes no allegiance to Gwydarioc. Did your fine tutors fail to teach you anything besides how to look down your overly long nose at others?"

The Banneret bristled and his retainers tensed, hands not quite settling on their weapons. Torbjorn noted that all were poised to draw. The tension thickened between the two elves, and Torbjorn wondered what he would do if things broke down between svartalfs. His practical side said that Gwyllie, for all his pretensions, was more valuable, but really, the choice was already made.

If steel was drawn, the Banneret and his retainers would be dead on the ground. Torbjorn would craft a convincing lie for the lady marshal. *Given their scheming, it wouldn't have to be that convincing.*

"Torbjorn!"

The commander turned and saw Clahdi coming over the crest of a ripple of hills to the north.

"Lads, behave yourselves," Torbjorn warned as he left to meet the hustling dwarfess. "We've got plenty that needs doing without putting knives in each other's backs."

"Oh, rest assured, Your Majesty," Utyrvaul murmured through bared teeth as he caressed his sword hilt. "I won't be putting a knife in any back."

"Does an Urivianoc even know what to do when an enemy is facing them?" Gwyllethon asked. "As far as I know, they've never settled anything that way."

Torbjorn offered a prayer to the Shaper that the pair wouldn't murder each other by the time he returned.

Clahdi puffed toward him, and he met her near the base of the hillock. "Any sign of outriders or other land-based escorts?" Torbjorn asked, wondering what could've made the dwarfess come back from her reconnaissance in such a state. "Anything that would give us away?"

The young dwarfess shook her head and swallowed another mouthful of air, pointing back the way she'd come.

"Moved down the river path," she panted, leaning on her long-handled axe. "At their current speed, in an hour, they'll pass near a stretch of gravel and sand that is barely more than a handsbreadth below the surface. They might not even know it's there since it is pretty loose."

Torbjorn blinked as he took in the former ranger's words, then stepped forward eagerly and took her by the shoulder. "You said an hour?"

Clahdi nodded, wincing at Torbjorn's grip. "Aye." He released her. "Though it's a narrow stretch, so they'll clear it quick. If we're going to make a go of it, we'll have one chance. Then there's not going to be another chance until Greyshelf, as far as I can see."

Torbjorn nodded and ran a thumb over his scarred cheek, then shot the dwarfess a grim smile.

"Tell me true, ranger. Can you lot shoot the wings off a crow in flight from two hundred paces?"

Clahdi paused, surprised by the question. Then a dangerous smile spread across her flushed features.

"With fair weather, I could shave a bumblebee bald from that distance. If all you want is a gimpy crow, I'd just need to be within three hundred paces."

Torbjorn's smile broadened at the boast. "I'll hold you to it, lass." He clapped her on the shoulder. "Let's fetch the others before they kill each other. Then I'll set out the plan."

CHAPTER ELEVEN

"You all right, sis?"

Tomza raised one hand from a thick tree bole to flash a rude gesture at her brother. The ride on the backs of the wosealf skinchangers had not been long, but they had woven through dense timber and bounded over many rough hillocks. By the time Bella and Hukka had deposited them at the edge of a glade, the dwarfess was gray in the cheek, and her brow was too sweaty for the cool air in the trees' shadows.

"Fair enough," Ober replied, remembering having similar feelings the last several times he'd ridden on worcsvines or blotferows. The young dwarf might have pondered why he found clinging to Bella's heaving form less strenuous, not to mention less frightening than riding a beast that had been domesticated by his ancestors over a millennium ago, but what lay beyond the tree line commanded his attention.

Gathered like a group of canvas-backed primeval beasts was a collection of covered wains. They'd formed a rough circle around a central fire pit that showed signs of recent use, though only a small mound of smoldering embers remained, trailing thin wisps of smoke that vanished the second they rose above the treetops.

There were no signs of the wains' owners or the beasts that drew the wagons other than the grass around the wagons being stripped.

The peculiar scene was made even stranger by the prickling in Ober's mind. It set the spirit sharing his skin to snuffling and rumbling.

"Wains with no wain dwarfs," Ober muttered as he moved to keep watch without being exposed. "Something is going on here."

"Why do you think we brought you?" Hukka growled as he stalked up in elfin form. "The wandering stonehearts are not unknown to us. Perhaps you know why they are here."

Ober thought "not unknown to us" was a delicate way to describe how the savagelings had butchered and eaten every dwarf in their territory, even the heretical ones. Since that had happened within the living memory of the short-lived humans in the Vale, it made the statement seem darkly amusing. Before he could comment further, he heard soft footsteps. The other wosealf sibling was nearby.

"We know they should not be here," Bella whispered from behind a tree to his right. "The wanderers come in the early spring and are on their way south again well before the first frost. To find them this far north at this time is strange."

Ober nodded, but the truth was that being Vale-born, he knew very little about the movements of the heretical nomads. Wain dwarfs avoided the dwarvish settlements they came across. Imperial edicts technically gave them protection, but even in the most civilized cities in Central Wyrmspines, it was weak at best. In the far wilder Vale, a wain dwarf caravan that came to a dwarvish settlement or attracted the attention of a garrison was asking for trouble they were unlikely to survive.

That did not speak to why these wain dwarfs were here. Ober's frown deepened as he scanned the perimeter of the glade.

"I'd like to know how they even got here," he muttered and pointed at the timber ringing the area. "There's nothing like a track or path between those trees, much less a road wide enough to bring their wagons through."

His sister's approach was a wince-inducing racket compared to the stealthy movements of the elves as Tomza fetched up against a tree near Ober's shelter. She had recovered some of her color, but the less-than-grateful look she shot Hukka suggested full recovery would be an extended process.

"Don't you remember the secret paths they took us on?" she asked, meeting Ober's gaze. "Remember what they were actually doing?"

Ober had made a concerted effort to forget that trip. Not only had it been a confusing beginning to the most confusing time in his young life, but Tomza's behavior during that time had not helped. Seeing the excited gleam in her eyes, he realized his sister fondly remembered their time with the wain dwarfs.

"I remember you said some nonsense about the path not being a path," Ober snapped. When the eyes of the wosealfs and his sister turned to him, he added, "It was something about us moving through the world differently. Are you saying that was how they got in here with those wagons?"

"Absolutely." Tomza nodded. "That might also be why we can see the wagons but not the dwarfs and their animals.

Their charms allow them to hide, not by tricking the senses but by letting them slip into that space between worlds."

The young dwarf's eyes swung back to examine the wagons, not liking the suggestion that what he saw might not be all there was. He knew that was ironic, considering that one would never guess he was carrying a thunderblood spirit in his body, but that did not dismiss his unease.

"That explains why we nearly missed them," Bella hissed to her brother. "I was wondering how we failed to scent so many, especially the draft beasts, while we were scouting."

Hukka produced a wet snarl as he sniffed the air, clearly aligning with Ober's take on the situation.

"Unnerving to think stonehearts would have such power, but that's not the issue. The question is what to do with them. The army will not pass through here, but if they are spies, they could easily take the measure of our forces. Leaving them here makes us vulnerable. We can't—"

"That's ridiculous," Tomza interjected, heat in her voice to go with the sharp words. "There's no way that any wain dwarfs would work with Ashfer's forces, and even if they would, there is even less of a chance that Ashfer would trust people he'd call heretical scum."

Ober wanted to ask why she'd qualified the description of the wain dwarfs with "people he'd call," but staring at the vacant camp was making the spot between his shoulder blades itch. He felt like they were being watched, and the blow from the unseen foe could fall at any moment. They had to make some decisions and act quickly before his paranoia was proven right.

"Trust is not the same as use," Hukka countered. "And given our success, would it not make sense that our enemy would seek new allies in his desperation?"

That made sense. Ober even wanted it to, but deep down, the wosealf didn't understand the depth of the animosity. Even Vale-born dwarfs with deviant beliefs like him and his sister were hostile toward the wain dwarfs. A mountain-raised dwarf like Ashfer would find the very idea of cooperation cause for violence. Still, something had to be done about the inconveniently positioned caravan.

Tomza began another rebuttal to Hukka, but Ober silenced her with a wave. He earned a cold glare for it.

"Is there a way we can get them out of that in-between place?" Ober asked, looking at Tomza. "That, or is there a way for us to go in there?"

His sister's eyes narrowed. "What are you thinking about doing?" Her expression was pinched.

"What we have to," Ober snapped. More venom had seeped into his voice than he'd intended. "Hukka's right. They can't stay here. It's too risky."

"So, what's your plan?" Tomza asked, bristling. "Drive them out of hiding and slaughter them?"

At the mention of a violent confrontation, the spirit within Ober roused, but he eased it back down. It might well come to that, but not yet.

"Not if we don't have to," Ober told his sister, forcing his voice to remain even. "First, we try to reason with them. If that doesn't work, Hukka and Bella try to spook them. If *that* doesn't work, I could change and raise a ruckus. Maybe destroy a wagon or two to let them know we mean business. We're a lot of steps away from violence."

"But they aren't harming anything," Tomza insisted, looking at her brother and the elves. Her eyes lit up with a thought. "Besides, Torbjorn wanted us to avoid hurting the residents of the Vale, and given the path he told us to take to

Greyshelf, we should do that. He might not have known about this caravan, but I expect he'd want the same protections extended to them as we're giving Klavoburg and Jorsburg."

"Klavoburg didn't spring up overnight," Bella stated, her voice gentle but firm as she met Tomza's eyes. "We roamed out this way a few days ago when the army first set out, and they were not here."

Tomza's face looked hunted. "You yourself said you missed them before," Tomza began, her voice tight and her words hurried. "Maybe they've been here this—"

"Tomza, that's enough," Ober growled with a force that made even the wosealfs recoil. "I don't know why you are so worried about these heretics all of a sudden, but we have a duty to Torbjorn and the dwans serving in his army."

Tomza looked as though she was ready to argue further, but she had to gather herself after his forceful rebuke. He didn't plan to give her the time.

"We're driving these vagabonds out of here, and that's that," Ober declared. "Now, tell me how we get to wherever they're hiding."

Just behind them, a rustle was followed by a statement made in a full, buttery voice. "Well, for starters, you could ask."

Dwarfs and elves spun to see a mature shapely dwarfess standing between two trees half a dozen strides from them. Her hair was bound up in the winding scarves common for wain dwarf females, and the skirt of her robe was pleated and bore the brightly colored tassels associated with her kind. Among those tassels were pendants and charms of many metals and polished stone, twinkling as they swung.

Her face was tanned and weathered by a life on the road, which did not mar the beauty of her open and honest features.

Her lashes were darkened and her lids had a smoky sheen, framing keen black eyes. Those sharp eyes scrutinized the dwarfs and elves.

Ober didn't like how quickly the dwarfess had taken his measure. They hadn't even spoken directly. However, standing there gawking wouldn't give her a good impression of him.

"Do you speak for your caravan?" he asked, looking over his shoulder. "We have things to discuss."

The dwarfess smiled as if to suggest she was being very patient with him. "I currently speak for them, and I heard the gist while I was waiting."

"Waiting for what?' Tomza asked.

"To see what your plans for us were. It seems you've got concerns about where we are located and would very much like us to move on."

As she answered Tomza's question, she slowly turned to Ober. When she finished speaking, she was gazing at him. Ober felt like she was looking into him deeper than she had any right too. The power in her stare set his teeth on edge, and when he finally spoke, his words were hard and cold, her opposite in every way.

"Will you parley with us, or are you going to make this difficult?"

A chest-deep rumble emerged with the words like a storm on the horizon.

"We would welcome you to our fireside for a chat as friends," the dwarfess replied, her tone and expression unchanged. "But you will come unarmed and seeking fellowship, not to threaten or harm."

Ober felt the spirit who shared his skin stirring at her declaration, and a brutal laugh rose in his throat. Who did this heretic think she was? Could she even comprehend who she was talking to? He was the breaker of armies, the hammer that shattered opposition. The dwans feared him. Wasn't that what Torbjorn had chosen him for?

"I'm never unarmed," the young dwarf crowed, stepping toward the dwarfess. "And I'm not going to pretend I won't do what I have to to get you and yours out of our way, no matter what that takes."

The dwarfess eyed him, but she was not intimidated. Rather, she was sad, or maybe disappointed, as though she'd expected better. The beast bristled within him.

"Ober, what are you doing?" Tomza hissed in his ear, having stepped over to his shoulder. Ober left off glaring at the wain dwarfess to look into his sister's eyes. The concern and fright he saw there filled him with as much rage as anything the heretic could have said or done.

"Aren't you tired of this?" Ober growled, rounding on his sibling, his voice low and urgent. "Things are changing, and we are at the heart of it. It's about time we got some respect for what we do. We bent and scraped while we were chained and beaten, but things are finally being set right. I'm done begging, and I'm not going to plead with that blaspheming bitch."

Tomza reached a trembling hand toward her brother, but he twisted away from her with a snarl. The wain dwarfess watched, her expression neutral, but he thought he saw laughter in her eyes. He stalked forward, raising a clenched fist.

"Kak on you and your fireside and your fellowship," he spat. "You and your degenerate mob are going to clear out now, or I'm going to turn your wagons to kindling, and anyone who tries to stop me won't live long enough to know how big a mistake they made."

The wain dwarfess' head cocked to one side as she eyed Ober, the sadness in her expression now more than a suggestion.

"I'm sorry to hear you say that," she replied. "But you will do no such thing, Ober Draulson of Clan Jaln."

Tomza gasped, but hearing this stranger speak his full name further fueled the fire that was burning in him. The heat made the thunderblood drag himself closer to the surface.

"Please, he's not himself," Tomza called over her brother's shoulder. "Ober, please stop."

"Do you know this stoneheart?" Hukka asked, concern and suspicion in his voice.

"She can't know me," Ober growled, a prickling itch spreading over his limbs as dark hair sprouted. His voice was impossibly deep and guttural. "Otherwise, she'd know she is facing death!"

Before anyone could move to stop him, Ober lunged forward, the bestial changes sweeping through his form. He would not be wholly transformed when he reached her, but he was already twice his original size and now had dagger-sharp claws. The wain whore would flee before him, or he'd flatten her. She'd been warned, so he was well within his ri—

SLEEP, BEAST

The words came from the dwarfess, but they were not spoken. They were more than sound waves in the air. The words rang through the world and the living things within it. Through Ober as well. Her will surged against, over, and through him. The young dwarf struggled against it, finally emerging out the other side like a cork popping out of a bottle.

He was still moving toward the wain dwarfess, but the changes wrought by the thunderblood were gone. No fangs behind his lips, no claws on his hands, no doubled mass. Not even a pelt except what any member of his hirsute race would have.

"W-what did you do to me?" Ober asked as he stared at his fingers.

The dwarfess shook her head. "Not to you. To the one you carry with you."

Ober gazed at her, mouth working but no words coming. He reached within himself, and for a wrenching second, he thought the thunderblood was gone. His heart hammered and his breath came in ragged gasps as he tried to understand what it meant, and in that shocked stillness, he felt a rumble of slumbering power. He was still there, only resting deeper and stiller than since the first contact.

"What did you do?" he demanded, looking at the wain dwarfess with a mixture of hate and fear.

"I lulled a beast to sleep," she explained as though it was the most natural thing in the world. "And not just the one that lies beneath your skin."

Ober heard elvish cursing behind him. When he twisted around, the wosealfs were gaping at the heretic.

"That is deep magic," Bella murmured, wrapping her arms around her narrow shoulders. "I've never seen it before."

Hukka alternated between staring at his hands and feet and looking at the dwarfess in horror.

"Mailevong," he whispered, pointing a shaking finger at the dwarfess.

"Anything but, good elf," was her smooth, sure reply. "My people have known for a long time how to speak to beasts."

Silence descended as every other soul stared at her. After a moment, she nodded as though she'd come to an agreement none of the others were privy to. She then moved past Ober toward the glade. As she passed, she set one strong, square hand on his shoulder and gave it a gentle squeeze.

"No hard feelings," she murmured, eyes still pointed ahead. "Let's break bread together and chat for a bit."

They heard dwarvish voices laughing, chatting, and singing. Bovine lowing underpinned the bustle and commotion.

CHAPTER TWELVE

"You remember that time Barro Morrson nearly got us killed by taking a piss?"

Torbjorn fought the urge to clench a gauntleted hand around the haft of his cwellocs as he watched the barge come around the bend. He would've felt better gripping it in full Sablestone armor, but given where they were, that wasn't the best choice. Reflecting on that, he realized this was why Gromic had recalled the aforementioned memory.

"We were landing at Adaelton when Barro felt like the old waterskin was full," Gromic continued. "Normally, I'd have made him let it run down his leg since we were coming in hard, but we'd been stuck on our barge for going on three hours, so I thought it wouldn't hurt to let him step to the rail and let 'er go. Better than all of us having to stand in formation for another hour or two with his piss reeking at our feet."

Torbjorn nodded but ground his teeth at the slowness of the swine-drawn barge. The sail was slack, an obvious if unhelpful explanation as to why the vessel was creeping along. If things continued like this, what were the odds that Gwyllethon would misjudge the timing of his charge?

"So, he goes to the rail to do his business, only there's a problem." The stout dwarf chuckled. "Barro's was a big ol' slab of a dwarf, near on to the size of Tweldwan Okmur or maybe even bigger, and he's not only got a cwellocs sized for him—great, ugly brute of a thing—but the nozzle for his danglers matches his size as well. Trying to make water in Sablestone armor is hard enough, but doubly so when your meat worm requires two hands to manage."

Hunched over his duabuw, Waelon snorted. Clahdi raised an eyebrow without taking her eyes off her target. The special on their duabuws gleamed with wicked promise, grinning crescents of steel.

"The big aurochs tries to juggle everything and finally pitches his weapon to one side," Gromic recounted, shaking his head. "The oversized grem-walloper hits the deck, and there's a thud like you wouldn't believe! Person at the helm of the tub was a nervous human lending us 'is barge. He hears that without knowing Barro's situation, and he thinks he's struck a rock or something. He cranks hard, thinking he needs to keep his overladen boat from getting spitted."

In moments, the two former rangers would take their shots. Torbjorn's gaze swept down the banks, fearing he might spy Gwyllethon's or his retainers' arms glinting in the mid-day sun, but so far, nothing. From their sheltered spot atop a low hill, the dwarf commander could see grem scuttling around, encouraging the recalcitrant worcsvines. The irregulars loped along a stone's throw from the goblins and their charges, spending more time jeering at the grem than watching the riverbank.

That suited Torbjorn fine.

"A good number of us went sprawling and sliding at the sudden turn, and Barro went into the river, one hand still clutching his meat worm. The rest of us redistributed our weight while that jittery longshanks sawed her back and forth, trying to regain control.

"In the end, we landed at Adaelton before the command came, so we had to take the town on our lonesome. Didn't get a chance to fish out Darro until the next day, and when we dragged his corpse up, we found that something had eaten off most of that impressive nozzle o' his. Some of the lads said he deserved that for nearly getting us all killed and setting us up for a hard-won fight, but I couldn't help feeling bad for the lad, even if he was dead."

Gromic lapsed into silence, and the former rangers readied themselves to launch their bolts—the most crucial point of this entire operation. Torbjorn was glad not to have to instruct the former fordwan to quiet down. Instead, he could spend his time watching to see if the Banneret bungled his part.

Another myrkling set his teeth on edge as his high voice pierced the stillness.

"I'm sorry, Gromic, but you are peculiar, to say the least," Utyrvaul chided from where he crouched in the scrub, Reeve family blade drawn. "Did you share this story because you somehow think us assaulting a barge relates to your dear comrade having his member eaten by river scavengers?"

Torbjorn might've wheeled around to club the elf into silence, but he caught a glint up the bank. His heart lurched, and his gaze snapped back to the approaching vessel and entourage to see if anyone had noticed anything amiss.

"I suppose," Gromic acknowledged, his voice pensive. "Maybe I'm just nervous."

"About what?" Utyrvaul spluttered. "That you'd suffer a similar fate today?"

"Maybe." The stout dwarf frowned. "Depending on how this goes, any of us could end up in the drink."

Torbjorn's gaze darted to the north bank. He could now see people, not just glints of metal. Certain that would not go undetected, he glanced at the water and saw a few of the skiff-borne svartalfs pointing at the advancing riders.

It was too soon, and every stride Gwyllethon's adyrclaf took narrowed the window of opportunity. The skiffs changed course, and Torbjorn's blood froze when Gwyllethon blew a hunting horn to signal his cadre's charge.

"Well, I suppose there are two points to consider if we are to allay your fears," Utyrvaul began, but someone on the water yelled before he could finish speaking.

"Keep your nozzle in your trousers," Clahdi muttered as her finger tightened on the trigger of her duabuw.

"I don't expect there's any fish small enough to bother with you, tub," Waelon finished, and both duabuws sang their throaty songs.

The razor-steel heads flashed over the water. There was a dull twang as they struck the wrist-thick ropes that ran from the barge to the worcsvines on the far shore. The ropes drew taut, and for a strained instant, it seemed as if the effort had been for naught. Then they heard a pair of snaps as the partially sheared ropes surrendered. The worcsvines on the far shore stumbled forward, suddenly free of their burden. The barge groaned and listed hard to one side.

"*MOVE!*" Torbjorn thundered as he sprang to his feet and pelted down the hill, cwellocs in hand, earth spraying behind him with every lunging footfall. Beside him were Gromic and

Utyrvaul, and half a stride farther back were Waelon and Clahdi.

As they vaulted toward the riverbank, Torbjorn saw Gwyllethon and his retainers closing on the swine team on their bank. The land-based squad of svartalf irregulars, who were conscripted criminals and debtors rather than mercenaries, according to Utyrvaul, stood frozen. The officer among their ranks seemed torn between squaring off with the quartet of svartalf cavaliers or moving to intercept the dwarfs who had appeared behind his squad.

In the end, neither option suited the svartalfs. They threw down their weapons and scattered like a flock of starlings before a falcon. The slowest were caught in Gwyllethon's charge and cut down as the Banneret rode through to tear into the grem and their squealing worcsvines.

At nearly the same time, the barge's broad belly fetched up on the gravel bar. The vessel shuddered, and those on deck had to fight to keep their feet. Finally, it came to a halt with a deep crunch that sent all hands sprawling. With a groan, the weight settled into the shoal, and the barge tilted farther over. The armored svartalfs nearest the rail spilled into the shallows with surprised shrieks, emerging on hands and knees.

They were met by dwarvish boots.

Torbjorn planted his in the face of one elf, and his momentum forced the myrkling's thin neck back with a pop. He planted his other boot on the bowed back of a svartalf in the water whose breath rushed out in a burst of bubbles as his weight bore down. Torbjorn launched off his back toward the barge's tilted rail.

Torbjorn knew he couldn't make it, so he slammed the bill of his cwellocs into the rail. Hauling with all his strength, he dragged himself onto the rail, and with another heave, he slid onto the listing deck. Like a steel-covered boulder, he rolled over a few svartalfs unlucky enough to have an arm or leg in the way, drawing piercing shrieks. Their screams signaled that the battle was joined in earnest.

Torbjorn swung, and the axe blade of the polearm bit into the face of a svartalf whose helm lacked a visor. The myrkling was too busy choking to scream as he toppled over, and Torbjorn followed him like a stabbing thunderbolt. The spear-tipped crown of the cwellocs took a second elf through the throat, ripping through the rings of his mail as the edge scraped the top of his gorget. The myrkling's legs folded beneath him as he reached up to paw at the weapon's head and shaft.

Torbjorn planted his foot on the svartalf's body and yanked his weapon free, and the pause gave some of the barge guards time to climb to their feet. Torbjorn ducked a hurled javelin that sailed by him, and a saber stroke glanced off his helmet. He chopped at the legs of the elf who engaged him, but the warrior danced back from the stroke, then lunged forward to take another swing at Torbjorn's head. The blow never fell since Torbjorn used the missed swing to swivel around and thrust up with cwellocs' butt spike. The hardened steel point passed under the myrkling's upraised arm and punched through gambeson into the tender flesh beneath. The dwarf yanked the point clear as blood ran down the elf's side. Then he collapsed on the deck.

The world was suddenly full of stabbing weapons. Torbjorn was driven back to the rail when a trio of elves came at him, glaives thrusting and sweeping. Torbjorn tried to fend them off, hoping he might snare one with the bill or beard of the cwellocs, but the elves were too quick and their spear work was too deft. Another series of slashes and probing stabs put Torbjorn's back to the rail.

He was trapped, and he found himself remembering the sorry fate of Barro Morrson.

Well, if you go over, you're all buttoned up, he reassured himself, batting at another glaive point.

The sunlight flickered, and Torbjorn thought another javelin had sailed by. When one of the glaive wielders staggered back, axe wedged between pauldrons and cuirass, he realized the projectile had been going the wrong way. He didn't have a chance to look around before boots hit the deck beside him.

Waelon and Clahdi flanked him, and a moment later, looking for all the world like he'd been dredged up from under the barge, Gromic rolled over the rail and got to his feet with his perpetually shocking alacrity.

"Where's the elf?" Torbjorn asked, but something soared overhead. Utyrvaul was a lithe silhouette arcing through the air to snatch a bit of loose rigging, blood-stained sword flashing. With a ringing laugh, the svartalf struck a guard who was attempting to creep around the side of the dwarvish formation, then landed on the deck and came up in a flurry of slashes.

"I do believe time is of the essence," the myrkling called over his shoulder as he traded blows with a pair of svartalfs. "Let's dispatch this lot before we have to fend off their lackeys, eh?"

Torbjorn gave a steely laugh, buoyed by the elf's enthusiasm. "You heard him, lads and lassie," he growled, gripping his cwellocs. "Time to mop up the deck. *BAD BADGERS!*"

CHAPTER THIRTEEN

"In truth, more than one of us would like to leave as much as you want us to."

The wain dwarfess' confession came after they'd settled around the fire, which was far more impressive than a mound of embers. Huge logs crackled and snapped, flames springing up and around the wood. It was not unlike the energy that filled the glade now that charms had been lifted.

As rowdy and colorful as any other gathering of dwarfs, wearing clothing of the east and south that seemed peculiar and eccentric to their guests, the wain dwarfs went about the business of preparing food with vigor. A couple of young goats had been dressed, skewered, and seasoned before the camp was revealed, and they were being spitted over the fire to roast by a cadre of stout dwarfs. As this was happening, several dwarfesses prepared a bed of coals on one side of the fire and set pans to warm before stretching greased dough across the sizzling iron. The glade filled with the scent of herb-crusted roasted goat and frying flatbread.

Tomza watched them all work, chattering in a dialect of

Dwarrisc she'd only heard when they'd partnered with the wain dwarfs at Jorsburg. It was a faster, more fluid version of her tongue, and while she recognized many words, the speed and variety of inflections were too much for her to handle. What was clear was that, despite her brother's aborted display, the wain dwarfs would feed them well.

"We can't leave without speaking to your prince," the dwarfess explained. "He and Caravan Master Heshut struck a bargain, and we were told to seek him."

Tomza glanced at Ober, who was still shocked by the ease with which the dwarfess had overcome his beast. The rumors said all wain dwarfs were connected by a vast network, but this was the first evidence she'd seen. Tomza's stomach knotted, and she wondered if her previous protests about heretical dwarfs had been ill-advised.

"So, that's how you knew Ober?" Tomza pressed, unable to keep an edge out of her voice. "He and Heshut concluded their arrangement. Then the caravan master spread a rumor that Prince Torbjorn is soft on your kind."

The wain dwarfess just laughed. Tomza was ashamed of her petulant tone, feeling like a child whose attitude was beneath an adult's dignity to chide.

"That's one way to put it." She met Tomza's gaze levelly. "Our people are always glad to hear we have a chance for more than violence and hate among our kin, but your prince's indulgence is not what I'm here for. I'm here to give him information that might prove useful."

A pair of young dwarfs strode over to the meeting beside the fire, carrying trays on which rested steaming bowls that perfumed the air with mint and honey. They offered bowls to Tomza and her brother first. They both took one, though slowly.

When the bowls were offered to the elves, both sniffed before leaning back and gesturing them away. Finally, the wain dwarfess took a bowl with a grateful nod, and the young dwarfs bowed themselves away.

Tomza and Ober sat frowning into the tea. Their hostess smiled, lifted her cup to her lips, and drank deep.

"It might not mean much to you," she nodded at the waiting bowls, "but among our people, hospitality is sacred. Our clans would not have survived as long as they have without the hospitality of others, so we honor them by extending that hospitality when we can and abiding by its strictures even with our enemies."

She took another sip, still smiling. "Which, to be clear, you are not."

Tomza eyed the bowl. It smelled like something her mother would have brewed. She glanced at her brother, who nodded, and with a shrug, she took a sip. It tasted even better than it smelled. Her brother's frown deepened, and he contemplated the bowl's contents.

"If you are not a foe," Hukka piped up, crossing his arms, "why do you hide using strange magics?"

"And why have you not told us your name?" Bella added. "You do much skulking and sneaking for someone who claims to be a friend."

"I never said we were friends," the dwarfess replied, setting her bowl to one side. "And in regard to us secreting ourselves in this glade, I would think wosealfs and Imperial dwarfs need little explanation for why. Our cousins are known for being less than gentle with us, and as to your elven kindred? Well, saying that you are familiar with the taste of our meat since Randsvich is explanation enough."

The wain dwarfess squared her shoulders and stared into her guests' eyes in turn, her gaze intense.

"This caravan is not composed of my people but my family," she continued, her voice firm but not harsh. "These are my brothers and sisters, nieces and nephews, children and grandchildren. They are every soul I hold dear in the world gathered together, and I've led them here to the very belly of the beast. I hope you understand what I've risked to bring word to your prince and your people."

Tomza's breath caught in her throat as the implications settled over her. If what the dwarfess said was true, Tomza had trouble imagining she would risk so much for anyone, much less those who would not speak of them without spitting and cursing.

"But I *will* give you my name." The wain dwarfess sighed, her posture and tone softening. "I am Mehk Dolla Furrodottr of Clan Omru, and I've come from the shadow of Cer'Kest with word and warning for Prince Torbjorn."

Dwarfs and wosealfs raised their eyebrows and exchanged concerned looks at the mention of the wight's impregnable citadel in the south. Cer'Kest was rumored to be where the dead had first risen, and it had become the main threat to imperial dwarvish power in the Vale. The great necropolis, which had only seemed like a majestic if grim oddity from the past, had discouraged legions of the living from its unplumbed depths, and it was the heart of the wight counterclaim to the valley.

"You've been to Cer'Kest and lived to tell the tale?" Hukka queried doubtfully. "You say you risk much by coming here, yet you came from the Rock of the Dead?"

Dolla Furrodottr's eyes glittered as she met the incredulous stares.

"How quick you all are to forget the differences between us when it comes to such things." She laughed, and a hint of sharpness crept into her tone. "As sad as it is to say, the wights are more tolerant of us than wosealfs or our own kin. We offer no challenge to their rule, and our caravans bring trade and news to their human and goblin subjects, so we are tolerated."

"You've allied with the Blind Giants?" Bella hissed, baring her sharp teeth.

A few of the dwarfs preparing food turned, utensils gripped tightly, and as one, they looked at Dolla. When she just chuckled, they turned back to their tasks, the tension leaving them, but the implication was not lost on Tomza. Though they had been gentle and patient thus far, the wain dwarfs had a limit to their tolerance, and the outnumbered quartet would be wise to remember that.

"Oh, lass! You might as well ask if I've made compact with an avalanche or an earthquake." The wain dwarfess smiled. "The dead kings could care less about us, and if they suspected we threaten them, they'd be all too happy to kill us like the dwarfs. Given what I will be telling your prince, that might happen soon."

"You keep talking about what you have to tell Tor...Prince Torbjorn," Tomza began, trying not to watch a burly dwarf gripping a long carving knife who stood nearby. "But you still haven't told us what is so important that you'd risk all this."

Dolla nodded and seemed ready to answer, then raised her chin and sniffed the air. Above the fragrant tea, the smells of goat and bread were reaching a crescendo. Even the wosealfs couldn't help but eye the meat turning on the spits. Mehk Dolla shot them a sidelong glance and a knowing smile before turning back to Tomza.

"You are right that I've not told you, but seeing as you are not the prince, Tomza Drauldottr, I can't imagine that is a shock. You and your brother are among his inner circle, but what I have to say is for him before all others. Still, you are here, and the food is ready, so I see no need for you not to enjoy it before we send you on your way."

Tomza wanted to press the issue, but the dwarf with the large knife returned bearing a huge platter laden with prime cuts of roasted goat. Lying around the steaming meat were rounds of fried flatbread, some spread with goat cheese, others a crispy brown. Behind him was a dwarfess bearing a bowl of fresh autumn greens, and at her heels came two younglings. One clutched a collection of drinking horns in his little arms, and the other hefted a jug that was nearly as big as she was.

Further conversation stalled as the dwarven and elven siblings were plied with food. Ober ate mechanically, hardly seeming to notice what was put in front of him. Tomza tried to pretend that she was being cautious, still suspicious of what was being offered, though it was a thin ruse since the robust food soon claimed her attention. The second the goat meat was brought to Bella and Hukka, they set to it with a will. Tomza, like all dwarfs, was not particular about table manners, but even she found the zeal with which the savagelings tore into the meat to be uncomfortable.

The jug was filled with a crisp cider whose sharp flavor went well with the roasted herbs, pungent cheese, and fried bread. Water was also offered, but cider was the preferred beverage, though Ober spent more time sipping cooled tea than savoring the cider.

When the company had eaten and drunk their fill and a touch more than that, the sun was just past its zenith. The day was as warm as it would be, and combined with the heat from the fire, the siblings experienced a soporific effect. Tomza felt it tugging on her eyelids, the weight of good food in her belly leaching her ambition to return to the conversation about Torbjorn and the news from Cer'Kest.

The world was going soft around the edges, and her head felt heavy as she turned it. A small burp of surprise escaped her lips when she saw the wosealfs leaning against each other, pointed chins resting on their chests. On the other side of her, Ober was lying on the soft meadow grass, head cushioned on his folded arms. A long blink later, a low snore reverberated from the depths of his impromptu pillow.

Tomza tried to shake off the lethargy, but her body seemed to be against her. Her arms hung limp at her side, her feet could barely drag across the ground, and her neck was incapable of keeping her head from hanging. Why was she so tired? The food and the warmth and...

She was finding it hard to focus.

Something apart from the pressing call to sleep brushed her mind, yet it nudged her toward the desire for rest. She didn't feel it with the senses bound to her physical body.

Fear prickled in her mind when she felt the lulling caress of subtle magics.

"Ober," she slurred, though she tried to shout. She couldn't make the effort. "Ober, there's...there is m... It's magic."

In a final effort to seize control, she tried to lurch toward her brother, thinking to shake him awake, but her limbs betrayed her. Her feet tangled and she fell, her body surrendering to Erduna's grip. Surprisingly, she was not perturbed by the loss of balance. She descended to the earth, even as part of her screamed that she needed to wake up, shake it off, and save herself.

That tiny voice didn't win, but Tomza's freefall was arrested suddenly but not roughly by a strong pair of arms. Her descent was managed by someone else.

"Easy there," Dolla cooed in her ear, a hint of strain in the smooth, rich tones. "Easy does it."

The magic was soft but heavy, like an impossibly thick blanket settling over her.

"You've a strong will, lass. I'll give you that," Dolla murmured as Tomza came to rest on the soft grass. "That's why you've recovered as well as you have from the corruption. There's much to be proud of in that."

Tomza nodded, though the angry voice hurled recriminations and questions at the wain dwarfess. Sunlight framed Dolla's face.

"We're leaving the glade to wait for your prince elsewhere," the Mehk of Clan Omru told her. "You'll not find us until we are ready to speak with Torbjorn. Do not be afraid. You should be safe until you wake up."

Tomza thought Dolla turned to look at the others sleeping around her. It was hard to tell since things got fuzzier.

"There's not much we can do for your brother and the elves, nor is there much they'd let us do. The beasts are part of them now. But you, Drauldottr? You, we might still be able to help and heal."

Tomza's eyes were shut, but she could feel as well as hear the wain dwarfess' presence.

"Think on it, lass. Before we depart the Vale, there is much we can offer you, I think."

With that, a warm and welcome darkness came over Tomza, and she slept.

CHAPTER FOURTEEN

"You'd think they'd get tired of dying."

Shoulders and back burning, Torbjorn drove the point of his cwellocs at another svartalf coming over the rail. The myrkling irregular twisted away from the blow, so the point ripped through his cheek but failed to gain purchase. Teeth flashing beneath a curtain of blood, the elf sought to press past the extended weapon, one long-fingered hand seizing the haft for leverage.

Torbjorn used his attacker's efforts to pull himself forward, and the elf choked on a scream when the dwarf's helm smashed into his face, splintering teeth and pulping lips. Despite this punishment, the elf continued to grip the polearm, so Torbjorn rocked back hard, then threw a flat-footed kick at the svartalf's chest. There was a wet crack and some gristly pops, and the myrkling toppled overboard with a wheeze.

Torbjorn leaned on his cwellocs and looked at Gromic, his face slack with fatigue. The stout dwarf had just tugged the blade of his cwellocs out of another myrkling, who limply slid over the rail.

"Don't suppose it has anything to do with our newest additions," he rasped as he nodded at the mast. "Seems like they're very interested in him."

They glared at Gwyllethon, who stood near the center of the barge, far from the fighting, as he shouted challenge after challenge at the svartalfs wading through the shallows. His retainers, along with the Bad Badgers, raced to wherever their attackers made to board while Gwyllethon stood with sword bared, shrilling like a hawk.

"Is that all you've got, you spineless eels?" the Banneret keened at a detachment of irregulars coming in via skiff. "You dare to come at me with only five? You're not worthy to lay bleeding at my feet, much less wet my blade with your bastard blood, you worms!"

Torbjorn knew the only blood wetting the young aristocrat's blade was that of the poor grem handlers and their terrified worcsvines, though Torbjorn doubted Gwyllethon had the courage for even that.

"Why don't we just pitch him overboard?" Gromic asked, moving to intercept the new attack. Utyrvaul and the two former rangers were hacking at some coming from the shallows. At the stern, svartalf retainers were locked in combat with another batch that had come via skiff.

"For all I care, they can have him," the stout dwarf groused. "It would give the rest of us a few moments of respite from his shrieks."

Torbjorn agreed, but lacking the will to prevent it from happening, he charged toward some elves leaping onto the barge rail. The ship had settled onto the shoal, no longer as sharply pitched, making Gromic and Torbjorn's rush not as laborious. Despite that, two elves were able to reach the deck.

Coming in low and hard with their polearms, both dwarfs took the attackers' first strokes on their mailed shoulders and helmeted heads. Trusting dwarvish steel, they bore the blows and stabbed the elves' abdomens. Their padded doublets and leather jackets would have warded off shallows cuts, but the spiked heads of cwellocs drove up and through them, and the gory points tented their backs.

With near-mechanical efficiency, Waelon and Gromic set their feet, then punched forward, then yanked the polearms back, freeing their attackers' bloody heads. The dying myrklings slid toward the rail. One tangled with a would-be boarder, while the other was used as a stepping stone by his comrade.

That spring-footed svartalf nearly caught Torbjorn by surprise as he leapt off the corpse and brought a two-handed axe sweeping down. The heavy weapon nearly refuted Torbjorn's confidence in his helm, but the dwarf commander instinctively raised his cwellocs crosswise and caught the axe haft to haft.

The elf bore down, needle-sharp teeth bared. No sooner had Torbjorn pushed back than the force reversed, and the beard of the axe threatened to yank the weapon out of his hands. Torbjorn released one hand from his weapon and let the polearm swing out, and the axe head slid down the haft. The myrkling stepped inside Torbjorn's guard to hammer Torbjorn's head with the butt.

The blow drove Torbjorn back a step, ears ringing from the impact.

This blade ear is no joke, Torbjorn thought, gritting his teeth through the pain. *Better than any of those knights from earlier.*

True to the dwarf's estimation, the irregular came at him, axe sweeping out. Torbjorn backed up and warded, trying to create enough room to get his cwellocs back into play. Despite his efforts, the svartalf was too canny to let him do so. It was all Torbjorn could do to ward off the axe head and not let his feet tangle beneath him.

An axe stroke whistled overhead, and the elf turned too far into the swing. Seeing his moment, Torbjorn rallied and brought his cwellocs around, butt spike stabbing. Too late, the dwarf commander realized it was a ruse to draw him forward. The elf used his momentum to come around with an overhand chop to cleave Torbjorn's head.

The blade flashed like Grimmoth's grin, and Torbjorn watched his end come.

It was delayed when Gromic appeared at the elf's side and launched his own chopping blow. The ferocious svartalf sensed something was awry and tried to twist toward the new threat, but Gromic's axe blade met his snarling face.

The elf's weapon tumbled from his nerveless grip as the heavy blow split his skull. Gromic tried to yank his axe free, but the head was wedged tight, so the weapon went to the deck with the dead elf.

Torbjorn would've thanked his faithful dwan, but the remaining irregulars from the skiff were making their play. Luckily for the commander, both were as unskilled as they were unsure of their assault. Torbjorn's polearm swept left, then right.

One was left with a torn throat, while the other clutched an axe-notched arm. Torbjorn would've followed the blow with something more final, but the wounded myrkling fled back over the rail with a squeal.

Heaving a sigh, Torbjorn moved to the elf writhing on the

deck, ruined throat pumping blood. One hard thrust to the heart, and the svartalf stilled.

Gromic finally ripped his cwellocs free.

The dwarfs exchanged weary nods and turned to face the next onslaught, only to find that a strange calm had settled over the deck. Even Gwyllethon was silent as the remaining boarders fled on foot or by skiff.

Torbjorn leaned on his cwellocs with one arm and tugged on the straps of his helmet with the other. The battered metal bucket came free, and he sucked in a breath. It stank of blood and urine and feces, but it was better than his stale breath.

"Seems like they finally got tired of dying." Torbjorn coughed, forcing back the bile that threatened to rise. "Though I'll be honest. I didn't expect them to fight that hard. Never seen a mercenary fight that hard for, well, *anything*."

"That's because they know that if they lose the Scroll, there will not be a payday," Utyrvaul explained as he strode forward, cleaning off the blood clinging to his blade. "Only nobles are permitted to negotiate contracts. The commoners in their employ are bound by those agreements. It keeps them loyal even when far afield since they know that if they betray their masters, they will never be hired for any other svartalf mercenary operation."

Gromic frowned. He was picking at a fresh notch in his cwellocs axe blade.

"But if they're far afield, what's to stop some lads from saying their master caught a bolt in the neck or got eaten by savagelings or the like?"

Utyrvaul shrugged as he examined the sword.

"The circumstances of their liege's death is of little importance to most. Whether they died through treachery or simply the failure of the commoners to lay down their lives for their master, who wants warriors who fail?"

Waelon and Clahdi trudged over. The dwarfess was limping and had a bandage bound around her calf. Torbjorn was glad to see the pair and even happier to see them exchange disgusted looks before glaring at the svartalf.

"Let me get this right," Waelon began, his rough voice even more hoarse from the battle. "You mean to tell me that any svartalf soldier who doesn't die with his liege is…what, an outcast?"

Clahdi shook her head, then spat a red-streaked stream over the rail. "I knew you myrklings were decadent," she grumbled through split lips. "But I never imagined you'd be that wasteful."

Utyrvaul furtively looked around, then leaned forward and winked.

"It's been said that it isn't always so," he whispered. "Some have suggested that a desperate or very enterprising noble might find a way to *rehabilitate* such dispossessed souls—at an extremely discounted rate, you understand. This is just gossip, especially for those commoners who need motivation to serve their betters."

The four dwarfs looked at the elf, shaking their heads.

"Every time," Waelon muttered. "Every time I think you blade ears can't get worse, I learn something new, and I discover that you really *are* the worst."

Utyrvaul chuckled and seemed ready to retort or, given his grin, perhaps agree, but a commotion from the stern drew all eyes. Gwyllethon was animatedly instructing his retainers to hurry and drag a large chest out of a cabin at the stern of the vessel. One of the poor wretches was gray from blood loss and tottering on his feet, but the Banneret demanded they bring the stout container out onto the deck.

"You don't suppose we still might find an excuse to pitch him overboard," Gromic growled as they moved toward the stern. "Just have to make sure we put him on the side that's deepest."

"Tempting as that is," Torbjorn muttered, rolling his shoulders as he considered the sweet splash Gwyllethon might cause, "we're remaining neutral through all this, remember?"

Waelon stood next to Torbjorn, eyes fixed on the tall svartalfess. She looked even more dangerous now that she was covered in blood and her armor bore fresh scars.

"Neutral, but we're still killing the she-elf, right?"

Utyrvaul rolled his eyes as he languorously strode alongside the dwarfs.

"Please say it louder," Utyrvaul grumbled under his breath. "How many times must I remind you our delicate ears are not just for decoration?"

Waelon scowled at the myrkling but held his peace.

"Fair point, Utie," Torbjorn replied, glad to see that the nickname still irked the elf. "But yes, Waelon. That's still the plan, though we will wait until she makes her move."

"Sounds dangerous," Clahdi observed.

"Welcome to the Bad Badgers." Torbjorn snorted. "Dangerous is the way of it."

The chest skidded across the deck after one of the retainers fell back with a shriek. The others recoiled. The shrieking retainer stared in horror as his gauntleted hand shriveled, the metal buckling and twisting while emitting smoke. On a large brass plaque affixed to the chest, a constellation of runes glowed a sullen red. When the afflicted svartalf swooned and collapsed to the deck, the runes ceased to glow.

"Careless fool," Gwyllethon hissed as he stepped past the senseless retainer to examine the chest. "If any damage was done to the Scroll, you'll be lucky if the only thing I do is cook your other hand."

Two of the retainers moved to the fallen elf's side, intent on administering aid, but the Banneret would have none. "What are you doing?" he demanded, continuing to examine the chest. "Leave the wretch alone and do something useful. I'm sure this isn't the only plunder on this tub."

The retainers looked at each other but said nothing as they stepped away from their fallen comrade.

"My lord," the tall, stern retainer standing behind Gwyllethon interjected. "If we wish to save his hand and thus preserve his usefulness, succor is required. If aid is not given, then by his contract, he—"

"All right, all right, Nissari!" Gwyllethon glared over his shoulder at the retainer. "I suppose if we have to be practical about such things."

Turning from Nissari, the Banneret shooed his other two retainers away. "Go attend to whatever leechcraft is required," he snapped, then turned back to the chest. "But keep a record of every resource you use so I can take it out of his share."

The retainers hastened to oblige, dragging their wounded compatriot to the far rail.

"And just like that," Utyrvaul whispered at Torbjorn's shoulder, "our wee lamb is separated from the herd. Are we certain his charming existence is worth preserving in light of the consternation it might cause the good lady marshal?"

Before Torbjorn could answer, Gwyllethon shouted, "Torbjorn! Damn your eyes. Get over here so we can open this thing."

The svartalf aristocrat bent over the chest like a miser

counting coins while retainer Nissari stood to one side, cleaning blood from the finely wrought falchion she carried. It only required a moment for the dwarf commander to form the image of the exquisite blade cleaving Gwyllethon's outstretched neck.

Torbjorn tightened his grip on his cwellocs until his knuckles popped and took a breath. "The plan hasn't changed," he grumbled out of the side of his mouth, then quickened his pace. "On my way, Banneret. It's a bit farther for my short legs, is all."

CHAPTER FIFTEEN

"So, you're telling me they're still out there?"

Tomza and Ober nodded in unison as the driver looked at them. Haeda frowned at the siblings, fidgeting as though she was unsure what blistering rebuke to heap on them. She gave up with an irritated splutter. Throwing up her hands, she looked at the new lardwan with the air of a beleaguered parent.

"I'm at my wit's end. These two idiots headed out with those savageling idiots without telling a soul, and now they stagger back with nothing to show for it but tales of vanishing wain dwarfs. I'm not sure whether to pummel 'em both or just tell them to get out of my sight so I can drink away the headache I've developed from listening to them."

Mordah nodded, her face grave, and when she finally spoke, her tone was even and calm. "I don't like it either, but now that we know they are out there, we can take precautions. Also, though I don't pretend to know what such heretics would have to say to the prince, if they planned real mischief, they wouldn't have let them return and warned us about them being here."

Haeda shook her head and leaned against the map table in the command tent. Tomza could tell from the driver's sour expression she was not convinced by the argument.

"Maybe, or maybe us knowing they're out there isn't going to keep them from doing whatever they planned. Or maybe it was an attempt to make them seem harmless so they could get close to Torbjorn and stick a knife in him because we let our guard down. Really, the more I think about it, letting these two kak-for-brains go free would help me if I wanted to get up to mischief."

Tomza opened her mouth to refute the suggestion but found that she didn't have much to say in her defense. What could she tell them? That she believed Mehk Dolla, as though that was evidence? Was she going to tell them about the offer they made her? Would that make them listen and believe her, or just grow more suspicious?

The dwarfess looked at her brother for assistance, but Ober just shook his head. Apparently, her sibling had accepted that they were just going to have to endure this chewing out. Tomza choked back a frustrated splutter and gazed at the pair standing in judgment.

"I agree that it is not how I would've wanted things done, and it has exposed all of us," Mordah began, her words cutting deep despite their mild tone. "I'm also sure that both of them understand there will be consequences for their behavior, but we must deal with what they saw and plan accordingly."

Haeda frowned and gestured at the map table she'd been leaning on. "What plan? We don't have a clue where they are now and little information to let us find them. Worst of all, we don't know what they intend to do next."

"No," Tomza interjected, drawing all eyes to her. She had to fight the urge to wilt under their combined stare. "That is, it's not true that we don't know what they intend. They told us they've come to talk to Torbjorn because at Jorsburg, he proved he was willing to consider amnesty for the wain dwarfs."

"A point we'd be wise not to discuss outside this room," Mordah responded quickly, her eyes darting to the open flap. "Things have been radical enough, what with us opposing tradition by rising up against the ondwan. Throw in amnesty for the heretics, and things are liable to come apart at the seams."

Tomza didn't agree, but now was not the best time to contradict the lardwan.

"That's Torbjorn's business, and I'll leave him to it." Haeda spat as though the thought had fouled her spittle. "But we've got an independent operator, and we don't know where they are or how to isolate and deal with them. I mean, we're supposed to be Torbjorn's eyes and ears, for Shaper's sake, and we're blind and dumb to boot!"

The driver rounded on the siblings, green eyes flashing with fury.

"If you two idiots had alerted a ranger patrol, this might be a different story. At least with the rangers, we could have moved on the bastards in force. Taken some of them in for questioning. Instead, we only have word that they're out and about, and we won't know where they are until they show themselves. Just perfect!"

Tomza wilted under the dwarfess' scrutiny, her shoulders slumping and her chin settling on her chest. There was little point in denying the truth, and Haeda wasn't wrong. Tomza wasn't sure if the rangers would've helped, but they'd taken enormous risks without thinking them over.

Ober's head was down, and he was chewing his lower lip. His opinion was apparently the same as Tomza's. There was nothing they could do now but accept whatever chastisement lay in store for them. The young dwarfess wasn't sure who she hoped would administer the punishment. Mordah was exacting and particular. Haeda was far more inventive…and petty.

Tomza squared her shoulders, then fixed her gaze in the middle distance. "We'll accept whatever consequence you deem worthy," she told her superiors, straightening as she thumped her fist in salute.

Haeda eyed Tomza like she was a recalcitrant worcsvine. Then the driver looked at Mordah. "I'm not going to pretend to know what to do with them," Haeda declared, shaking her head. "The lass is supposed to take shifts tending the wounded, both ours and prisoners. Her brother? Let's just say that whatever we do to him, it is because he lets us, so that seems like a waste of time. You got any thoughts, *Lardwan*?"

Mordah gazed at the pair, lips pursed and brow furrowed. Eventually, she too shook her head. "I agree. You were both impetuous. I expect better of you in the future, but for the time being, there is no reason to draw any more attention to this situation since we can't fix it. If anything, punishing you would further complicate the situation."

Ober looked up. "So, does that mean we're dismissed?" he asked, eyes wandering from the lardwan to Haeda and back.

"I suppo—" Mordah began.

Haeda cut her off. "Get out of my sight, you. Go do your actual job for once!"

"Where are you going?"

Tomza didn't bother to turn around when she answered her brother's question. "Doing what I'm told," she replied, trudging toward the infirmary wagons parked beneath a low hill. "There's patients that need tending."

There was only one who she was explicitly responsible for, and given that she'd already seen him that day, her statement made no sense. She *could* find something to do, attending to the wounded and stricken, though if she was honest, she was just looking for a chance to be away from people who might ask questions. There were so many thoughts buzzing around in her head that she was afraid if she opened her mouth too wide, some would fly out.

"Is it because of Haeda?" Ober pressed, shuffling around a group of dwans pushing handcarts loaded with supplies. "As far as that goes, I thought we got off pretty easy. A few kak-brains and a loud dismissal? She must be busy keeping the army on course and has no time for us."

Tomza grunted and quickened her pace as she closed on the wagons, or tried to. Small personal tents had been erected around the wagons for those in care, so the dwarfess was obliged to carefully watch where she stepped. Ascedwans walked around with satchels over their shoulders and lanterns swaying at their belts. Some had lit their lanterns since the hill blocked the setting sun.

"Is this about what happened in the glade?" Ober asked.

Tomza wheeled around to give him a sharp look.

Her brother's face crinkled in confusion, clearly not imagining that mentioning the glade was indiscreet. "Does it have to do with what Dolla said to you?"

Tomza's stomach plummeted, and her heart clenched. "I don't know what you are talking about," she hissed, then ran over to the nearest ascedwan. "What needs doing around here?"

The dwarf frowned and hefted his lantern to get a good look at her, which left Tomza blinking away stars.

He answered gruffly, "We've got this lot covered, and we've got a rotation working." His tone was defensive. "You missed a meal, which is when we administer medicine and tend to anything else that needs doing."

Tomza got the point, but Ober was behind her, and her mind raced for any excuse to get away from him. Her eyes roved across the deepening shadows and spied the caged wagon set a little way the infirmary train.

"What about the tweldwan of the 6th? Was he tended to?"

The ascedwan looked at the caged wagon and shrugged. "Since when is that our job?"

Tomza bit back the angry reply that sprang to her lips, forcing her voice to be steady. Some of the attending ascedwan were looking her way, their expressions less than friendly.

"Is there anything left from the evening meal?" she asked. "Anything I could bring to him?"

The dwarf seemed ready to turn his back to her, but he heaved a sigh and nodded at a lean-to that had been erected against one of the wagons. "Doubt there's much left, but if there is anything, it'll be there." He resumed his route among the tents.

Tomza walked toward the lean-to, but Ober appeared at her back. It took remarkable restraint not to launch a backward kick into his groin.

"What did the wain dwarfess say?"

"Would you please just shut up?" Tomza groaned. "I don't know what you are talking about."

Ober followed her as she went into the shelter and pawed through it for something that resembled food. "I heard her talking," he insisted, doing nothing to assist except block the meager light. "I thought I was asleep, and maybe I was, but I heard her talking to someone and knew it wasn't me. I was so tired it was hard to turn my head, but I did, and I saw her holding you and whispering."

Tomza picked up a cask that was so light she nearly pitched it aside, assuming it was empty. Then she heard something rolling around in it. Lifting the lid, she groped inside and drew out two small, hard apples. They were not a fitting meal for her, much less a brute like Okmur, but there were no soft spots. She'd been remiss with her charge already. No need to give him spoiled food.

"I couldn't hear what she said or if you said anything back," Ober admitted, eyes glittering in the gloom. "But you've been different ever since. What happened now?"

Tomza drew up sharply and glared at her brother. "Happened *now*?" she hissed, thrusting her chin toward her brother defiantly. "What is that supposed to mean?"

Ober faltered, one foot sliding backward when he heard the threat in the question. He stammered out an apology, then he stopped. His expression hardened as he straightened and met his sister's glare.

"Last time, a wheezer speaking to you nearly broke you," the young dwarf stated, his voice cold and flat. "Now some wain dwarf whispers in your ear, and you go into your own head. I'm not sure what is going on, but you're moving away from me, sister. I'm not going to pretend I don't see it."

Tomza paused, a thousand thoughts racing around her

skull. Some were insistent on getting out, while others were content to keep buzzing around. Her body seemed to be caught up in it as well, her muscles tightening and her bones aching as a lightning-like current of anxious energy coursed through her.

How could she explain? What could she possibly say?

The apples were still in her hands, and she realized she would crush them if she held onto them. Fingers trembling, she put them in her satchel before looking up at her brother.

"Please move," she requested. "I've got to go feed my charge."

She could barely make out Ober's frown in the dark, but she felt his eyes boring into her. It was all she could do not to scream and rant or collapse before that gaze, but she held, then with a growl that resonated from a chest that wasn't his, Ober stepped aside.

It took Tomza a moment to recover from hearing the thunderblood speak through her brother, but when no claws appeared and no fur sprouted, she convinced herself it was safe and walked out.

"You were losing yourself to our mother's magic," Ober whispered, freezing her in place as she passed him. "Then a dead man convinced you to give it all up, though it nearly broke you. What did the wain dwarf tell you? Come and learn some new witchery? Forsake everything and join their wandering caravan?"

Tomza forced herself to take a step, then another. One more, and she'd break free of her sibling's gravity. It was a hopeful yet lonely feeling.

"If taking to the caravan could heal whatever is broken inside me," she whispered, barely trusting her voice, "would it be so bad?"

She waited, desperately hoping her brother would speak. Sweet and understanding, he would reassure her, telling her that no matter what, he would stand by her side and support her decision. She wanted it so badly that she thought her desire would manifest that response.

But no words came, and Tomza felt as though she was beside a statue, not her only living relative.

The silence stretched, and with nothing to fill the emptiness, Tomza moved off to fulfill her duties.

CHAPTER SIXTEEN

"Finally."

Torbjorn nodded at Gwyllethon as he came to stand before the chest. The dwarf commander didn't trust himself not to shout at the irksome Banneret, so he said nothing.

"They seemed to move well enough before," Gwyllethon grumbled to Nissari, rubbing his hands together in anticipation. "It is a wonder that those stunted creatures get anywhere on time without having to do the little waddle-run."

He's really full of himself, Torbjorn mused. *Never learned that those who get that swollen are likely to be popped by something sharp.*

"All right, here we are." Torbjorn huffed and worked at loosening his gauntlet. "We'll open this thing and hope to the Shaper and whatever passes for gods in Arawuvasc that the Scroll is in here."

"Oh, it's in there. I can practically taste it," Gwyllethon murmured as he worked off own glove and pitched it to Nissari. "Hold this."

In a display of dexterity, the retainer flicked the oiled rag into the air, caught and tucked the hurled gauntlet under her arm, and caught the rag on its way down. Torbjorn gave a small nod of appreciation, which drew the svartalfess' eyes to his. He attempted to hold them with all his will.

Don't do it, he thought, hoping against all reason that the elf would understand. *You can make all sorts of excuses, but let this one go. You shouldn't have to die here.*

"*Prince* Torbjorn," Gwyllethon drawled, the title sounding as foul as the speaker's mood. "If you enjoy ogling my retainer so much, I'm sure we could arrange something later. For the moment, could you please focus?"

Torbjorn's gaze broke from Nissari's and he yanked his gauntlet off, fighting a deep and abiding desire to batter the Banneret senseless.

"Let's get this over with," he growled. He stepped to the chest and slapped his hand on the brass plaque without ceremony.

Careful not to touch Torbjorn's hand, Gwyllethon reached out, his hand trembling, and pressed it to the ensorcelled engraving. Heat bloomed within the brass to the point of discomfort without reaching pain.

Torbjorn felt the baelgeld within the runes tasting his flesh like a rasping feline tongue. He suppressed a shudder, wondering why his people scorned witchery of all sorts but found using baelgeld acceptable. The plaque gave a sharp snap, and he stopped thinking about ancient traditions when pieces of the rune lock fell away.

"Finally," Gwyllethon cried, seizing the lid of the chest and throwing it back.

The interior of the chest contained orderly stacks of heavy

golden coins whose center bore a platinum-plated image of Torbjorn's father's face in profile. The stacks were stored in wooden sleeves so they could be easily counted. At a glance, Torbjorn guessed there were a hundred coins to a stack and nearly as many stacks, which put the wealth in this chest squarely in the realm of the astronomical.

Torbjorn had been born in a palace, but most of his life had been spent as a dwan on campaigns, so he'd learned the value of currency. A dwan would receive a single coin for every two years of service, and even then, his wages were only paid after ten years on the line. The wages increased as one climbed the ranks, but an honored ondwan who served to the last day of his few centuries of life would not have accumulated a quarter of this wealth.

If I take this, the Badgers and I could leave this cursed valley and never look back. There's enough here that we could live like fat nobles wherever we landed. South to Aruhkham, or... No, Scadish, or across the Caged Sea to Verenvar. It wouldn't matter since these coins would last all of us three lifetimes of excess.

Gwyllethon seemed nonplussed. "What is this?" he demanded, glaring at the fortune like the coins were lead. "I don't need coins! Where is the Scroll?"

The shrill cry brought Torbjorn back to the matter at hand. The fantasy of a life far from war, politics, and treachery vanished into the aether. Torbjorn frowned when he too realized there was no sign of the Scroll.

"Perhaps the lady marshal was misinformed," Nissari offered, unable to hide the hope in her voice.

Torbjorn shot her a look of pity. As he did, he noticed the lid of the chest with its plush interior. At first glance, he thought it was just one of the eccentric touches the svartalfs always included in objects they crafted and almost dismissed it. Then he remembered that this chest had been made by dwarfs, was filled with dwarvish coins, and had been sealed with dwarvish runes.

Would any dwarven craftsman allow his practical and utilitarian work to be soiled by elvish affectations, even if it had been crafted for the creatures?

"I don't want theories," Gwyllethon ranted. "I want what is mine. I want the Scroll!"

"Doesn't my lord mean, 'What is the lady marshal's?'" Nissari asked, steel in her voice to match the steel in her hand.

Before Gwyllethon could answer, Torbjorn touched the lid. The snorri birch his left hand was crafted from bit through the chest's softer oak. He snared a few fingers full of the trim and tugged. The cloth ripped, and half of the cover came away in his fist. Balls of down spilled over the stacked coins, as did a round case of polished wood a little thicker than an elf's dainty wrist.

"Aha!" Gwyllethon crowed and reached for the scroll.

Things got complicated.

Nissari was already in motion. Her falchion whistled in an arc that would've opened the Banneret's neck to the spine, but Torbjorn caught the blade with his left hand. It struck his palm with a dull thud and dug a thin furrow in the wood as his fingers clamped down.

The retainer's red eyes widened in surprise, but to her credit, she recovered quickly. She tugged on the sword, but when Torbjorn maintained his hold on it, she released the weapon and spun around. Her dexterous hands had unsheathed daggers during the movement, and she sent one hurtling toward the Banneret.

Torbjorn tried to intercept the dagger, but he couldn't

move fast enough. Time slowed as the razor-sharp blade sheared the air, sunlight flashing along its length. If not for its destination, the dwarf would have called it beautiful.

Time resumed its normal pace when another blade intercepted the dagger, and both clattered to the deck. Torbjorn barely had time to appreciate Utyrvaul's deflection before the svartalf sprang past him to meet the advancing Nissari.

"Terribly sorry, darling," Utyrvaul called, sword licking out.

Nissari's scream would have shamed a wild cat as she fought to check the reach of the much longer blade with her dagger. Had she still had her falchion, Torbjorn thought she would've matched Utyrvaul's exceptional skills. As it was, she tried to press toward Gwyllethon without the heirloom blade finding her throat.

"Kill her!" Gwyllethon shrieked as he staggered back, cradling the Scroll to his chest. Eyes roving like a hunted beast's, he glared at his other two retainers and hit an even shriller note. "She betrays us! Kill her *now*!"

The retainers had their weapons in hand, stalking forward, but their postures screamed a warning to Torbjorn.

"Kill them all!" Nissari shouted, fending off another swipe at her face. "Quickly!"

The other retainers moved with slightly less alacrity than the svartalfess since they were faced with four armored dwarfs instead of one cringing lord. Their hesitation proved fatal.

One took two steps before Waelon's hurled axe dented his helm, staggering the elf. The other made it four strides before Clahdi's duabuw spoke. The svartalf's knees buckled, and a bolt jutted from his shoulder.

Like an armored avalanche of dwarven muscle, Gromic

rushed forward, cwellocs swinging. The pierced elf couldn't raise his saber, but it wouldn't have mattered since the back bill of the polearm smashed down with meteoric force. The hardened point punched through the helmet into the myrkling's skull, and the retainer twitched out his last moments.

The svartalf with the battered helm dropped his spear and desperately dragged his helmet off. Thus, he had a clear view of Waelon as the dwarf drove a magsax into his face.

That ugly business done, Torbjorn pitched the falchion in his left hand to the deck and glanced at the dueling svartalfs. Utyrvaul, mercilessly pressing his advantage, had driven Nissari toward the rail and was menacing the retainer with shallow thrusts.

"Come now, darling," Utyrvaul chided, the needle point of his blade dancing before him. "There's no need for this to go any further."

Torbjorn almost missed a step when he heard the words. *That elf never mucks about. Lass must be more special than he let on.*

"He...has to...die," Nissari wheezed, then snarled when Utyrvaul's blade nicked her cheek. The heirloom blade had given it half a dozen such steely kisses.

Very special indeed.

"I know you're being well paid, and he's a rotten scamp," the elf declared with a knowing nod. "But he's not worth dying for."

"I would've killed him for free," the retainer growled, then launched forward in a desperate flurry of slashes. Utyrvaul's blade licked out and Nissari staggered back, clutching her hand as blood welled. The dagger she'd been wielding clattered to the ground along with the ends of two of her fingers.

"Please," Utyrvaul murmured. His outstretched blade hung between them. "Stop."

Nissari looked up at him, and Torbjorn saw a will and defiance he couldn't help but admire, yet also something… broken. This wasn't just about money, and given the despicable way Gwyllethon treated his subordinates, the dwarf could only imagine the indignities he had foisted upon the retainer.

Torbjorn almost shrieked at him to stop but turned to look at the coin-laden chest beside him.

"I can't," Nissari whispered. "I just can't."

The svartalfess began to advance, still clutching her wounded hand.

"Don't," Utyrvaul pleaded, but his stance stiffened in preparation for the killing blow. "Please."

His blade was nearly at her throat when Torbjorn gave a battlefield bellow. *"HOLD!"*

Both elves froze and turned their eyes to the dwarf commander.

"What are you doing?" Gwyllethon hissed, still cradling the Scroll. "Kill the bitch!"

Torbjorn ignored the Banneret and scooped up as many coins as he could hold in his hand.

"What is the meaning of this?" Gwyllethon shrieked. "That is—"

Gromic and Waelon flanked the elf, weapons in hand. "Shut it, blade ear," the former ranger growled.

The Banneret gaped, and Gromic chuckled. "That's right. Quiet, now. Prince Torbjorn's working."

Behind the elf stood Clahdi, duabuw primed.

Torbjorn nodded his appreciation to the dwans and advanced toward the cornered retainer, coins in hand. Utyrvaul gave him a quizzical look and after a nod, lowered his blade and stepped back a pace.

"Right," Torbjorn began and eyed Nissari, including the severed ends of her fingers. "You're a little banged up, but you'll mend. That's just as well since I've got an offer for you, lass."

The she-elf's eyes narrowed, but she didn't initiate a suicidal charge. Torbjorn took that as a good sign. He held up the coins and turned them so the sunlight played off their edges, then lowered them. When he addressed the elves, his tone was measured and sensible— business-like.

"Now, I'm not going to suggest that your honor is for sale, but we've got a bit of commerce to conduct here. I understand that you've a host of incentives to kill that bastard behind me. Perhaps the least is money, but the fact is, you're in an impossible situation because I'm afraid I can't let you do it. Not even if he deserves it a hundred times over."

Nissari's shoulders squared, and she opened her mouth to say something defiant, but Torbjorn beat her to the punch. "Again, I'm sure there are all sorts of reasons why you feel the way you do about him, and between you and me, the world might be a better place without the prick. It would make me happy to hand you your sword and let you finish what you started. Honestly, it would."

Gwyllethon spluttered a protest, but a low growl from Waelon made him pipe down.

"We both know soldiers rarely get what we want," Torbjorn continued, meeting Nissari's gaze. "So if neither of us gets what we want, what's the next best thing, eh? Money."

Torbjorn held up the coins and was glad to see that the svartalfess' eyes lingered on them for a moment.

"It's not the Banneret's head hanging from your saddle, along with whatever the lady marshal promised you," Torbjorn observed. "That's well beyond your grasp now, and nothing's going to change that. However, these *coins* can change what happens to you since Gwyllethon is going to live."

Nissari stiffened at that assertion, her skin turning a deep blue.

"Do you know what he intends?" she asked, leveling a condemning finger at her former liege. "Do you know what he is planning to do now that he has the Scroll?"

Gwyllethon protested, but wordless warnings from the dwarfs silenced him.

"I can well imagine." Torbjorn sighed, shoulders bowing. "But I'll tell you that he won't be pulling a fast one, at least not until we reach the camp outside Greyshelf. He and the lady marshal are going to have it out, and there will be no further dispute about who's leading the svartalf mercenary companies. Then we can bring this business with Greyshelf to a close. I've no intention of this turning into a siege that lasts all winter, and svartalf squabbles, either over betrayals or botched blood magic, will waste time I don't have to spare."

Nissari's hatred when she looked at Gwyllethon was incandescent. Then she closed her eyes and took a steadying breath. When she opened her eyes again, she fixed her gaze on Torbjorn.

"Even if I don't kill him, my life is over," she stated, her stare unfaltering. "I'm the last of my family, and no one will protect or even vouch for me now. Even if I was to pay my way out of my contract of service to House Gwydarioc, I would be set upon by anyone who fancied the boots on my feet."

"Aye, I don't doubt it," Torbjorn nodded. "But the world is a wide place, and you've shown yourself more capable than most. I'd say that with these coins and a few more if you have a bag to put them in, you could ride that lizard-chicken of yours to someplace far from the Vale and start anew. Given how long your kind live, I'm not sure this would be enough to last you for your entire life, but it would start you off well. Given your skills, I don't doubt you could sort things out from there."

Nissari held his gaze for a long time, but eventually and inevitably, her eyes fell on the stack of coins in his hand.

"Once you bring him back to the lady marshal, she will send others after me."

That would happen even if he protested. "I don't doubt it." He shrugged. "But you'll have a head start, plenty of money, and a notion of where you are going that none will share. Her hounds won't chase you to the ends of the Earth, and even if they do, a smart lass could keep them chasing their tails for a long time. Either way, it's much better than bleeding to death over something you can't change."

Nissari's chin dropped to her chest. "All right," she muttered, sounding more pained than when her hand was struck. "It's not... Well, it's more than I could hope for."

Torbjorn grinned as he pressed the coins into her uninjured hand.

"There we are." He beamed up at her. "Feels good in the hand, doesn't it? Dwarvish gold always does. Now, find yourself a stout sack, and we'll see how much it can hold without bursting, eh? Send you off proper."

Torbjorn turned to Gwyllethon, intent on acquiring the Adamant Scroll. After all this, the dwarf commander planned to keep the over-important scrap of parchment with him until they sorted this business out once and for all.

When he heard Nissari speak behind him, he spun back, only to discover that she was not addressing him. "You could come with me," Nissari offered, holding the coins up in front of Utyrvaul, not unlike what Torbjorn had. "With what the prince is offering, the two of us together could go anywhere. Start over and have something together."

Utyrvaul stared at the retainer, incapable of a jaunty smile or a witty rejoinder for once.

"I know you were just using me," the svartalfess continued, refusing to look away though tears formed in her eyes. "Despite that, you can't deny that there was something there, even if it was not yet fully formed. With this, we could find out what that something is."

Torbjorn stared at Utyrvaul's back, wondering what he would say if the elf turned to look at him. If the svartalf really wished to leave, could he keep him there? Did he really want to? Did he have any right to hold the elf back?

The silence seemed to stretch to the edge of Torbjorn's composure, but finally, Utyrvaul stepped forward to take Nissari's injured hand. His movements tender, he raised the limb he'd wounded to his lips and gave it a soft kiss.

"Nothing would please me more." He sighed. "But I began this journey with Prince Torbjorn some time ago, and though it might kill me, I will see it through. I've little hope we will survive, but for now, my path lies with him."

Nissari bowed her head, opalescent trails on her skin where her tears touched it. "I understand."

Utyrvaul kissed her hand again.

"Among all our people, I believe you truly do," Utyrvaul

said. "And that more than anything else is why I wish to go with you, but as Torbjorn said, we soldiers rarely get to do what makes us happy."

Torbjorn sniffed and turned away, shaking his head.

Just goes to show you can always be surprised.

CHAPTER SEVENTEEN

"Well, isn't that a sight?"

Torbjorn looked around to see Greyshelf looming overhead. Although he knew the defenders within numbered substantially fewer than when he'd been the acting ondwan, there were far more torches and lanterns gleaming in and around the fortress. Whoever now commanded it had raised a defiant display. The citadel in the cliff face cast its light on the surrounding stone and the valley floor like the burning eyes of a watchful deity ready to pass judgment.

Torbjorn might've been daunted if he wasn't planning to put out the eyes of the looming god. "It's just a fortress. It's an obstacle to be overcome, nothing more, nothing less."

Gromic was standing on the crest of the flat-topped hill they'd just climbed. "Beggin' your pardon, my Tweldwan, but I've seen Greyshelf enough times not to be impressed. I was talking about that."

Torbjorn joined his companion and looked down at a vast military encampment. Like scrub, it sprawled around and beneath trees whose leaves were surrendering to autumn's glory. Dwans were going about the business of a siege with the industrious vigor few but dwarfs could muster. Earth work had been initiated, temporary palisades were being erected, and ammunition was being distributed. Every dwarf seemed to know precisely where he was going and what he was doing, just as planned.

Although Torbjorn knew it was a ruse, he understood why Gromic had drawn his attention to it. Dwarvish military forces at work on such a scale were an incomparable sight. In moments like these, he could almost believe that what the Rune-Speakers said was true and the dwarfs were indeed destined to refashion the world as the Shaper intended. Seeing his people working toward a powerful goal convinced him that there was little they could not accomplish, given enough time.

"Aye." Torbjorn looked at Gromic. "That is a fine sight."

"Even finer, knowing who commands them," Gromic replied staunchly. "I've seen armies enough times, but knowing that those dwans are here because they believe in Prince Torbjorn fills my heart up."

Torbjorn's cheeks burned, and he forced a smile as he looked around for Waelon.

Get 'im, you ol' cuss, Torbjorn thought, eager to avert further adulation. *Start with the fat jokes, and don't stop until he's pummeled into silence.*

Thinking about it, Torbjorn realized he hadn't seen Gromic react to Waelon's jibes about his size with anything but laughter. "Nothin' to say, Waelon?" He was desperate.

When no answer immediately came, Torbjorn turned and saw the former ranger with an arm around Clahdi's shoulder. Torbjorn smiled, glad to see that something more than the damned scroll had come of their little detour.

As though summoned by the thought of the Adamant Scroll, Banneret Gwyllethon came trotting up on his adyrclaf. Utyrvaul stayed conspicuously close to him. Torbjorn wasn't sure if Utyrvaul's presence had kept Gwyllethon from fleeing or if he'd had a vain hope that things would turn out in his favor. Either way, Torbjorn was surprised that the myrkling had made no attempts to escape, though they'd made the whole trip north with him whinging.

"What is the point of all this?" the svartalf aristocrat groused, reining his mount around. "Why drag me back here just to watch Annuvel kill me? Your stomach not strong enough to have a true noble's blood on it?"

The entire company laughed at the questions.

Gwyllethon remained indignant. "Mock me if you want, cowards," he snarled, hands trembling as he clutched his reins. "But none of you've dared to harm me, so I've every reason to question you."

Torbjorn laughed louder. The Banneret had tried bribes, flattery, and threats, but all had failed. He'd spent the last day trying to find a vulnerability or insecurity among his "escorts." Torbjorn knew that would fail too.

That was apparent when Utyrvaul's gauntleted hand smacked the indignant svartalf on the cheek. Gwyllethon raised a hand to his welted cheek, mouth stretching into an O of shock.

The elvish addition to the Bad Badgers was still laughing, though Torbjorn saw a dangerous edge to his smile.

"What does that do to your theory, my sweet lord?" Utyrvaul asked, grinning.

"H-how dare you?" Gwyllethon trilled. His mount shuffled nervously to the side, sensing its rider's distress. Torbjorn watched Utyrvaul carefully, sensing the svartalf's bitter edge.

"Oh, I'd dare quite a bit more than that," Utyrvaul promised, his armored fist a threat and his words dripping venom. "You'd do well to remember that the only reason you are still here, my *dear*, *sweet lord* is because a prince I respect wishes it so. The second that ceases to be so…well, that will be a very interesting time, won't it?"

To emphasize the threat, his hand settled on the hilt of his sword and caressed it gently.

Never seen Utyrvaul taking anything so seriously, Torbjorn mused. *Maybe that elf lass made a bigger impression than he let on. And since when does he respect me?*

Seeing Torbjorn's attention on them, Gwyllethon urged his mount toward the dwarf.

"Prince Torbjorn," the Banneret whined. "I must protest. This brigand you keep in your service has menaced and hectored me the entire journey, and now he is making threats on my life. As one aristocrat to another, you must surely see that cannot stand."

Torbjorn shook his head. "I'd save my breath, friend." He nodded at the encampment below. "Of all the elves within a mile of here, Sir Utyrvaul is the only one with a reasonable dwarf keeping him at bay. Down there is many a svartalf who's planned your death because they knew you would betray them."

He patted the case that hung from his belt. "Instead of spending your time pestering us, you should've been coming up with something convincing to say to the lady marshal. She's the one soul in this valley who can save you, and she is the one you betrayed."

Svartalf faces were not the easiest to read, but Torbjorn had no difficulty seeing the raw terror in the Banneret's eyes. If it had stayed terror, Torbjorn might have found it in him to pity the wretch and possibly press for clemency. However, the fear became malice.

"What of you, Prince Torbjorn? Who is looking after you?" Gwyllethon hissed and leaned down in his saddle. "What will happen when the lady marshal learns you thwarted her assassin and then sent the bitch off with a significant amount of the money that was going to be used to pay her and those in the company?"

Torbjorn made a show of clearing his throat, then shifted his pack on his back. It clinked dully. "If anyone told her, she'd think it was good fortune that *any* of the coin came to her. Especially when she remembers who has the bigger army and is feeding hers. That's what I expect to happen, but I appreciate your concern."

Gwyllethon leaned down farther, his position in the saddle untenable but for elvish agility.

Fool doesn't know when to leave well enough alone.

"Perhaps, but I don't think you understand how unreasonable my *aunt* can be," the Banneret pressed as he peered into Torbjorn's face. "You don't appreciate the situation you are in, Prince, but I'm not so proud that I can't see my way to assisting y—"

Torbjorn's hand caught Gwyllethon across his other cheek. Luckily for the elf, the blow was not delivered with his left, but it landed with enough force to pitch the elf out of the saddle. The skittish adyrclaf gave a throaty squawk and tore back down the hill the way it came.

Gwyllethon came up on his elbows, shaking his head to dismiss the discombobulation of the fall. Torbjorn's boot stamped on his chest, flattening the elf, and the dwarf leaned into the svartalf's face. His weight drove the breath out of the elf.

"I am where I am now because of scheming and politicking," Torbjorn growled. "I'm sick to death of it, so I'm going to suggest you shut up, stand up, and haul your arse down to the camp. Otherwise, I just might find out what sort of witchery the lady marshal has planned with your blood after all. Understand?"

Gwyllethon didn't have enough wind to answer, but he managed to cough out an affirmative, bobbing his head. Satisfied, Torbjorn removed his boot from the svartalf's chest and thrust his chin toward the encampment.

"Get moving."

Breath coming in quick, tight gasps, Gwyllethon scrambled to his feet and almost ran down the slope.

Utyrvaul and the dwarfs around him nodded their approval. Torbjorn might have laughed since they all had a reverent look in their eyes that set his teeth on edge, but he still remembered that night in the throne room at Mount Smarthdun.

"Enough gawking," the dwarf commander growled, adjusting the straps of his pack to more clinking. "I'd think you lot would be eager to get back to camp and eat something more than trail rations after all this."

The dwarfs exchanged knowing looks and shuffled down the hill. Utyrvaul nudged his mount alongside Torbjorn.

"A leader uninterested in schemes or politicking," Utyrvaul mused as he lounged in the saddle. "Wouldn't that be something! Why, that might start a revolution. Someone like that would find plenty of eager fellows looking to join up."

"I'm not looking to start a revolution. I was just making a point."

Utyrvaul's belly laugh jangled the dwarf's nerves. "When other leaders make a point, they don't do so with an entire army. Leave it to a prince to think the way to make a statement is by inspiring mass defection and then laying siege to a citadel. Oh, Torbjorn, you are too much!"

Torbjorn wished Utyrvaul was close enough to slap. He'd use his left hand. "I wasn't talking about that. I was talking about Gwyllethon."

Utyrvaul cleared his throat and straightened. "Oh, I'm sure you were, but I wasn't. I've demonstrated that I'm invested in this little escapade, so I hope you will listen to me as though I was one of your stunted, hairy kindred since I believe I've earned that right."

Arguments welled up, blustery, angry things meant to drive the svartalf back and silence him. Then he remembered the pain in Utyrvaul's voice as he bid farewell to Nissari, his outrage deflated. He nodded reluctantly.

"Oh, well, good. Er, here it is, then," Utyrvaul began, clearly unprepared for Torbjorn's acquiescence. "You've stumbled your way through this since we gave the lass up by being your charming, morose, masochistic self, but very soon, that's not going to be enough. You and I formulated the plan to take Greyshelf without a protracted siege, and I know it will work, but after this, things are going to become complicated. You're going to have to make a choice."

Torbjorn thought he knew what the svartalf was going to say, which filled him with dread. Wasn't the unknown supposed to be the greatest horror?

"You pretend otherwise, but you are the scion of a mighty dynasty," Utyrvaul continued. "You've been prepared to rule from birth, and though you don't believe it, your failings and tragedies only make you *more* qualified. After Greyshelf falls and the whole dwarven territory in the Ysgand Vale is under your rule, things will balance on the edge of a knife. You began this fight to stop the excesses and callousness of a cruel conflict, but are you ready to lead after the rebellion is successful? Are you ready to be the ruler you were always meant to be?"

Torbjorn's chin had sunk as the elf spoke, weighted down by the words. The last question pierced his fatigue.

Ruler? he thought, the word painful in his mind. *Ruler of the Ysgand Vale? Is the elf mad? All this time in my company and he doesn't know me at all. I'm no ruler. I can hardly keep my army from tearing itself apart.*

"You are probably rehearsing all the reasons you are unfit," Utyrvaul continued, which drew an irritated scowl. "And you can hate me for it, but I think it's past time you stopped lying to yourself. Are you flawed? Most certainly, but with the exception of yours truly, that is the condition of all creatures on this wretched mudball.

"You need to see that because this army…no, no living soul in the Vale can afford for you to cling to your self-deprecating delusions any longer. If you wanted to, you could not only stop this wasteful war but bring peace to the Vale."

A hundred refutations entered his mind. He thought about what might go wrong with the wights, the savagelings, the humans, the grem, and the bloody dwarvish empire, yet a cold, honest part of him whispered, *And who has faced all of those? Who knows the measure of each? Who's survived the worst and seen the best of each?*

"But I…" the dwarf began, but his voice failed. He suddenly felt very tired. "I can't…"

These words trailed off too, and he looked at the encampment. They had been moving toward it as they spoke, and they were getting close. Torbjorn watched the dwans on sentry duty hurry to move the palisade. They were young to be in the meat grinder. They hadn't even had time to grow proper beards before they came to this bloodbath. They looked at Torbjorn and his Badgers with eager faces.

They trust and believe in me. They believe I'm leading them somewhere better than into battles without purpose and wars without end.

His heart hammered and his eyes darted around, but there was no escape. No avoiding what was coming to him. It wouldn't be denied, no matter how many times he conjured the Great Hall at Mount Smarthdun or the cold back of his father. He felt like he was spinning through time and space.

You know what you've got to do. Since when does a Bad Badger not do his duty?

Utyrvaul was smirking at him.

"What are you grinning about, you needle-toothed blade ear?" he asked, though they both knew the answer.

The elf stretched. "Oh, nothing. I just never tire of being right. That's all."

CHAPTER EIGHTEEN

"This was not the resolution I expected, considering our original arrangement."

Indigo blood heated Lady Marshal Annuvel Arouveth's cheeks, which belied her dulcet tone. Since they'd brought the mercenary leader into the command tent, she'd done an exceptional job of hiding her irritation at seeing Gwyllethon alive and Nissari nowhere to be found, but in the end, her complexion betrayed her.

As Utyrvaul had revealed the results of their mission, the blood vessels around the albino svartalfess' eyes had thickened. Now her face was covered with blue spiderwebs.

"Well, I'd say that goes for both of us," Torbjorn replied, speaking for the first time since the meeting had begun. "The truth is, you weren't honest, so as a result, I had to make several revisions to the plan. You played a dangerous game, Lady Marshal, and if I hadn't learned the truth, things might have gone differently and very badly for you."

She did not reply, only sat quietly as she glared first at Torbjorn, then at Utyrvaul, and finally Gwyllethon.

"This does not change your fate, little one," she told the latter, her voice all the more chilling for its almost maternal tenor. "Your penchant for treachery and schemes was known to me, and I swear that no matter—"

"Easy, now," Torbjorn interjected, ignoring the myrkling's threats. "Before we go swearing to this thing or that, let's get our business settled. It might have some bearing on all that."

The lady marshal's voice was as cold as the glare she shot at him. Her eyes looked like bloody chips of ice.

"Do tell," she purred. "What do you have in mind, Prince?"

Torbjorn slouched in his chair and met her gaze without flinching. "Most of it is unchanged from the original arrangement," the dwarf began, nodding at the wood-encased scroll on the table. "Gwyllethon does his due diligence with the Adamant Scroll, and then it is handed over to you for safekeeping. I'll throw in all the coin we hauled back."

"What is left of it, anyway," Annuvel observed pertly, her gaze darting to Utyrvaul.

"Aye." Torbjorn nodded, then stifled a yawn. "And since you're getting all that, I expect your cooperation in the effort to take Greyshelf."

Her eyes narrowed. "I would agree, but given our dealings to date, I feel I must be specific. I'm not going to use my knights and their forces as bolt fodder for your siege. Having the entire company signed over will do me little good if I lose them all right away."

Torbjorn shook his head and allowed a small chuckle to spill from his lips. "We wouldn't want the mercenaries to actually have to do any fighting," he rumbled, then waved off her withering look. "Oh, don't worry. I've got a plan that doesn't involve any of that meatgrinder business. In fact, I think you'll like it. It's daring and devious, and if we're lucky, you'll hardly have to raise a blade to see it done. Just the sort of thing to suit your taste. I'm sure you knew this, but as it turns out, I was unaware of all of the uses for elf-draught. It's fascinating stuff, isn't it?"

Annuvel raised an eyebrow. The elf was intrigued. He obligingly paused for her to nod.

"That *does* sound interesting," she purred. "Though we *will* want to discuss the rest without the others." She tilted her chin at the Banneret, who was sulking in a chair near the tent wall.

"Too right, my Lady." He sat forward and put a hand on the Adamant Scroll. "Gwyllethon, get over here and certify our lady marshal."

Utyrvaul shoved the cringing svartalf, and he staggered forward a few steps. He was nearly to the table when he glanced at Annuvel and recoiled.

"Come on, Gwyllie. Don't be like that," Torbjorn chided. "Chin up. What would your uncle think?"

The Banneret looked ready to crumple, but at the mention of the late Lord Gwenmaelon Gwydarioc, a fiery light came into his eyes.

"It's *mine!*" the Banneret screeched, and Torbjorn winced. "She stole what should've rightly gone to me, and you want me to legitimize her with the very blood in my veins!"

The svartalf's voice broke, and the fire turned into a feverish light.

"And for what? So you can capture some ruin while she has my throat slit and my body thrown to one of your filthy pigs?"

Utyrvaul's hand dropped to his blade, but Torbjorn waved him off and turned his grim gaze on the Banneret.

"You're a liar like the lady marshal. I'm not going to

pretend I know who the rightful leader is, so I'll go with what I *do* know. I know that you, Gwyllethon Gwydarioc, are a spoiled, feckless, cowardly creature I wouldn't trust to tend one of those swine whose hygiene you just maligned. The lady marshal might be as devious as you say or even more so, but she's managed to keep the greater part of the mercenary company together despite a lack of food and pay for months now. To boot, she also doesn't make me want to ram my hand down her throat every time she opens her mouth, so she's way up on you, you sniveling lil shit!"

The long-restrained words flew off Torbjorn's tongue, and after the initial onslaught, he took a steadying breath.

"However, setting all that aside, I don't see any profit in the lady marshal killing you right after you were so kind as to hand leadership of the whole enterprise over to her. I'm thinking in return for your cooperation, you'll get a promise —a sincere one—from the lady marshal that she won't do the throat-cutting bit."

Torbjorn turned to the svartalfess. "Think of it as an extra service you're doing in return for the coin, such as it is."

She held very still, and the web of blue crept back into her features, but then her eyes settled on the scroll case. Her nostrils flared, and her clawed gauntlet scraped the table's surface as her hands closed into fists.

"I suppose I could extend that mercy to him as a courtesy to *you*, Prince Torbjorn. A display of benevolence in response to your generosity."

Torbjorn bowed his head in appreciation and turned back to the fretful Banneret.

"There you go," he declared, hands spread wide as though he was presenting a gift. "Not a single svartalf on the Lady Marshal's payroll will harm or hinder you in any way."

"What about the svartalfs in your employ?" Gwyllethon asked, though he refrained from turning around and leveling an accusing glare at Utyrvaul. "Will you speak for them?"

Torbjorn heaved a sigh as though he was wounded by the suggestion and shook his head. "Of course. No elf in my employ will harm you. No dwarf, either."

Gwyllethon's gaze narrowed with suspicion, sliding from Torbjorn to Annuvel and back. It was several heartbeats before he spoke again, his tone wheedling and his words carefully chosen.

"When you sent my retainer away, you gave her coin to start her new life. Since I cannot return home due to my disgrace, perhaps you will give me something as well?"

Torbjorn felt as much as saw the glare on the lady marshal's face, but he kept his gaze on the Banneret as he spoke.

"As you might have heard, I just gave away a fortune to ransom your life," he replied, his face and voice neutral. "So I'm afraid I'm a little low on liquid funds, but you could hang around to see what plunder we get from Greyshelf. Of course, that does mean being here during a siege, and that's a dangerous business. No telling what sort of accident might befall an unlucky creature like you."

Gwyllethon frowned but nodded. "It was worth a try." He sighed, shoulders slumping. "Fine. Let's get this over with."

Torbjorn couldn't help smiling as he removed the lid of the scroll case and gingerly tapped the scroll out onto the table. He wasn't sure what he'd expected, but the mundane-looking roll of vellum that slid out was not it. It just looked like a rolled-up scroll with much of its surface covered in spidery scribbles. If Torbjorn had placed it on Mordah's desk, it would've taken only moments to get lost among the reports, missives, and other documentation already occupying it.

"Well," Torbjorn muttered as he slid the scroll across the table to Gwyllethon. "Have at it, then. Will you need a stylus and some i—"

Torbjorn stopped speaking when Gwyllethon bit his finger, then squeezed until a big dot of blood formed. Apparently the remark about "with my very blood" was more literal than Torbjorn had thought.

As a result, it took several moments to write the statement since the Banneret had to pause and squeeze out more blood. He did *that* after searching for a section of the scroll uncluttered enough to accommodate the inscription.

When all was said and done, the letters smoked and hissed on the magical vellum, and thin curls of crimson smoke furled up. Looking as though he'd rather be handling a worcsvine's teeth, Gwyllethon brandished the Adamant Scroll, then set it on the table.

Torbjorn kept the fact that he couldn't read the scrawled, insectile language of the myrklings to himself since the lady marshal was satisfied.

"You can go now, Banneret Gwyllethon Gwydarioc," the dwarf commander announced. "Your duty has been discharged, so you are free to leave."

Gwyllethon's breath emerged in short, sharp gusts. Torbjorn thought the fool might attack the lady marshal, but eventually, the Banneret forced himself to take a deep breath. When he exhaled, he turned on his heel and headed toward the tent flap. Utyrvaul stepped aside to let him pass, though he followed a few steps behind.

At the entry, the svartalf aristocrat turned back to throw a disdainful glare at the occupants of the tent. "My memory is long," he snarled with a hard smile. "I want you all to remember what you've done to me and how you've wronged me because I swear that someday, I will even the score. It might take me years, but one day, you will all find yourself at my mercy. You shall just have to hope I extend the same 'courtesies' you've shown me."

Gwyllethon's eyes settled on Utyrvaul, and his lips quirked in disgust. "And don't think that little whore Nissari won't receive the same. I'll pay her in kind first and foremost."

The Banneret was reaching for the flap when Utyrvaul spoke, his voice light and conversational. "On that note, there's one clarification I'd offer you, Lord Gwydarioc."

Gwyllethon's fingers gripped the canvas as he called over his shoulder. "And what is that, derelict?"

"Torbjorn's never paid me," Utyrvaul stated, his voice icy. "Not once."

The Reeve family blade flicked out, and Gwyllethon's body hit the ground half a heartbeat before his head did.

Torbjorn frowned at the corpse twitching and oozing on the rushes that covered the floor. "You couldn't have waited until he was outside the tent to do that?" the dwarf complained, kneading his temples.

CHAPTER NINETEEN

"I'm supposed to wait around for a magical dwarfess to wander out of the trees? You do know that with winter coming, we *are* on a schedule, don't you?"

Tomza glanced at the other Bad Badgers. They'd gathered in the communal tent beside the command tent for a debrief and a discussion of what lay ahead. Now, after Tomza had told the tale with reluctant input from Ober, the meeting had come to a sticking point.

"I, uh, well…no, that's not what I'm, er, saying," Tomza floundered, her gaze swinging to her brother for help. Ober's expression was flint hard. The young dwarfess fell silent, feeling like a child and angry at herself for feeling that way.

What might have been tears softened the edges of her vision, but she drove them away by sheer force of will as she gathered herself and finally spoke. She forced herself to hold Torbjorn's gaze. "All I know is that they are out there, they spoke of having a message for you, and though we were at their mercy, they did nothing but give us good food and make us take a nap."

"Brought on by witchery," Waelon observed. Ober grunted in affirmation.

"Maybe," Tomza nodded and met the red-haired dwarf's frown. "But they were keeping us from knowing where they were headed, and sleeping with a full belly is better than being clobbered unconscious or left trussed up with sacks over our heads. They're not harmless, but I don't think they're dangerous. Not to us, anyway."

The Badgers' faces were not convinced, but Tomza refused to give ground. "What are we afraid of?" she demanded, meeting their eyes in turn. "They marched a caravan into the middle of a tree-ringed glade without even breaking a stray branch, and they left it the same way. With a few words, they kept Ober and the woself skinchangers from transforming, and with less than that, they put us to sleep. If they'd wanted to do us ill they could have, and there was little we could have done about it."

None of the other dwarfs could muster a reply, but Utyrvaul, who was lounging at the back of the tent to afford his long legs the space to stretch, spoke. "Well, as one slightly more familiar with supernatural matters, I'd say that even if the aforementioned displays of magical prowess were not exaggerated, there are limits to what any charm, hex, or spell can accomplish."

Tomza started to protest, but the svartalf raised a forestalling hand. "That is not to say that the young lady doesn't have a point. If these wain dwarfs do intend mischief, they could easily make themselves a nuisance. All indications are that they intend no such thing."

Tomza nodded, and the elf added, "Their potential danger so noted, we should meet with them. If for no other reason, so you can capture them to ascertain their motives in a place of safety."

Tomza stared at the elf, lost for what to say.

Several of the Bad Badgers nodded.

"It's always scary when the elf makes sense," Waelon stated.

"Chilling," Utyrvaul agreed with a yawn. "Absolutely petrifying."

Tomza wanted to scream or throw punches. "What's wrong with all of you? They did us no harm, and they're offering to help us in their way, and you want to run them to ground like a bunch of animals."

No one showed remorse or embarrassment.

"They're wain dwarfs," Clahdi declared in explanation, and as one, the Badgers, sans Tomza, spat. "We all know you can't trust them as far as you can kick them with a broken foot."

Tomza met the eyes of every dwarf in the room, her mind racing. Deep within her, something ignited, and the flames climbed her throat and seized her tongue before she could stop them.

"For just one second, could you just think about this?" she snarled, her body trembling. "We're taught to hate and mistrust these people, who by our own traditions are kin to us, because of something that happened so long ago we don't even remember when! We curse them, shun them, drive them out, and even kill them when they so much as cross our paths, yet when have any of you actually heard a credible account of wain dwarfs raising a hand to any of us?"

Under Tomza's burning glare, the usual rumors seemed foolish. Grunts echoed through the tent.

"That's what I thought," she snapped. "It's bad enough that our people behave this way, but for us to cling to that ancient grudge is beyond stupid. It would be funny if it wasn't so sad."

She received sharp looks and angry frowns, and Haeda voiced the group's displeasure. "What is that supposed to mean?"

Tomza glared into the driver's eyes, uncowed. "Just think about it. Think about us," she shot back. "For our actions, our associations, and things beyond our control, we've all been outcast, mistreated, and more than abused. Even when we were serving the Holt'Dwan, our fellow dwarfs treated us like garbage or tried to kill us."

"Not anymore, though," Gromic said around the pipe he held in his teeth, arms crossed over his broad chest. "Thanks to Torbjorn, that's being set right. We're no longer outcasts. We're on our way to being respected dwans again."

"Exactly!" Tomza cried, exasperation making her voice hoarse. "If we, who've done things we're not proud of but are still trying to do what's right and honorable, can be redeemed, why not them? If every dwarf who cursed and beat us was wrong, why can't we be wrong about the wain dwarfs? If there's a chance for us, then why not for them?"

With that, the burning animus within Tomza winked out. Her shoulders slumped, and her arms dropped to her sides. It was all she could do to stay on her feet as she looked around the tent, finally settling on Torbjorn.

The dwarf commander's brows were furrowed. Clinging to a desperate, half-formed hope that some part of what she'd said had overcome years of tradition and suspicion, Tomza stared at Torbjorn, eyes pleading even if her voice had left her again.

One by one, the other dwarfs looked at the leader, their expressions torn between confusion and concern. For several seconds, no one spoke.

Finally, Torbjorn ran his thumb across his scarred cheek.

"I'm not going to pretend I like what I just heard," he began, his gaze fixed on Tomza. "But I can't deny that what the lass says makes sense. More than once, the wain dwarfs could've served us a bad turn, and they didn't. All we've seen them do so far is help, and that's a damn sight more than most dwarfs have ever done for us until the last few months."

Torbjorn lapsed into silence, and several of the Bad Badgers began talking at once. Not even those speaking could've said which protest was theirs.

"What about the traditions?"

"What if it was all an act?"

"How can you trust a bunch of heretical witches?"

More emerged, some repeated, others rephrased. Torbjorn allowed them to wash over him and gave Tomza a surreptitious wink. He coughed, and when that didn't quiet them, his voice rose in an ear-battering shout.

"*ENOUGH!*" To a dwarf, the Badgers fell silent. "Look, I'm not saying we should offer them command positions or divulge our operational plans to them or anything like that. I'm just saying that giving the witchy little heretics a chance without us planning to slaughter their children and burn their wagons sounds reasonable. Unless you think it's reasonable to act like every dwan who spat on our food and pissed in our water just for existing?"

An uncertain rumble ran through the group. To Tomza, it sounded like a stone wall giving way. The Bad Badgers glanced at one another, their eyes speaking when their mouths didn't, remembering every unwarranted blow, every unearned curse, every unjust deprivation.

"Well, when you put it that way," Haeda grumbled at last. "I suppose it's not mad."

The rest of the Badgers nodded.

"Aye," Gromic agreed, throwing an arm around the driver. Eyebrows went up when Haeda didn't seem to mind. "If Torbjorn says we should give 'em a chance, that's good enough for me. He saw somethin' in each of us, didn't he?"

More nods were accompanied by grunts and mutters as the Bad Badgers looked around with something like hope.

Tomza heaved a sigh of relief, but that sigh caught in her throat when she saw that one Badger was still scowling.

"We both know what this is about."

Tomza started at the sound of her brother's voice so close and nearly spilled the bowl she was using to prepare Okmur's ointment-soaked bandages. She'd known this conversation was going to happen after the meeting in the tent, but when he had not immediately come to her, she'd thought—hoped, even—that he'd chosen to let it go until after the business with Greyshelf was done.

As she stood in front of the wagon in which Okmur was caged, she was unprepared for her brother's sudden appearance.

"You just pop up like that and expect me to know what you are talking about?" she snapped, carefully drawing out another strip of infused fabric.

Okmur's deepest wound had shown remarkable signs of improvement lately, and she'd devised a new ointment to try to accelerate his healing. She wasn't sure what the rush was since after the former tweldwan recovered, she'd have fewer things to occupy her time and keep her from the nagging thoughts that had begun to plague her.

"That's not true." Ober sniffed as he sauntered over to peer into the wagon bed. Okmur's massive frame sprawled across it, and he appeared to be sleeping, his breathing steady and even.

"You always remember exactly where we are in a fight." Ober sighed as he leaned against the side of the wagon. "Used to frustrate me. I'd think you'd forgotten about something, and you'd spring on me like a cat on a mouse."

Tomza couldn't hold back a small smirk.

"I don't remember it ever being quite like that," she muttered, eyes still on the bowl in her hands. "I *do* remember you standing there with a slack look on your face. Used to make me want to smack you upside the head."

Ober nodded and scratched the back of his skull.

"If my memory serves me, you often did. At least until I got big enough to swing back."

"Yeah." Tomza sighed. The memory of the day when Ober was no longer a runt to be pushed around sparked equal parts loss and pride. "I wore a stupid expression when you swung back that day. Caught me totally off-guard."

"Yup." Ober snorted, then his face settled back into a scowl. "But here's the thing. You don't look like that now."

Tomza looked at the gray sky as she fished out the last bandage. "What do you want me to say?" No sooner had the words left her mouth than she wished she could haul them back.

She knew what her brother was going to ask, and if he did, she could not escape answering. If she ran, she would have to abandon the bandages, which would throw off the cycle of care for her special charge. Ober had chosen the time and location of this confrontation well.

"I just want what we've always spoken," her brother began,

his voice hard but not angry or sharp. "I want the truth, Tomza."

Tomza felt like her chest was in a vise. Every attempt to get a full breath left her shorter on air. After a few seconds, she had to grasp the table next to the wagon for support. Her heart thudded as she blinked to clear the spots from her eyes.

"The truth is…" Tomza began, her throat tightening. Each new word felt more impossible than the last. "I think I might…need to go…soon."

The effort of the confession left her gasping, and she peered pleadingly at her brother. Ober just looked at her, his jaw clenching and unclenching, something in his eyes burrowing into his sister's heart. As difficult as it had been to speak the truth, it was nothing compared to seeing the hurt it caused her brother.

"But…" Ober began. He halted when tears formed in his eyes, then swiped them away and began again. "But why?"

Another question she had known was coming. It was the same question she'd been asking herself. Why was leaving the only answer that made sense to her? Why couldn't she just shake the thought of it from her skull? Why did it keep coming back, no matter where she was or what she was doing?

"I don't know," she admitted, sure the answer would be as unsatisfying to her brother as it was to her. "I've thought about it a lot over the past few days, and I don't have a good answer. I just don't know."

Ober looked away. Tomza's heart ached. She wanted to drag him into a hug like when they were children, so she moved toward him but settled for leaning against the wagon next to him. Their shoulders touched, and Ober didn't recoil. That was as much contact as she dared at that moment.

For several heartbeats, neither spoke.

"Do you remember when Bella taught you about the thunderblood?" Tomza asked, staring across the encampment at the base of Greyshelf. "Until that moment, could you have believed that this wosealf, this savageling, this creature who'd been part of the war against our people and against us, could be so important to you understanding who you are now?"

Ober winced as though the thought had caused him pain. "No, and if you'd told me so, I would've told you that you were crazy."

Tomza nodded.

"But when I was there and she spoke to me," the young dwarf continued, looking beyond the fortress at that day in the woods beside the wolf den. "When I looked into her eyes, I just understood what she was offering to me, and I knew I-I needed it."

"I think this is like that," Tomza offered weakly. "Like Bella had the answers you needed, some of them to questions you didn't know to ask, I think Dolla and her people can help me understand who I am after all the… Well, after everything."

Ober pursed his lips and wrinkled his nose. "As I remember, you were far less understanding when I was going through this," he observed.

Tomza laughed. "Well, as usual, you get to learn from my mistakes. One of the benefits of being a younger brother, I suppose."

"Lucky me." Ober chuckled, then asked, "Are you going to tell anyone else?"

Tomza realized that what had been in her head was much more real now that she was saying things out loud. "I'll tell Torbjorn. See if he wants me to wait until after Greyshelf. To be honest, given his plan, I'm not sure there'll be much for me to do, and if there *are* wounds to mend…"

"Then something's gone very wrong," Ober finished, heaving a sigh. "You're right. Do you…"

His voice caught in his throat, and tears welled in his eyes. Tomza's hand found his, and they clung to each other.

"Do you know…" Ober began again, fighting to force the words through hitching breaths. "Do you know when you'll come back?"

Tomza's eyes glistened as she shook her head. She buried her face in her brother's shoulder. "No." She was grateful that, despite everything, he stood strong for her to lean on. "No, I don't."

Ober nodded again and forced out another few words. "You promise to come back, right? Someday?"

Tomza swallowed around the lump that blocked her throat and looked into the eyes of the only family she had. She had not been away from him for more than a few hours since their parents had died, barring abductions and incarcerations. Matching gray eyes locked, and Tomza willed him to accept the promise she was about to make.

"You better believe it," she declared with a tearful smile. "You *will* see me again, probably looking like I just fell out of a tree and need a bath to wash off the road dust. When that happens, you'll know I'm back for good. Then you'll be looking for a way to get rid of me."

Ober forced a laugh. When he spoke, his voice was steady but soft. He sounded like the little one she'd loved and watched over her entire life. "You promise?"

Tomza nodded as she worked to force the words out with the same steady voice. "I promise."

Ober heaved a sigh, then wrapped his arms around his

sister. Caught off-guard, Tomza froze, then melted into his strong embrace. She was comforted by the strength and sureness of his arms around her. Despite how badly it hurt, she couldn't tell herself she was leaving a child this time.

For a time, brother and sister just held one another. Then, as though both knew the time had come, they separated, drying their eyes as they exchanged bashful smiles. Ober squared his shoulders and headed back to the central encampment. After watching him depart, Tomza turned back to the bandages.

Some had stiffened, so she applied more ointment to make them pliable, then made for the back of the wagon. She was an expert at juggling medical supplies while opening the cage door, so it was only a matter of moments before the metal bars swung open and she was clambering inside.

She'd expected to have to wake the hulking dwarf with a gentle shake of the shoulder, but when she sank down next to him, he was staring at her. The intensity made Tomza aware of how close they were and how far the wagon was from the central encampment. To make matters worse, she remembered that only a few days ago, she'd removed the chain that bound his hands to his feet to allow him greater freedom of movement so he could exercise to promote his healing. He wasn't free, but in these close quarters, he could quickly overpower her. Maybe even fast enough to keep her from crying out.

"Good morning, Okmur," Tomza said, acting like this was part of their normal routine. "I've got more of those treated bandages for you. How about you roll over so I can—"

"I heard you talking," the hulking dwarf interrupted. "Heard what you said about leaving. Going to find somewhere to fix yourself."

Tomza's heart hammered so loud she had trouble hearing what the former tweldwan was saying.

"There was a lot you didn't understand," she began, willing her mind to craft an explanation.

Before she could come up with anything resembling a coherent sentence, a massive mitt closed around her wrist. She told herself to scream and fight like a cornered animal, but when she looked into Okmur's pale eyes, she was paralyzed by his piercing stare.

"When you go," he said, his voice a hoarse whisper, "I want to go with you."

Tomza's jaw dropped. "What?"

CHAPTER TWENTY

"I'm going to be honest. This was not how I saw this all going."

Torbjorn stared at Okmur "Peak-Breaker" Kallson, whose shackles jangled as he hunched in a seat that was comically ill-suited, given his proportions. Torbjorn hadn't intended it to be so, but if they brought out the spindly things designed for the elves, the huge dwan was likely to flatten the thing. It would be bad form to send the nearly mended Okmur shambling back to Tomza with broken bits of chair stuck in his bum, so they'd gone with a stout dwarven chair. The former tweldwan looked as comfortable as an ogre taking tea in a grem's hut.

"I wouldn't have thought so," Okmur replied. "But since we're being honest, I'm not sure why you kept me alive."

Torbjorn frowned as he poured half the leftover schnapps into one of two stout wooden steins.

He'd just found the re-stoppered bottle when Tomza had come in with her "news," and Torbjorn had thought about downing the contents to help him cope with this most recent revelation while she was talking. It wasn't until he'd seen to the young dwarfess, given a command to have Okmur brought in, fretted over the seating issue, decided there was nothing to be done about the seating issue, and seen the former tweldwan ushered in that Torbjorn realized he'd been walking around with the bottle in hand the whole time.

No more of that nonsense, he promised himself as he poured the remaining liquor into the other stein.

"I suppose part of it was a point of order," Torbjorn explained as he moved a stein within the shackled Okmur's easy reach. "I was not going to execute a dwan I'd just gone to the trouble of saving. Didn't want anyone to get the impression that I agreed with that ugly business in any way."

The huge dwarf accepted the stein with a bob of his head. It looked like a teacup in his hand.

"That wasn't the only reason, though," Okmur stated, pausing to sample the spirits' bouquet before taking a hearty swallow. "Ah, good stuff, that. Good as any I can remember." He frowned and lapsed into silence.

Torbjorn took a few sips before deciding his guest wasn't going to resume the conversation without prompting.

"No, that wasn't the only reason," Torbjorn acknowledged. "I also wanted to set a precedent for those under my command. We'd thrown out the book, as it were, and I knew we'd collapse into something worse than what we'd left behind if I didn't lay out some rules. You are the first example of that. We don't kill prisoners without cause."

Okmur nodded and took another sip. When he spoke, his voice was barely above a whisper, and his eyes were unfocused. "Didn't you have cause? I'd tried to murder you under a flag of truce. I hated you so much that I was willing to cast aside my honor and the law to kill you. Isn't that enough reason?"

Torbjorn took a few pensive sips before answering. "Maybe, but that's also why I wanted you to survive." The cool burn of the drink sliding down his throat felt good. "I wanted to prove you wrong, for one thing. You aren't the first one to think that because of this or that thing I did, I deserve to have others act dishonorably toward me. I wanted to show you that whatever else you or anyone else did, *I* would do what was right. Not because I had to but because I chose to."

Okmur's head bowed, his expansive beard draping over his bandaged belly. "Then you've accomplished everything you set out to do with me." His deep voice was as hollow as a bell. "You've proven you aren't doing this for vengeance, you've shown you will lead with honor, not blood, and you revealed my shame that I was less honorable than the lowest of criminals."

Torbjorn looked at the sullen dwarf over the top of his stein and felt sorry for him. He knew what it meant to be crushed under the choices you made and be convinced that nothing you could do would ever make things right. Torbjorn still felt that way.

"Well, I'm not going to pretend it wasn't a bastard trick," the commander admitted, throwing back a hearty swallow. "But the way I see it, this war in the Vale's dragged on for so long that it was bound to twist any dwan.

"That's why I started this little rebellion, if that's what we're calling it. I was sick of seeing dwans broken in body and mind in a fight that had no real purpose and no clear objective. I think it warped many of those dwans who attacked you and the other officers like it did you."

Torbjorn eyed the contents of his stein and was disappointed that he only had two more gulps left. While trying to decide if he wanted to make it last longer by sipping, he downed half.

"Maybe it's a curse for waking up the wheezers, or maybe it was just bad leadership." Torbjorn sighed as he swirled the contents of his stein. "Either way, things couldn't go on as they were."

"I see that now," Okmur agreed and set the cup in front of him. Torbjorn saw a fair amount of liquid move within the stein, or more than was in his.

"Particularly the twisted part," the former tweldwan continued. "I think I felt it before I saw it, and I saw it before I believed it, but now there's no way around it. My time here did not serve me well. It blinded me to what was in front of me, even about myself. That's why I wish to leave it."

Torbjorn took another sip that turned into a hearty pull, leaving him with an empty stein. He looked at the one Okmur had abandoned.

"You think that signing up with the wain dwarfs is the way to do that?" Torbjorn asked. "I suppose I get where Tomza's coming from. She wants to trade one set of dwarvish witchery for something that doesn't seem as awful, but what is *your* reason for wanting to join the heretic parade?"

Okmur winced at Torbjorn's tone, but when he spoke, he looked Torbjorn in the eye.

"First, from all I've heard, they never wage war. That is a source of hope," Okmur began. "Also, going with them will take me out of the Vale, which would help heal my mind and spirit. And last, they're a group I've spent my life hating."

Torbjorn frowned. "Most would consider that a reason to avoid the wheel-totting buggers."

Okmur shook his head. "Don't you see, Torbjorn? I've become something I hate," Okmur's voice was urgent and pained. "I'm not who I thought I was and certainly not who I want to be, so I now stand equal to them. If they are willing to take me in and I can abide with them, I can hope for restoration and redemption."

Torbjorn nodded and set his stein down. Without ceremony, he took Okmur's and drained it as well. "Well, it's not the most sensible thing in my estimation, but maybe it will turn out. Also, seeing as Tomza's looking to jump on that wagon train, it will be good for her to take some company, though I might be a fool for thinking you've reformed. Still, being broken and almost dying has a way of shaking a dwarf up, so this makes sense if you look at it sideways."

Okmur was silent. Torbjorn inspected the schnapps bottle to confirm there was nothing more within.

When Torbjorn set the bottle aside, Okmur squared his shoulders. "So, are you agreeing to my request?"

Torbjorn nodded, and the first smile of the evening appeared on Okmur's face. That smile vanished when, without warning, the commander seized the shackles on Okmur's wrist and hauled the big dwarf eye to eye.

"There's just one thing you need to know before you go," he growled. His tongue tasted foul, but he thought that would enhance the message he wanted to relay.

"I've grown quite attached to the lass during her time with us, so I need to make this very clear. Any harm comes to her and I hear about it, you can bet every bone in your body that I will come for you, and I'll leave those bones crushed to powder."

Torbjorn saw the old Okmur surface, his shoulders bunching and his brows thunderous, but like smoke before the wind, it blew away.

"You don't have to threaten me, Torbjorn."

"That's good to know." Torbjorn released the shackles and slouched back in his chair. "Still, I'll probably keep doing it until your wain mother comes to abscond with you. Consider it the first step on your penitential road."

Okmur smiled as he folded his shackled hands in his lap. "That seems fitting."

"Fitting." Torbjorn chuckled. "Aye, that's the word for it. So, now all that's done, we just have to wait on your wain dwarfs to mosey on in. How long will that take?"

"You lot must keep a close ear on things."

Mehk Dolla of Clan Omru cocked her head as Torbjorn came over to sit beside her fire. As was their wont, the wain dwarfs had appeared on the fringes of the camp a few days ago. Torbjorn had been deep in conversations with the svartalfs and Tomza when word had come from the wosealfs that a lone wagon was just out of duabuw range from the encampment. It had settled against an old solitary snorri birch, and the occupants were making camp there.

When the scouts had been questioned as to why they hadn't approached the wagoneer, their response had been a befuddled "Yes, why didn't we?" That, as much as the wagon appearing, convinced Torbjorn that the time had come.

The snorri birch was a nice touch.

"I'm not sure what you mean," the wain dwarfess admitted. "Since we were waiting for your arrival, we were paying close attention to that. Is this what you're referring to?"

Torbjorn shook his head as he held out his hands to the warmth of the crackling logs. The night's chill had turned his breath to white plumes and set an ache in his bones, but here beside the wain dwarfess' fire, the pain receded. Remembering what Tomza and Ober had spoken about, the dwarf commander stamped his feet and rolled his shoulder to ward off sleepiness.

"I'm talking about how you don't just wait until I arrive." Torbjorn chuckled. "You bide your time until I don't have just one dwarf but two coming to me, asking for permission to follow you back to your people."

Mehk Dolla straightened from adjusting the kettle on an ember-heated stone and frowned. "Two?" Her dark eyes glittered in the firelight. "Draul's son and daughter have both decided to heed our call?"

Torbjorn cocked his head. The dwarfess had not guessed it was Okmur who'd spoken of joining the wain dwarfs, but it struck him as odd.

Maybe I've made too much of them and their strangeness, he admitted to himself. *Maybe they're more like us than I was willing to believe.*

Torbjorn shook his head and rose to offer the dwarfess a hand as she made for her seat. Dolla took the proffered hand gladly, giving him a grateful nod and a smile as she sank onto a small camp stool that had been set out. Her hand was weathered and hard but warm to the touch.

"Thank you." She sighed as she settled herself and adjusted her tasseled skirt. "I'm glad to see that you not only bear the title of prince but also the manners. So, it is not brother and sister who wish to join us?"

"No, the second is not Ober," Torbjorn stated, returning to his stool. "The other dwarf is a former tweldwan of the 6th Division—the one who was sent to crush my little rebellion. It seems his defeat shook his understanding of the world and himself, and word of what you offered Tomza appealed to him."

The wain dwarfess pursed her lips pensively, and her eyes bored into the heart of the fire. "He is welcome," she began but paused, her gaze shifting to Torbjorn. "Assuming you permit it and believe he is speaking in good faith, not in an attempt to avoid judgment. All can be called, but the caravan is not a refuge for fleeing criminals."

Torbjorn nodded as he leaned toward her.

"That makes sense, given what you told our scouting party in that glade. The caravan is your family, your kin, and you wouldn't want to let in some miscreant who'd end up causing trouble."

"There is that," Dolla agreed. "Also, we try not to interfere with the laws of the lands we pass through. We are taught that it is good and right for the magistrate to keep the peace and would never wish to be seen subverting such institutions if it can be helped."

Torbjorn couldn't keep a smile from appearing.

"I'm amusing you." Dolla chuckled and took a long rod from beside her stool to shift the embers around the cooking stone. "Tell me what this silly old dwarfess has done now, my prince."

Torbjorn sniffed at the title, then cleared his throat, remembering the conversation with the elf a few nights before.

"I mean no disrespect," he offered. "I just find it funny that you talk about honoring magistrates when you are here to aid a dwarf who rebelled against those magistrates and killed their deputies."

When she raised her eyes from the fire, Torbjorn laughed. "Hardly seems like you're keeping the faith, good Mehk."

Dolla met his stare for three heartbeats. Then her dark lashes fluttered and she looked back at the kettle. "I don't expect you to know much about us, Prince Torbjorn. Nor do I plan to give you a detailed precis of all we believe, at least not tonight, but you strike me as a smart, even clever dwarf, so I think sharing this tidbit might help. Among our kind, there is a saying—a stricture even—gleaned from our faith, that explains this best. *An unjust law is no law, and a corrupt magistrate has no authority.*"

Torbjorn's brow furrowed, and he adjusted his seat on the stool. It wasn't watertight as far as philosophies of governance went, but he liked the sound of it. It cast their current struggle in a better light than the Imperial dwarfs' belief in conformity to the authority of clan and king over all else.

"So, you justify your meeting with an arch-traitor as taking action toward true justice, eh?" Torbjorn asked, raising an eyebrow. "Quite a lofty pedestal you've put me on."

The kettle whistled, so Dolla paused to use the rod's crooked end to fish it out. She poured the boiling water into a pair of bowls with silver infusers at the center, awaiting their bubbling baptism.

"I can't blame you for being cynical, Prince," she murmured as aromatic steam rose. "But ideals are not to be mocked, especially not when the war you've been waging is about ideals."

"Has it now?" Torbjorn asked curiously. "What a lofty view you hold of me."

Dolla fixed him with a stare. "You've marched from Tuvaloth to Greyshelf, yet there are no smoking ruins left in your wake or pits filled with executed prisoners or unfortunate civilians, something the dwarvish legions cannot boast of.

"We can waste the night pretending that you are someone you are not, Torbjorn Hralson of Clan Cyniburg, but you can't persuade me that you are a stony-hearted warlord. Far be it from me to tell a prince how to conduct his business, but if I believed half of what you are trying to convince yourself of, I wouldn't be here right now."

Torbjorn straightened and glanced at the fire. Half a dozen angry retorts came to mind, along with denials and accusations, but he knew what they were.

The old lass stung you. You like cutting to the quick, but it's not as fun when it's you getting the knife, eh?

Dolla was drawing out the infusers when Torbjorn heaved a sigh. "Perhaps you are right." He hoped the firelight would explain the glow in his cheeks. "Shaper help me. I'm a principled fool on a quest to set things right. What word do you bring from Cer'Kest? Is it a warning that the wheezers are coming, or perhaps a prophecy of an even greater and darker power that the wights know about or are preparing for?"

The wain dwarfess frowned. "Nothing so dramatic. In fact, this has little to do with Cer'Kest, the wights, or any of that. You managed to button that matter up soundly. What gave you that idea?"

Torbjorn opened his mouth to recite the words relayed by Tomza and Ober but stopped when he saw the sly smile on Dolla's face. He shook his head and leveled a narrow stare at her.

"Why, Mehk Dolla," he began, his tone reflecting in mock outrage. "I do believe you played your last guests like a fiddle. You mentioned Cer'Kest, and just like bairns hearing about a boogeycritter, their heads filled with all manner of frightening phantoms that never existed."

The caravan mistress lifted one bowl and held it out to

Torbjorn, smiling through the vapors still rising from it. "In my defense, I *was* near Cer'Kest when the word came to me," she explained as Torbjorn took the proffered bowl. "We were selling wool to human locals who dwell thereabouts, though I might have failed to mention that bit. That apparently set the impressionable young dwans to speculating."

Torbjorn felt the pleasing warmth of the tea seeping into his fingers through the clay as he shook his head mournfully.

"Just shameful." He sighed, staring into the bowl. "Well, let's have it, then. What do you want, a trade agreement? My word that if I secure the valley, I'll enact laws to protect you and your people? You've earned your chance at a request through gullible youths and sheer daring, so make it good."

Dolla took a sip of tea, savoring the drink. She was silent for so long that Torbjorn looked up from his tea with a frown. He was about to urge her to get on with it, his spirits sinking at the seeming futility of the meeting, when the dwarfess gave him a knowing smile.

"None of that interests me currently," Mehk Dolla began as she cradled her tea. "No, what I have for you is word, I believe, from the Shaper himself. It was intended for you and only you, and even those within my caravan—even my dear old husband, Speaker keep him—doesn't know. They've come all this way so I could deliver a message no other has heard and will never hear."

His anger rose. Did this vagabond heretic really think she could convert him to her petty cult? "Well, let's have it, then," he urged with an angry rasp in his voice. "You came all this way. Let's have it."

Dolla gave him an indulgent smile and set her bowl on the table.

"The message is this, Prince Torbjorn." She set her shoulders and stared into his eyes. "Forgive your father."

Torbjorn blinked. "Is that it?"

Dolla nodded and retrieved her tea.

Torbjorn heaved a sigh and looked around, then scratched his head and ran a thumb over his cheek. "You came all this way to say that?" He sounded incredulous. *"Forgive your father."*

Dolla gazed at him over her tea.

Torbjorn composed a thunderous rebuke for wasting his time, but then he looked at the surety in her face and reached the only logical conclusion: she was mad. And if that was so, lambasting her would be a further waste of his time. You didn't rebuke the mad, and you didn't try to teach a worcsvine to dance. You wouldn't get satisfactory results, and the likelihood of someone getting bitten went up the longer you continued the exercise.

Shaking his head again, Torbjorn gulped his tea and tossed the bowl on the table with a flick of his wrist.

"Fair enough. Consider it done," he declared, slapping his knees before climbing to his feet. "I forgive the cold, ruthless old bastard and revoke my juvenile declaration to piss on his grave when he dies. My, how you've changed me."

Mehk Dolla watched him with hooded eyes as he stood over her, considering ignoring his own advice about teaching worcsvines to dance. If she sensed his anger, she gave no sign; she remained infuriatingly placid. In the end, Torbjorn threw his hands up and stalked away from the fire.

"Have a bloody fine trip back to Cer'Kest, Scadish, or where-the-hell-ever-else!" he snapped over his shoulder.

"Your father will be glad to hear of your forgiveness," Dolla called after him. "You should tell him when he arrives at the Lake Gate in Greyshelf in three days."

Torbjorn froze, his anger evaporating as the implications of the wain dwarfess' words sank in. "Three days," he muttered, the words burning on his tongue. *"Three days."*

Torbjorn was invaded by the cold autumn wind, and he realized that the only light came from the crescent moon. Spinning, he watched the old snorri birch claw its way into the air. The wagon, the fire, and Mehk Dolla were gone.

"Well, shit!" Torbjorn hissed and raced back to camp.

CHAPTER TWENTY-ONE

"What in Grimmoth's name is goin' on down there?"

In various permutations, the question echoed across the turrets and ledges of Greyshelf as sentries squinted into the mist that blanketed the ground and the camp around the fortress. In the gloom before dawn, word had come from the fortress' watch that a commotion was taking place down below. That had resulted in a general call to arms since all suspected this would be the first assault on the fortress.

In theory, it would only be a probing effort to assess the relative strength of the defenders, but that was uncertain, so the dwans anxiously watched from their posts. Veteran wisdom aside, the name of the enemy commander was at the forefront of every dwarf's mind. Prince Torbjorn the Kinslayer defied conventional wisdom, and from the highest officer to the lowest dwan, all knew it.

Hadn't he single-handedly driven out the wights? Then he had conquered the savagelings with fewer dwarfs than a ranger patrol? Hadn't those who just escaped the fall of the

Sufstan Holt'Dwan said he commanded demons that had laid waste to the entire army?

Let any dwan try to pretend he wasn't scared of what Torbjorn Kinslayer might unleash, and his comrades would know he was a liar.

Time dragged on and the ruckus in the foggy valley continued, but no attack came. The sun's rays peeked over the Central Wyrmspines, promising to dispel the mist, but it would be a slow thing.

Nearly as slow was the response from those who commanded the fortress. Lardwan Yorm had been roused from his bed when the commotion below the fortress started, but he had been slower to bring news to the ondwan than to drag himself out to walk the wind-chilled walls.

"What am I supposed to tell Assface?" the pugnacious dwarf had demanded when his staff had suggested waking the ondwan. "'There's a lot of noise in the valley, my Ondwan. No, I don't know what is causing it. Why am I waking you up from your drunken, overstuffed stupor, my Ondwan? Because I'm an idiot, that's why!' Now shut up and find me something to report before I pitch you off this wall!"

The scramble to discover more information without leaving the shelter of the fortress dragged on until the sun was high in the sky. Not until after the ondwan emerged from his chambers in a flurry of braying shouts and scrambling attendants did Yorm have anything resembling actual information to share.

Clutching his fur-lined cloak around him, Ondwan Ashfer stepped onto the walls of Greyshelf. "Yorm, you slack-jawed fool!" the ondwan bellowed as the dwans on the walls scrambled to get out of his way. "What is going on down there? Are we under attack or not?"

A pair of rangers reporting to the lardwan closed their mouths as they watched Yorm's face go through contortions. He finally affixed a properly deferential expression to it.

"My apologies, Ondwan. I've been laboring for hours to determine just that. My patrols that went out along the shelf of the mountain face are just reporting in. Please come and hear what these two have to report."

When the ondwan bustled over, neither ranger looked as though they liked the idea of standing before the commander. The pair shared a look, each urging the other to take the lead in this impromptu presentation.

They were spared his immediate scrutiny since, on his way over, Ashfer's ceremonial breastplate unseated. He appeared before his subordinates with the armor hanging oddly from his lumpy frame, so he tried to fix the problem. Assuming the expression that had caused his unflattering moniker, the ondwan grappled with the breastplate until an attendant, fearing he might harm himself, came to the rescue.

"Well, what are you waiting for?" Ashfer brayed, red-faced. He looked around for something to vent his spleen on. "You need to see me adjust my danglers too before you give the damned report?"

"Seems to be fighting in the enemy camp, Ondwan!" the first ranger explained. "Between the svartalf mercenaries and the traitor dwarfs, sir!"

Ashfer winced at the loud report, raising one hand to shield a jutting ear.

"No need to shout, Dwan. I'm right here." The commander turned a critical eye on the valley. "Fighting, eh? Sounds like the Kinslayer's having trouble keeping his sell-swords in line."

The second ranger, inspired but also cautioned by his comrade's example, snapped a salute before launching into his recitation. "Reports of fires and indications that the myrklings are striking camp, Ondwan," the dwan declared. "It also seems like the myrklings are raiding the wosealfs' supply depots as they go, prompting further chaos, sir."

Ashfer squinted at the ground before the fortress, but the mist was still too thick to make out much except many bodies among the trees. As the full weight of the rangers' reports penetrated the fussy and self-important dwarf's brain, he chuckled and rubbed his hands together, only partially because of the cold.

"Ho-ho. Are you scared because you might actually have to defend this place?" The ondwan sneered and shot a sidelong look at his lardwan. "Didn't want to wake me because you were afraid you might not be able to scamper away on the back of one of your beloved pigs, eh, Yorm?"

The diminutive lardwan's jaw clenched, but he forced his tone to remain calm. "I wished to avoid disturbing you without anything to report, my Ondwan. The fog—"

"Excuses!" Ashfer clucked, batting away Yorm's explanation like a fly. "By all rights, you should be out there right now, capitalizing on Torbjorn's calamity."

Yorm straightened to his full but inconsiderable height as he raised his chin. "Give the word, my Ondwan, and I'll gladly lead a squadron of chargers into the enemy camp!"

The ondwan swatted away that suggestion too as he stared at the valley floor through watery eyes. "Nonsense. What a stupid idea." Ashfer gestured at the churning mist. "In that soup down there, you're more likely to plunge butt-first into a latrine than close with the enemy. You wouldn't be much of a loss, but when the emperor arrives in barely a day, I don't want to tell him I squandered the cream of our forces on an ill-advised charge. Shaper knows this has been embarrassing enough."

"They're fleeing!" The cry came from farther down the wall. Sentries pointed at a cut in the mountain's shadow that allowed the sunlight to gnaw on the mist. In that thinner patch of mist, they saw armored svartalf knights streaming away from the fortress on their sharp-snouted mounts.

Ondwan and lardwan shouldered their way across the wall to a better view as more of the myrklings fled.

"Ha-ha. I bet the Kinslayer's pulling out his beard!" Ashfer crowed as he leaned against the parapet. "Those shiny elves decided they didn't want to join his little uprising after all. This is brilliant!"

"Look," Yorm cried as his finger jabbed toward other shapes moving in the mist. "They're not letting them go without a fight."

A ragged batch of mounted savagelings gave chase, their riders keening as they indignantly waved their lances and swords.

"Never knew a myrkling to leave empty-handed," the ondwan brayed. "Let them catch up and kill each other. They'll be scattered between Longsnout and Klavoburg by nightfall at this rate."

Everyone nodded, then someone shouted from the lower tier of the wall. Following the exclamations and pointing fingers, the ondwan and the lardwan saw people struggling on foot. This wouldn't have been remarkable, but those on the walls determined that the people were not fleeing from the fortress but approaching it.

"What are they thinking?" Yorm asked. He'd had to stand on tiptoes to see over the wall.

"Just turned around in the fighting, maybe," Ashfer offered.

"Cowards lost their heads and don't realize they're running right toward death."

"They look like they're carrying something," the lardwan said, pressed to the wall. "Plunder, maybe."

"Dwarvish riders are following them!" one of the sentries called, and a moment later, the first of the blotferows trotted out of the fog. Then several made their way across the broken ground.

"Not going to make it very far with that treasure, now are they?" the ondwan jeered, and an avaricious gleam came into his eyes. "Give the word at the gate not to loose until the swine riders have slaughtered them. Then we can pick off the riders and send out a few dwans to collect the spoils. It must be quite a prize if they're willing to risk so much."

"A clever plan, Ondwan," Yorm replied, nodding at a nearby dwan to relay the order to the dwans at the gate.

From their elevated perch, the dwarfs of Greyshelf watched the drama unfold as the small knot of lithe figures struggled on and finally fetched up against the Vale Gate. The riders behind them had been stalled by old broken wooden barricades, but they'd now reached open ground and were coming on fast.

"Nowhere to go now." Ashfer chuckled as he strained to get a better look. "Oh, this will be fun to watch."

With less glee but no less interest, the other dwarfs leaned forward with bated breath. When an urgent shout rose from the gate, several of the dwans jumped in surprise.

"They have the Kinslayer!"

The ondwan and the lardwan exchanged glances, then shouted in unison for a repeat of the report.

"They've got the Kinslayer. They've got him, and they're requesting protection in return for him."

Ashfer's eyes widened. The greedy light was now a blazing fire. "That *is* a treasure!"

"It could be a trick," Yorm suggested, scowling as he stretched to get a better look at the gate. "They could be trying to—"

"To what?" the ondwan spat, brushing past the lardwan. "Seize this fortress with a handful of winded elves? Don't be absurd! We're not going to miss this chance to hand the Kinslayer to his father on a platter when he arrives. That might be the key to recovering from this entire debacle."

The ondwan's harsh voice echoed down to the gate. "Get them inside quickly! I want the Kinslayer in the keep hall in short order!"

"Well, this is disappointing."

The two savageling servants who deposited Torbjorn's body on a hastily cleared table in the keep hall of Greyshelf exchanged confused glances. Supposing they only spoke their heathen tongue, Ondwan Ashfer shooed them away as he stalked toward Torbjorn. The wosealfs crept back to cower behind their svartalf masters, who were under guard at the back of the hall.

"How do we know he's dead?" Yorm asked as he slunk behind the ondwan, his suspicious glare shifting between the body and the elves. The Kinslayer lay flaccid on the table, one arm hanging free. He had ragged, blood-smeared holes on his chest.

"There's one way to find out," Ashfer remarked, snatching a carving knife from the table.

With a suspicious frown, he prodded the hanging arm. The

sharp blade bit into the flesh and blood oozed out, but the rest of the body remained inert. Not yet convinced, the ondwan dug at the wound, spattering blood on the floor and himself. Finally, he tossed the knife aside with a disgruntled huff.

"Well, that is substantially *less* valuable."

Yorm scooped up the blade to conduct his own tests. He was raising the knife to plunge it into the dwarf's throat when his commander turned a withering glare on him.

"What are you doing, idiot? Do you want to hand the mutilated corpse of a son over to his father? Even if the child was a treasonous piece of filth, I don't want to have to explain to the Emperor why we are handing his former heir over in pieces! Put that knife down before you end up doing something equally stupid."

Yorm's venomous glare at the ondwan's back could have curdled milk, but the diminutive dwarf pitched the knife behind him.

Waddling forward, Ashfer looked the svartalfs over. The leader of the group was a disturbingly evocative member of her species, an albino bedecked in silver plate to match her unusual skin tone. The regal disdain with which she looked at the world was daunting.

When Ashfer saw that, despite his orders for the elves to be disarmed, she still bore a sword upon her hip, he was not surprised. The blade was a crude piece of black iron, little better than slag slung across her hip. He imagined she'd grabbed it in the mad flight from the camp and clung to it as her only weapon. Looking at the Sablestone guards who flanked the elves, Ashfer could laugh at the ugly thing.

When he finally spoke, the ondwan directed his words at the albino, chin raised and arms crossed.

"I suppose you'll be wanting a reward for this poor excuse

for a gift," Ashfer began, looking down his nose at the mercenary. "For services rendered, I *could* find it within me to part with a few coins, but he would've been worth far more alive."

She took a step forward and the Sablestone guards around her tensed, but Ashfer waved them back. He expected she would haggle, as was the way of sell-swords.

"The Kinslayer was a dangerous one," she stated, her voice bearing the lilting myrkling accent. "We could not have reached you if he'd fought us the entire way."

Ashfer nodded since that sounded reasonable. "Even so…" He nodded at the corpse. "A living traitor in chains is far more useful than a corpse. Also, I'm not sure if you myrklings realize this, but the Kinslayer wasn't just a rebel but also a prince of the Cyniburg clan. His father the emperor will be here in a day or two, and there's no telling how he will react."

The elves stiffened at the revelation, whispering among themselves in their melodious tongue.

"Then we will take our pay and depart," the she-elf replied with a bow. "By your leave, Ondwan."

Ashfer shook his head. "No, you won't," he declared, rocking back on his heels. "I think I'll keep you lot around in case the emperor is distraught and wants someone to take it out on. If we make it through his visit and he leaves a few of you alive, I might part with some coin to see you on your way."

Ashfer basked in the sullen silence of the myrklings as they stared at one another, then at the guards around them. The ondwan didn't even bother to hide his smile when the mercenaries nodded at their pale leader.

The albino bowed nearly double to Ashfer. "We have little choice." She sighed. "May I offer something to complete the gift you wish to present to the emperor?"

Ashfer frowned, uncertain what else she could give him now that Torbjorn was dead. He was ready to relegate them to the dungeon for safekeeping, but then he recalled the elves' propensity for trophy-taking and cannibalism, and his heart lurched. The thought of presenting the Kinslayer to his father, only to discover some yet undetected desecration that could undo his plans to recoup the favor he'd lost, sickened him.

Wincing, Ashfer nodded.

The albino removed the sword from her belt and, despite the leveled weapons of the guards, slowly extended it toward Ashfer.

"This was the blade that took his life," she told him, head reverently bowed. "We believe the soul of the slain clings to the weapon that dealt the mortal blow. You may give it to the emperor so he will have part of his fallen son."

Ashfer looked at the ugly piece of metal. He would have liked nothing better than to cast it away, but the elf's anecdote might add panache to the tale of the Kinslayer's demise. Careful to avoid nicking himself, the ondwan took the proffered blade, which felt every bit as ugly and cruel as it looked. Under the eyes of his subordinates, Ashfer decorously deposited the weapon atop Torbjorn's corpse in what seemed a fitting funerary tribute.

"Thank you, I suppose," the ondwan said as he turned away from the corpse and sword. "But just so we're clear, I'm not going to pay you extra for that piece of sla—"

Yorm's sudden scream became a choked gurgle. Ashfer wheeled and saw his lardwan on his knees, clawing at a ragged slash in his throat that went nearly to the spine. Even more horrifying, ribbons of blood streamed from the gaping wound. Coiling and stretching, the blood wrapped serpent-like around the jagged black blade on Torbjorn's chest, and Ashfer saw the mangled slash on Torbjorn's arm healing.

His mind reeled. "*Guards! Guards!*" the ondwan screamed as he lurched back.

At a pair of wet growls, Ashfer whirled to see two wolfish horrors spring from the midst of the svartalfs. Despite their alchemically enhanced strength and substantial bulk, the Sablestone guards were knocked over by the lupine monsters. The beasts gained momentum with each impact until they were furry blurs and every last guard was on the floor.

Darting between the wolves, the svartalf mercenaries snatched felled guards' weapons.

Faced with wolves and armed myrklings stalking forward, Ashfer tried to escape. A hand seized his shoulder, and he was spun to face the pale but very much alive face of Torbjorn.

"Hey there, Arseface," Torbjorn growled, raising the jagged black blade. Rivulets of blood vanished in thin red plumes. "What do you say we all take a little trip down to the gate? Don't worry if we run into any dwans on the way. I'm sure they'll listen to their ondwan's commands."

The jagged iron blade was less than an inch from Ashfer's throat.

"At least, you better hope they will."

CHAPTER TWENTY-TWO

"You don't have to do this."

Torbjorn smiled.

"Not true, my fordwan," He sighed as he settled a hand on Gromic's shoulder. "We both know there's only one chance for this to turn out anything but bloody. I'm not saying it's a good chance, but it's the only one we've got."

The commander stood on top of the Lake Gate with his Bad Badgers, watching the end of the rebellion.

He had anticipated how quickly the fortress would come under their control since the dwans stationed there were all veterans of the Vale wars and not keen on the ondwan who'd ambled down from Heimgrud to salvage his reputation. Also, Ashfer had made it clear that he didn't care if their defense of the fortress cost the blood of every dwan in the Sufstan Holt'Dwan.

After Torbjorn and his infiltration team threw open the Vale Gate, the coup was complete. Torbjorn hadn't had time to deal with the aftereffects of the elf draught that had put him into a deathlike state.

"Do you suppose they'll use those things?" Clahdi asked, pointing at the baelgeld cannons mounted on the enormous ship's decks. "Any one of those could turn this gate to rubble."

"You'll be lucky to find anything that resembles rubble if one of those fires," Waelon replied, slipping a protective arm around her shoulder. "The baelgeld makes the shot tear and burn like no natural iron would."

The veteran dwans nodded, and Clahdi bit her lip as she leaned into the red-haired dwarf's embrace.

Ever punctual, Emperor Hral of the Cyniburg dynasty had arrived on the third day after the meeting with Dolla. His coming had been heralded by rangers' signal bolts from the cliffs surrounding Heimlagu, but his approach was slow and methodical.

For the last hour, the Bad Badgers and many of the dwans had watched the titanic vessels plod across the eternally cold waters. The ships were foreign to these waters. They were typically only deployed to the Umberdiepe below the Wyrmspine Mountains or the coasts of the Northern Wyrmspines and the subterranean Caged Sea.

Armed to deal with deep wyrms and coastal pirate bastions, their crews and dwan cohorts rendered them floating fortresses. Six of the leviathans churned the Heimlagu while smaller escort vessels wove between them like sharp-spined sharks.

Their dominion was absolute. The few deeplings who'd tested the matter had been treated to a reprisal that even those alien monsters understood. Now the only ripples in the water came from the emperor's flotilla.

"Do you think they know Ashfer's not in charge anymore?" Ober asked, his voice hard but welcome.

Tomza and Okmur had vanished not long after they'd taken Greyshelf, and in the two days since then, Torbjorn hadn't heard the lad speak. For a time, he'd been concerned that Ober would sink too far into himself, but he was finding his way back. Perhaps it was just determination to survive this new threat and see his sister again, but Torbjorn was glad to see the sturdy dwan staring clear-eyed at the approaching force.

"We know a few slipped out of Greyshelf after we took over," Torbjorn answered. "I very much doubt they weren't picked up, and they would have told their tale to whoever found them on the Lake Road."

Utyrvaul pointed a long finger at the paved road winding around the lake. "Speaking of which, here they come."

Division after division of the dwans beneath the banners of the Norstan and Jurstan Holt'Dwans marched down the Lake Road. Their gleaming arms and new boots spoke of a recent refit, and siege engines, some with pulleys and winches, others gleaming cylinders wound with baelgeld, advanced among their ranks.

Apparently, Emperor Hral was going to vent his displeasure on the new occupants of Greyshelf.

"We poked the bear. He had to come out of his cave eventually." Gromic sighed. He was leaning on the stones of the old fortress for support.

A moment later, Haeda's hand settled over the stout dwarf's paw. "He hasn't opened fire yet. Maybe that means he's willing to talk. To negotiate, maybe?"

Torbjorn nodded, though he couldn't find the strength to speak.

Dwarfs like Emperor Hral Rolloson of Clan Cyniburg didn't negotiate with rebels. They decreed, they proclaimed, they commanded, and they passed judgment. That was part of what made them who and what they were.

It was also part of the reason Torbjorn could never rule. He wasn't like that.

Now he was going to find out if he'd been wrong all this time, as the heretical old dwarfess had told him.

"They're sending an envoy!" Clahdi cried, pointing at the blocky vessel that peeled away from the lead leviathan. On its mast and prow, white flags of truce flapped. It cut a path toward the dock, moving steadily across the black waters.

Torbjorn forced himself to breathe. He knew it wasn't just some envoy on the boat. "That's my cue." He turned to his Bad Badgers. "Anyone want to say anything worth remembering before I do this?"

The dwarfs and elf gazed at the commander—their commander—eyes brimming.

"Didn't think so." Torbjorn smiled. "Pleased to serve with you, as always."

He headed for the stairs but was stopped by a hand on his shoulder. Torbjorn didn't resist as he was drawn into one embrace after another. Even Waelon wrapped his muscle-knotted arms around his commander. None spoke, understanding there was nothing they could say that their hands and hearts hadn't already said.

When it was his turn, Utyrvaul sank to one knee so he was eye to eye with the dwarf, and after a moment, he extended his hand. Torbjorn met the elf's eyes as he took the offered hand and gave it a hearty shake.

"I'll be waiting right here," the svartalf stated, his voice tighter than usual. "So don't dawdle. I'm liable to catch a chill if you do."

Torbjorn couldn't laugh, but he did smile. Before the elf could stop him, he drew the myrkling into a quick embrace.

"Best blade-eared Badger I've ever seen," Torbjorn whispered, then broke away and made for the stairs.

He couldn't stay there a moment longer. There was still something for him to do. Something they were counting on him to do.

"I'm surprised you still have your hair."

Torbjorn reflexively raked a hand through his shaggy hair, then let the hand drop to his side.

"This many years, and that's the first thing you say to me?" Torbjorn scoffed. The dwarf before him could have been confused for any armored officer who was fit for war, but the crowned inset on his helm and the fine detailing on his boots and belt suggested he was different.

Emperor Hral, his father, unfastened his helm and placed it under his arm, revealing his broad bare pate.

"Just noticed, is all." He shrugged and ran a hand across his smooth skull. "Must've come from your mother. She had a thick mane you could tangle your fingers in and not mind one bit."

"Can you even remember her name or just her hair?"

Hral frowned.

Torbjorn eyed the father he'd worshiped, revered, feared, and then hated during the long course of his life. Was this the titan he remembered, and if so, was how he remembered the dwarf, however vivid, wrong? For all his power, authority, and might, he was trying to remember the name of a wife from a hundred political marriages ago.

"I didn't think so." Torbjorn sighed, amazed by how the old dwarf seemed to shrink as he stared at him.

"Is that what this is about?" Hral asked, anger in his hoarse, worn voice.

The strange turns this conversation was taking threw Torbjorn off. He wondered if Utyrvaul's comments about family drama and politics being inextricably bound together weren't far from the truth.

"What do you mean?" Torbjorn asked, choosing his words carefully. "Are you asking if I deposed Ashfer because you don't know my mother's name?"

"No!" Torbjorn's father growled, then drew back and modulated his tone. "I suppose this is the most recent tantrum, but I meant all of it. The murder, the dishonor, the… the…*everything*. Everything you did to put a weapon in the hands of our enemies among the clans and make me wonder how I could be so wrong."

Torbjorn might have responded, but the emperor had hit his stride, and there was no interrupting.

"Of all my children, you were the only one who had the strength to bear the weight of the crown. I'd known that ever since you were born, but as I watched you, even as a whelp underfoot, I saw that strength, that will. Then there was that night with the throne, and I-I knew I and my favor endangered everything I saw in you, so I made sure you were properly trained without me. You got none of the frivolous things your siblings craved nor the distractions, but I gave you all you could ever need to be the greatest of our line."

Hral's expression hardened, and he spoke in the cold tone Torbjorn remembered so well. "And this is how you repay me. Dishonor, imprisonment, botched executions, and when I gave you a way out, you started a rebellion. A *rebellion*, Torbjorn, the likes of which our empire had not seen since its founding."

Torbjorn wanted to look down. He thought the shame would crush him, but somehow, he held his father's gaze without flinching.

"What did I do to make you hate me so much, son?" Hral asked, then stared at the Heimlagu. The last word had slipped free without the rime of cold contempt.

Torbjorn clung to that word and the pain and vulnerability in the others.

"I can't say I never hated you," Torbjorn began, still looking at his father. "But I *can* say that none of this was about hating or hurting you. All of it came from stopping the brutalities and cruelties of this war in whatever ways I could. Sometimes I succeeded, many times I failed, but not once did I set out to shame or harm you."

Torbjorn's voice betrayed him, thickening when he needed it to be strong and clear.

"I love you, Father. Even…even when I have reasons to hate you."

Hral gritted his teeth, still refusing to look at his son. "What is all this talk of ending cruelty and brutality?" he asked, voice dripping disdain. "War is cruel, and war is brutal. You went off to be a soldier, and you decided you wanted to make this war something it wasn't. Something it couldn't be. You've forgotten what a dwan does."

"No, Father," Torbjorn's voice rose like thunder in his chest. "*You* forgot. Just wars have a point and purpose defined by more than lines on a map and numbers in a ledger. You spent so long sending edicts from your throne that you forgot your aims should mean something to the dwans you are sending to die and the foe you are sending them to kill."

Hral's hand rose to brush off Torbjorn's words like motes of frost threatening to land on his shoulder. "I don't have the luxury of your ideals."

"*I've* never had the luxury of ignoring them!" Torbjorn roared. "You talk about my failures and shame, but you forget that on these very boards, I brokered the retreat of the wights that drove them back to their sepulchers without another bloody campaign, and for all that's gone on, the undead are *still* at bay. If you don't understand how that happened, you have forgotten *why* wars are waged, even if you haven't forgotten how."

The emperor continued to stare out across the water, eyes boring through the side of one of his ships into the mountain beyond.

In defiance of that silence, Torbjorn continued, hoping he could dig through the years and pain and reach his father. "Right now, Greyshelf is full of dwans and svartalfs and even wosealfs who stand with me because I haven't forgotten what it means to fight and bleed with them. They know that *I* know they want something more than more grinding war to hold some blot or scratch on a map."

Torbjorn paused to look over his shoulder at the Lake Gate. Though he couldn't see them, the Bad Badgers were watching him, willing him to a victory they didn't dare hope for.

"And since you mentioned that night in the throne room," Torbjorn began, feeling as though he was stepping along the edge of a precipice, "I remember the life you showed me. The lonely one that threatened every day to crush you under its weight. The one you were trying to harden me for. I remember it, and though I believe you were trying to protect me, you couldn't have been more wrong."

Torbjorn's father spun, his jaw clenched and his eyes narrowed.

"You were wrong to tell me it had to be done alone, and you were wrong to do it alone," Torbjorn pressed. "I've found that only by letting others in, trusting them, and serving with them have I been able to face the burden of leadership. You tried to teach me the most important lesson about leadership, but you had the wrong answer, and from that sprang so much wrong that I've had to spend all of my life unlearning it."

Hral's face was stony, but Torbjorn thought he saw cracks forming. "For that mistake, the one that shaped all the others, I've spent most of my time angry and fearful, but now? Now I can say something I could not have said in honesty before."

Father and son stood eye to eye and face to face for a moment the world forgot.

"Father, I forgive you."

Hral reeled back as though he'd been struck.

"I forgive you, and I want peace with you," Torbjorn continued. "I took the stand I did to end the war in the Vale, not to be your enemy. I accept responsibility for my actions, and I do not regret them, but you are not my enemy to fight. If you wish to punish me, I will surrender to whatever you see fit as long as you treat those within Greyshelf with the honor and respect due honorable dwans."

Torbjorn stepped forward and spread his arms wide as he sank to his knees, then closed his eyes. "I place myself at your mercy."

He was unsure of what would come, but he was certain that what he was doing was right.

When at last his father spoke, it was with an exasperated hiss Torbjorn was unprepared for.

"Oh, get up."

Torbjorn opened his eyes to see his father moving toward him.

The emperor dragged him to his feet. "I said, get up! Fine, have it your way. You say that the lesson of leadership is not in being alone, but who can I trust with something like this? Do you realize the impossible situation you've put me in, son?"

Torbjorn frowned, too bemused to speak.

"I need to choose someone to trust. Someone to serve with me so that maybe, just maybe, they can be for me whatever that pack of miscreants you have is for you."

Torbjorn squinted at his father. "So, what you're saying is…"

Hral groaned. "Oh, lad! You had heart, but you were never the brightest. I'm saying that you've cleared out a lot of loose rock and sand from the Sufstan Holt'Dwan, and you seem to have a plan for our territories, such as they are, and the will to enact it. Thus, I'm left little choice but to accept your offer of vassalage and declare you Thane of the Vale."

Torbjorn stared at his father, unable to believe what he had heard.

"You are serious?" He gulped and gestured at the leviathan his father had arrived on. "After all that, you are naming me Thane of the Vale?"

Hral shrugged, but Torbjorn could see pride burning in his father's eyes. It would have warmed the Heimlagu if he'd loosed it. "It's not what I came here to do, but it seems like the right thing."

Torbjorn's legs almost went out from under him. Seeing his son waver, Hral supported him with a steadying arm. For several heartbeats, father and son stood upon frigid boards above icy water but knew nothing of the cold.

"Oh, and one more thing," Emperor Hral said, turning Torbjorn with him to wave at the ship that had transported him to the docks. "I brought her for leverage, but now that we've settled things, I'm not quite sure what to do with her."

Torbjorn looked from his father to the dwarf who stepped gingerly across the boards. She had changed more than he would have thought since the last time he'd seen her, but the human part of her blood meant she was more prone to change in that time than a dwarf.

For all that, there was no mistaking the gold eyes that landed sun-bright on the dwarven commander.

"Torbjorn," the child whispered. Then she crossed the dock two or three boards at a time.

Torbjorn opened his arms and whispered, "Izze" when she flung herself at him and wrapped her arms around his neck. Heart full to bursting, he held her gently, fearing that if he squeezed too hard, she'd vanish and some terrible reality would crash in.

Hral was shaking his head but beaming. "I suppose since you'll be settling in Greyshelf to govern our holdings in the Vale, there is no reason you can't take this one back. At least you'll have a place to keep her."

Torbjorn nodded, his breath coming in happy gasps that robbed him of speech.

"Thank you," he managed at last, then looked at the head of Clan Cyniburg, his father. "Thank you."

"Just prove me wrong, Torbjorn," he murmured thickly. "I never thought I'd say it, but all I want now is for you to prove me wrong."

LEXICON

Military Ranks
—Enlisted—
Dwan - The base rank of the Holt'Dwan and also a term that generally refers to a dwarf serving as a soldier
Fordwan - A line officer, typically promoted from veteran dwan
Ascedwan - A dwarf soldier who has developed a useful skill (cooking, herbology, engineering, musical instrument, etc.), marking them out for additional pay/responsibility
—Commissioned Officer—
Dogordwan - field officer of a cavalry detachment
Frothdwan - commander of a cavalry squadron
Schildwan - quartermaster of a division
Tweldwan - commander of a division
Stendwan - commander of an established garrison, a castellan
—Command Staff—
Kuadwan - command staff, responsible for logistical matters

Lardwan - command staff, responsible for communication and intelligence

Vindwan - command staff, responsible for tactical direction

Ondwan - command staff, supreme commander of the Holt'Dwan

—Informal Positions—

Cubldwan - An unofficial position, represents when a soldier is selected to work under a superior officer, usually either a Tweldwan or one of the command staff

Military Terminology

Adyrclaf - a class of theropod typically used as a mount by the svartalf

Blotferow - a class of trained and bred pigs, suitable for use in battle

Cwellocs - a short-hafted dwarvish polearm intended for use in heavy armor

Duabuw - standard issue crossbow of the dwarven army

Holt'Dwan - A dwarven army, typically composed of between eight and twelve divisions

Magsax - standard issue sword of the dwarven army

Worcsvine - a class of trained and bred pigs, suitable for draft work

Slurs

Badger - Derived from drawing comparisons between the animal and dwarves

Clacker/Creaker/Rattler/Shuffler – a slur for the ambulatory undead who serve in the wight army given for the sounds they make

Grem - Derived from drawing comparisons between mythical gremlins and goblins

Longshanks - Can be used for any people group taller than dwarves but typically used for humans

Midges - An elvish slur regarding humans due to their much shorter life spans, though it can be applied to the like of goblins, halflings, and orcs

Myrkling - Derived from the dwarvish word for dark/dangerous forest (myrkvaul) and denotes an elf of svartalf or dark elf lineage

Savageling - a slur for the wosealf or wild elves of the Ysgand Vale

Wheezer - a slur for a wight after the sound of the undead voices

Miscellaneous

Cyniburg - the current ruling dynasty of the Dwarvish Empire

Dwarrisc - the dwarvish language

Svartalf - the dark elves of the Arawuvasc Principalities, a vassal state of the Dwarvish Empire

Wosealf - the wild elves of the Ysgand Vale, thought to be the original occupants of the Vale

AUTHOR'S NOTES - AARON D. SCHNEIDER

WRITTEN AUGUST 21, 2023

Dear Readers,

So we come to the close of another series. The Bad Badgers may have come apart, but they are set toward new horizons and what might be happy endings. Torbjorn may yet lead his people to a better future, Gromic and Haeda may yet find love, Tomza might find peace, and all the other brighter possibilities than death in some desperate battles. Call me a softy, but I just couldn't bring myself to do that to our stout friends. There's a good bit of love for the ol' doomed hero in me, but this time I wanted to hold onto believing that things could be better, that people (even stubborn dwarves) could change, or at least begin the long and painful process of doing so. I suppose that is just what I get for writing characters that I like; they join the cast of imaginary friends taking up space in my head and I just don't have the heart to watch them suffer too much.

Where do I go from here, then? Well, the future seems wide-open and with that free range there are all sorts of possibilities, both professionally and personally. I'll still be working with the great folks at LMBPN for various projects, but I'm also going to be delving into some of my one personal bits that should start coming out later in the year. I'm really excited to let you guys have a go at some of it, but things take time and I've so many things I'm getting into.

Speaking of things I'm getting into, I've got the little podcast that I've started with a friend that I'd love for you to check out. It is called The NerdFathers and it is a weekly show where we dig into all things Nerd discussing, dissecting, and disagreeing as we explore video games, film, tabletop, and of course books that we love and loathe. I'm so excited to get to share this new way to explore stories with all of you and hope you'll come join us as we plumb the depths of Nerdom to amuse ourselves and entertain you. You can find us almost anywhere that you get your podcasts, but if there is any question head on over to (https://www.aarondschneider.com/nerdfathers-podcast/) so you can make sure to get the latest and to make doubly sure that is the case you should sing up for the mailing list. That will help you keep up with the podcast and my other work.

Whatever the future holds I look forward to seeing you soon, Dear Reader, and always thank you for the precious gift of your time.

Sincerest Regards,

Aaron D. Schneider

AUTHOR NOTES - MICHAEL ANDERLE

WRITTEN AUGUST 22, 2023

First and foremost, thank you for not just delving into this story but also these authors' notes hidden away at the end. I appreciate you hanging around to let me chat with you just a little!

A World of Dwarf Adventures and More

Thank you for reading through this series! As our group of Dwarves figures out their own future, Aaron and I have many series together, and if you haven't read them all, I encourage you to jump on Amazon and check out what's available! We've had a blast creating these stories together, and it's a genuine pleasure to share them with you.

Cover Matters: Damsels or Dwarves?

I had a short talk today where we discussed the covers of this series. One of the ladies suggested we missed the mark by not having a couple of the lady dwarves really highlighted on the covers. I had to admit that personally, 'as a reader,' I go for the dwarven images of a hefty axe (no swords, no clubs), or perhaps I'd allow an occasional war hammer, but I'm not that interested in other versions with ladies dwarves on the covers.

I have a preference, ok?

Now, as a publisher, I'm open to whatever would sell the series male, female, swords, axes, etc. - so what do you think?

Do you prefer your dwarf stories featuring more traditional weaponry, or are you open to seeing some badass lady dwarves front and center on the covers? Let me know!

Tex-Mex Adventures: A Culinary Quest

I've been drawn lately to learning to cook Tex-Mex because (in Las Vegas) there aren't many options (Javiers in the Aria, and there is a location for Los Cucos THAT I JUST FOUND OUT ABOUT some 25 minutes from my house.)

When I have my taste fully back (medicines - that's another story), you will find me over there eating a lot. Assuming it's as good as the locations near Katy, Texas.

As an author, it's important to explore other interests and passions in life, and for me, that's been learning to cook Tex-Mex. I find it both therapeutic and inspiring, as it allows me to step away from the keyboard and immerse myself in a different creative process. Who knows, maybe the flavors of Tex-Mex might even find their way into one of my stories someday.

Until the next book, have a tasty and adventurous week or weekend!

I look forward to hearing your choice and diving back into the stories with you in our next story!

Ad Aeternitatem,

Michael Anderle

I have a couple of short stories you can read that I am sharing from my STORIES with Michael Anderle newsletter here:
https://michael.beehiiv.com/

OTHER BOOKS BY AARON D. SCHNEIDER

World's First Wizard

(with Michael Anderle)

Witchmarked (Book 1)

Sorcerybound (Book 2)

Wizardborn (Book 3)

The Outcast Royal Series

(with Michael Anderle)

Circle In The Deep (Book 1)

Voice On The Wind (Book 2)

Doom Under The Shadow (Book 3)

Incidental Inquisitors

(with Michael Anderle)

Last Gasp (Book 1)

Dire Song (Book 2)

Silk Webs (Book 3)

Hard Hand (Book 4)

Shot Dead (Book 5)

Dark Deed (Book 6)

The Warring Realm Series

War-Born

War-Torn

War-Sworn

Rings of the Inconquo

(with A.L. Knorr)

Born of Metal (Book 1)

Metal Guardian (Book 2)

Metal Angel (Book 3)

Join Aaron's Email List

https://www.aarondschneider.com/free-short-story-download-the-tops-tails-of-dreams/

CONNECT WITH THE AUTHORS

Connect with Aaron Schneider

Website:
https://www.aarondschneider.com/

Email List:
https://www.aarondschneider.com/free-short-story-download-the-tops-tails-of-dreams/

Facebook:
https://www.facebook.com/authoraarondschneider/

Instagram:
https://www.instagram.com/aarond.schneider/

TikTok
https://www.tiktok.com/@aarondschneiderauthor?lang=en

Amazon:
https://www.amazon.com/Aaron-D-Schneider/e/B07H8WZ2HT/

Connect with Michael Anderle and sign up for his email list here:

Website: http://lmbpn.com

Email List: https://michael.beehiiv.com/

https://www.facebook.com/LMBPNPublishing

https://twitter.com/MichaelAnderle

https://www.instagram.com/lmbpn_publishing/

https://www.bookbub.com/authors/michael-anderle

BOOKS BY MICHAEL ANDERLE

Sign up for the LMBPN email list to be notified of new releases and special deals!

https://lmbpn.com/email/

For a complete list of books by Michael Anderle, please visit:

www.lmbpn.com/ma-books/

www.ingramcontent.com/pod-product-compliance
Lightning Source LLC
LaVergne TN
LVHW041905070526
838199LV00051BA/2501